THE FIFTH STREETER

LoganHouse
Publishing

MMXVI

This is fiction. Similarities between the characters in this story and real persons, living or dead, are coincidental.

To my parents, Vincent and Mary Madden, who gave me every tool I ever needed.

Cover art, *Alone in the Dark*, by Daniel Dank, a photographer documenting urban ruins in Germany, Belgium and The Netherlands: www.Daniel-Dank.com

SPECIAL THANKS TO:

Carla Boccella, my beautiful wife, editor and muse,

and;

Carlos Eyster, screenwriter, film-maker, and friend, for excellent advice on plot, character and pacing,

and;

the cadre of court-appointed criminal defense attorneys in the District of Columbia, fighting for the rights of the indigent.

Note to Colleagues

This is fiction. As such, literary license was generously applied. While this story captures the essence of court-appointed criminal practice in the District of Columbia in the late 90's, factual liberties were taken, particularly with regard to *Lewis* disclosures as they apply to preliminary hearings, the *Brady* doctrine, interlocutory appeals, the District of Columbia Voluntary Sentencing Guidelines (which did not exist at the time) and a host of procedures at the Superior Court of the District of Columbia and the D.C. Jail. Nevertheless, those who feel the need to complain can connect with the author at: mikemaddenauthor.com.

THE FIFTH
STREETER

CHAPTER ONE

This all happened in the late nineteen-nineties when the homicide rate earned the District of Columbia its nickname, Murder City, and the drug wars were still generating three-hundred homicides a year. Addicts roamed the streets like zombies. To the honorable and decent, it was End Times straight out of Revelation.

But not to me.

I was a court-appointed criminal defense attorney and business was booming. How it worked was, you showed up at court and they handed you clients. No job application. No background check. All you needed was a pulse and a bar card. That's how desperate they were to have even the dregs of the legal profession lend a hand.

If you were smart, you stuck to the cases you could bill quickly, the misdemeanors and low-grade felonies. Murders you dodged. Ten years practicing law and I had avoided appointment to a single one. No small trick. The judges were desperate to dole out murders to the court-appointed stiffs.

Since then, I've represented dozens of men charged with murder. Some convicted, others acquitted and released. I don't even remember their names, except Alexander Bushill. They say you remember your first. Thinking back, he was more than just my first. Alex saved my life. Not like a firefighter or a surgeon, but in a more fundamental way.

I met Alex where I met all my clients, C-10, the auditorium-style courtroom in the basement of the Superior Court of the District of Columbia where new criminal cases were heard. I was getting ready to call it a day when Emerson Rathbone, an old-timer we called "Pockets," stepped to the podium.

"How's that, Yah Honor?" Pockets asked, tucking his shirt and giving his tie a quick choke. He swept a thin strand of grey hair across his polished dome, then cocked his head at the court defiantly, looking battle-ready in his coffee-stained blazer and corduroy slacks until the judge said something that had him scrunching his face in confusion.

Pockets killed me.

"The plea, Mr. Rathbone." Judge Bearmond gave him a wilted look. "There are two options here, guilty or not. How does your client plead?"

Pockets glanced at his client, as if the old man in the wheelchair next to him were capable of answering the question himself. A nappy afro sprouted from his skull, dark at the roots but topped a fine white. His hospital gown draped open in front covering his private parts, not much else. He had spidery legs, bony arms, and dark skin all dry and ashy. The best the old man could do was a head bob and a mindless stare about the courtroom.

After an awkward eternity Pockets announced, "The defendant pleads *not* guilty."

Excellent choice, I thought. Outstanding.

Pockets was a regular at Superior Court, had been there as long as anyone could remember, but the old buffoon hadn't handled anything more serious than a petty theft in ten years.

"My client waives formal reading of the charges, Yah Honor, and demands his *immeeeediate* release!"

Just hearing him draw out that word had every soul in the courtroom chuckling. The clerks at the bench, the spectators in the gallery, even the marshals were yucking it up by the Bullpen door. Not Bearmond, who hushed them all with an indignant scowl and a quick *rat tat tat* of the gavel.

Jeremiah Bearmond had the look of a judge, silver hair and a grim face, which at that moment was twisted into an ass-pucker clench. "The spectators will refrain from further outbursts and from disturbing the dignity of these proceedings."

I choked back a snort. Dignity? Bearmond was generous. Strike that: delusional. It was C-10, present-ment court, first stop on the judicial railroad for each miscreant arrested the previous night. The place stewed with every form of human poison imaginable. Wife beaters. Drug dealers. Prostitutes, their pimps waiting in the hall.

And that's not even counting the lawyers.

"That's release on personal recognizance," Pockets reiterated, stuffing the charging documents into his jacket, already bulging with the papers he'd collected at court that day.

No briefcase for Pockets.

Bearmond looked down at the file, then frowned disapprovingly. "This is a serious case, Mr. Rathbone. What's more, it's on *my* calendar. I'm vacating your appointment and am going to appoint someone –"

Puffing his chest, Pockets prepared to object.

Bearmond stopped him with an upturned palm. "Plenty of work for everyone, Mr. Rathbone. You've already been appointed to four misdemeanors by my count. I am going to pass this case and find another attorney to –"

"Your Excellency." The old man in the wheelchair executed a pretentious bow in the judge's direction. "May I be so bold as to ask a question?"

"That will be quite enough. Address any questions you have to your lawyer, not to the court."

"In that case, I ask the court for a *proper* lawyer."

Bearmond hammered down the sputters of laughter from the gallery with another triple shot of the gavel. The courtroom staff sobered quickly, but the spectators were giving him a run. Bearmond leaned forward and whispered, "Mr. Rathbone, do you think a forensic is in order?"

I thought he'd never ask.

Forensic examinations were required whenever a defendant's mental competence was in question. It was an elaborate process that took forty-five days, but almost always ended in a finding of competence, no matter how unstable the defendant appeared. I'd seen lawyers speak with deranged clients for twenty minutes then pass them off to a judge as competent just to avoid the delay. I suspected Pockets had spoken with this man for less than two.

"Ahhhh no, Yah Honor. Won't be necessary."

Bearmond eased back in his throne and made a theatrical production of perusing the courtroom for a "proper" lawyer. Simple math from my perspective.

Late in the day, only two court-appointed attorneys were left in the gallery, me and a fresh-faced newbie who couldn't have been more than a year out of law school. He looked straight off the cover of Ebony in a pinstriped suit over a starched white shirt with a black bowtie. The newbie seemed intent on catching the judge's eye and was vying for his attention like an eager grade-schooler. I was intent on putting as much distance between the judge and myself as was humanly possible.

Forensic clients are an attorney's worst nightmare. The last one I represented claimed to have an AM transmitter implanted in her head broadcasting her thoughts to the FBI. The only way she would speak with me was with an FM radio blaring static in the background. To scramble the AM signal, she said.

I was up the aisle and halfway through the door when Bearmond boomed, "Mr. O'Brian! You available to take an appointment?"

Friggin' Bearmond.

I considered pushing through the door as if I hadn't heard, and squandering the remainder of the afternoon at the coffee shop, or at Madam's Organ, my favorite watering hole. Happy hour started in twenty minutes.

Two-dollar drafts, three-dollar shooters, and all the chips I could scarf down. A pleasant alternative to the white-hot mess Bearmond wanted to gift-wrap for me, which he'd then have to present to the unsuspecting newbie.

"Yes, Your Honor," I heard myself mutter, heading toward the well of the Court.

Dodging the appointment would be acceptable, standard operating procedure even. Turning it down would be bad form. Bearmond would have seen that no cases were sent my way the rest of the month. "The Bear" could ruin a Girl Scout picnic.

The prosecutor stepped up and leaned casually against the courtroom rail. It was Shelly Jarvis, a well-built woman with mocha skin, long cornrows, and bright green eyes that've always looked cat-like to me. We started at the Superior Court at the same time, both fresh out of law school, but while I squandered the intervening ten years pounding out a living as a court-appointed defense attorney, Shelly spent them scraping her way to the top ranks of the U.S. Attorney's Office. Last I heard, her efforts had been rewarded with a plum assignment: Major Crimes, the section handling Felony One cases.

If Shelly was prosecuting, it was a Felony One, which was another thing that bothered me about this little gift from Bearmond.

As a court-appointed attorney I billed by the hour and didn't get paid until the case was over. Misdemeanors like possession of cocaine and simple assault were easy money. Finished and billed in weeks. I'd done my share of Felony Twos: narcotics distribution, burglary, the occasional robbery. They took longer, but within a few months a check was in the mail. Felony Ones, like murder and rape, could drag on for over a year. Felony Ones didn't pay the bar tab, at least not on time.

I could feel the blood gush through my head, that thump-and-pump sound in my temples getting louder. Give me a nice liquor store robbery, a carjacking, an aggravated assault. But a Felony One? I'd spent my career weaseling out of them, and if given ten minutes alone with the defendant was pretty sure I could weasel out of this one.

"Need a pass, Your Honor," I said. "To consult with the defendant."

Bearmond scowled. "Five minutes. Marshal! Step the defendant back to the Bullpen."

Shelly smiled as she handed over a copy of the Gerstein. I took one look at the document and froze. A murder. My first. Damn it to hell.

The victim was a cop.

CHAPTER TWO

A television murder case typically begins with the prosecutor showing the defense attorney a pile of incriminating evidence and saying something hackneyed like, "We'll let your client plead to Murder Two." In the real world, the only information the defense is given at the start of a case is a bare-bones description of the crime called a Gerstein.

No witness names.

No access to physical evidence.

It can be up to nine months before the defendant is indicted and the defense attorney is given "discovery," the evidence on which the government's case is built. Nine months of flying blind, with only the client to provide information, before being given so much as a police report.

So a case begins with a trip to the Bullpen.

Imagine the stench of a locker room after a game but before showers, picture a steel cage separating a herd of criminals from a thin line of rumple-suited attorneys, and add the maniacal screams of addicts incarcerated for twenty-four hours without a fix. That would be the Bullpen.

The same as always. Some were asleep, slumped against the walls or sprawled out on the grimy floor. Others milled about like cattle. The steel-bar door clanked shut behind me and announced to everyone in the cage that a lawyer had entered the Pen.

"Yo, yo, yo . . . You got lockup seventy-two?"

"You my lawyer?"

I ignored them as I reviewed the Gerstein. *Just before midnight, two detectives entered an abandoned rail tunnel near the Fourteenth Street Bridge to make an undercover drug buy...*

"Five minutes, counselor." The marshal muscled the wheelchair through the crowd and deposited the defendant in the front of the cage.

The man was a wreck, his face pitted, his eyes dull. The reek of sour wine on him blocked out the body-odor stench pervading the pen. The bandage wrapped around his thigh looked in serious need of changing.

"Roman O'Brian," I said, handing him my card and turning back to the Gerstein. "Be with you in a minute."

The suspect was a black male. . .

Check.

In his late fifties . . .

Check.

Disheveled and mentally unstable . . .

Double check.

The suspect screamed "Get out of my house!" and opened fire. He dropped one of the detectives with a shot to the forehead. The other detective returned fire and hit the suspect in the left thigh. The victim was pronounced dead at the scene. The only ID found on the suspect was a library card bearing the name, Alexander Seymour Bushill. The suspect was placed under arrest and . . .

"Rooooman Oooooh Brian." Bushill held my card to the light as if checking a counterfeit twenty. "You French?"

"Lawyer," I told him. "Be right with you."

The suspect was arrested and transported to George Washington Hospital. A search of the crime scene revealed . . .

"Look here, Frenchie!" He flicked the business card back in my face. "I don't have all day! I'm a busy man. You going to get me out of here, or what?"

I dropped the Gerstein in my briefcase. "Let's start with the basics. You are Alexander Bushill, correct?"

"Sorry." His eyes locked on the wall behind me. "Not at liberty to reveal that information."

Most defendants would be chomping at the bit to explain how the police had gotten the wrong man, how they'd acted in self-defense, or just plain hadn't done it. Bushill acted like a man who didn't care, which was fine with me. If he wouldn't speak to me, I couldn't represent him and Bearmond would let me out of the case.

Perhaps the newbie would have better luck.

"Excellent." I stood and yanked open the Bullpen door. "Let's get back in there and have the judge find a *proper* lawyer to –"

"Wait! Good God, sir. Does your hypocritical oath mean nothing to you? I'm innocent!"

"Didn't ask you that," I scolded.

Whether a client is guilty is not high on the list of questions to ask. It surprises most people to learn that the initial meeting with a criminal client is not about the facts, or the law, or about anything as trivial as whether the client committed the crime. It's all about establishing a rapport, a relationship based on trust and mutual respect, or at the very least on lies and loyalty.

Either way, if the man wouldn't tell me his . . .

"Alexander Seymour Bushill," he blurted. "Born March twenty-third in the Year of Our Lord, Nineteen-Hundred and Forty-one. There! I said it, be damned you. And I didn't kill anyone. Least I don't think so. No way to be certain, of course, things being as nebulous as they are. What with circumstances . . . acts of God . . . forces majeure and . . ."

I stood there with Bushill muttering incoherently at the wall and with the Bullpen door half open to the corridor. My only way out of that nightmare.

A goddamned debacle. A detective murdered. A wing-nut defendant. A police officer witness and the entire catastrophe on Bearmond's calendar. And the greatest injustice?

I'd work the case for a year before getting paid.

I let the door slam and squatted on the floor again. What the hell. Maybe there'd be a defense.

". . . the relativistic nature of it all . . . the fabric of the universe and the uncertainties inherent in –"

"All right," I said. "Tell me what happened."

He raised an eyebrow and stroked his chin as if pondering the complexities of life. "Afraid we may have an issue there. I feel compelled to inform you, I have a drinking problem."

"Uh huh. What happened?"

"As you can plainly see, I was shot."

"How?"

"Don't remember."

"Who shot you?"

"That I don't know."

"Why did they shoot you?"

"Excellent question."

"Who else was there?"

"Sorry, can't tell you."

"What *can* you tell me?"

Bushill considered the question. "Other than the drinking problem?"

It's called a Black Box case when the defendant is unable, or unwilling, to provide information. It's better to have a client who admits to the deed and can provide a blow-by-blow description. At least then, the attorney can get a jump on the investigation.

"What do you remember after being shot?"

"Not much."

"Remember being placed in the ambulance?"

"Nope. Blacked out."

"Remember anything?"

"I remember . . ." He stroked his chin. "Nothing of consequence."

The interview was getting me nowhere. I was on my feet, signaling to the marshal when Bushill looked at me for the first time.

"Except, of course," he said, "for the ninja."

Perfect.

I'd represented plenty of whacked-out clients, but Bushill was in a shiny new category of strange. And now he was talking about ninjas.

"Fine. Tell me about the ninja."

"I was in the tunnel, sleeping. Someone shot me in the leg. Then *he* appeared from out of the darkness. All black, mind you. Head to toe."

Bushill held his arms out all cockeyed and started waving them, left to right. "He crept across the tunnel, silent . . . stealthy . . . like a ninja! I was frightened at first when he grabbed my leg, but then he tied a rope around my thigh to stop the bleeding."

Bushill let his arms down with a flap. "He was my dark angel. My savior."

"I see. So you and the detective were shot by a person –"

"Or persons," he corrected.

"Or persons, unknown. Then a ninja appeared, tied

a rope around your leg, and what? Disappeared into the night?"

"As best I can recall . . . on the whole . . . yes."

Bushill's eyes glazed as he fixed them on the wall. The peculiar thing about the man was, as crazy as he seemed, he didn't have the manner of someone who'd spent a lifetime on the streets. The stately way he held his shoulders erect, the grandfatherly features of his face, actually made him look dignified.

The marshal reappeared and yanked Bushill back. "Time, counsel."

The other defendants filled in the space and the barrage started again. "You got lock-up thirty-two?"

"Yo, man! You my lawyer?"

"Am I going home?" Bushill called over them.

I did my best to give the impression I was contemplating every legal angle of the situation. "I'll do what I can, Mr. Bushill, but I gotta be honest. That's a pretty wild story."

"Right on, Frenchie. I don't trust you either."

I made my way through the maze of steel gates toward the bail report office to do a little checking on Bushill's background. Judge Bearmond was expecting me to head straight back to the courtroom where Shelly and I were supposed to lock horns over whether Bushill would be released, but there was no way I was going into a battle like that without a look at the man's bail report.

I should have mentioned to Bushill that, since he

was charged with Murder One, it was unlikely The Bear would release him no matter what his bail report said. In fact, with a dead cop, no defense and no defense witnesses other than a ninja, there was little hope he'd be going home anytime soon, even if he had a home to go to.

But the poor bastard would find out soon enough.

CHAPTER THREE

In grade school we're told to behave, admonished repeatedly that our transgressions would end up in our permanent record. Gullible children, unfamiliar with the ways of the world, do not believe this.

It's true.

In every courthouse across the country there is an office that compiles reports on new arrestees. Every encounter a defendant has had with law enforcement is at their fingertips: arrests, convictions, traffic offenses. A bail report is a lifetime of misbehavior reduced to a single document and the one thing a judge can be counted on to review.

A copy of Bushill's bail report was waiting for me in the courtroom, but knowing how Bearmond felt about delays, I figured he wouldn't give me time to read it.

Shelly Jarvis stepped out of the bail report office as I approached. "Roman! What are you doing? The Bear sent me looking for you, man. He's pissed."

"Be there in a minute, Shells. Don't mention you saw me."

She rolled her eyes and disappeared down the hall.

I liked Shelly. She was a hard-nosed prosecutor, but a soft-looking woman. Bearmond I could have done without.

Hunkered over the bail report counter was Shaniqua Moore, a burly woman with wild tangled hair and a nasty disposition, but a heart of butter.

"Whadaya say, Nini? That boy of yours keeping you busy?"

"Mr. O'Brian! Yeah, he runnin' me ragged. How you doin'?"

"Darlin'," I said, leaning on the counter, treating her to my best slick smile. "If I was feelin' any better they'd have me in the Bullpen."

As Bushill's attorney I was entitled to a copy of his bail report, but that's not how a courthouse works. If you need a clerk to go to the trouble of printing up a special copy, you have to toss a little sugar out there.

"Humph," she grunted. "Miss Jarvis was just here, sayin' the Bear is lookin' for you bad. You might end up in the Pen yet."

"Funny you mention that. Know what I need?"

"Knew it was somethin'."

"I've got a guy, Alexander Bushill."

"Lockup sixty-six?"

"That's right, how'd you –"

"One that killed that detective?"

"Allegedly . . ."

She slapped down a copy of the Washington Post,

its front page screaming *Officer Slain by Homeless Man in Railway Tunnel.*

"Reporters been callin' all day. Camera crews are settin' up out front." She treated me to a smile of her own. "You might wanna duck out the back when you're done."

Public scrutiny is the last thing a court-appointed attorney needs next to an IRS audit or a Bar complaint. The only high-profile case I'd ever handled was a dipper-head charged with smashing his car into a White House security checkpoint. The City Paper didn't have room to mention I'd won the case, but found space to note I'd been fined by Judge Waterman for showing up at trial without a tie.

It had been a rough night.

"Duck out with me," I said. "We'll run off to the islands together."

"Humph."

"Of course, I'd settle for a copy of the report on my guy, Mr. Sixty-Six. Whadaya say?"

"If Bearmond wasn't lookin' for you, I'd make you stand there and beg some more." She turned to the computer, printed the report and slid it across the counter. "Now go on, before he sends Miss Jarvis after you again."

I reviewed the report while weaving through a mass of lawyers and recently released defendants on my way back to the courtroom. Bushill had two priors for drinking in public and a conviction for pan handling.

No surprises there.

It was his personal background that was unusual. Although unemployed for the past seven years, Bushill once worked as a substitute English teacher.

Hardly your typical cop killer.

"Glad you could rejoin us," Bearmond announced as I burst into the courtroom, now empty except for Shelly, my client, and the newbie in the front row, still gawking at Bearmond as if hoping he would throw him a case. "Are we ready to proceed?"

"Yes, Your Honor."

"Very well. I've read the Gerstein and am ready to find probable cause that the defendant committed the crime, and to hold him without bail. Unless, that is, you have some sort of argument?"

"I do, Your Honor."

I had nothing, of course, and sure wasn't going with the ninja defense.

"Be brief, Mr. O'Brian."

"Your Honor, there is no physical evidence that the defendant was involved in this –"

"Says here," Bearmond whacked the Gerstein with his finger. "A handgun was found at his side."

I cursed myself for not reading the whole thing. "That may be, but . . . Court's indulgence."

I scanned the rest of the Gerstein, looking for a loophole of any kind. At this stage, the only evidence admissible was the Gerstein itself, but the damned thing was tight as a tick's ass. "Ah! There is no indication of any possible motive. Now, if my client was responsible for –"

"Irrelevant. The defendant was at the scene of the crime, armed with a gun, and pulled the trigger. Motive is not an element of murder. You are aware of that, Mr. O'Brian?"

"Of course, Your Honor. I . . . mention it only in passing."

"Anything else? In passing?"

"I'm asking that the defendant be released, at least to a halfway house, so he can participate in his defense. My client is an educated man, Your Honor." I waved the bail report at Bearmond. "With no prior history of violence."

"Your client is a homeless alcoholic," Bearmond waved his Gerstein at me, "with an immediate history of violence. The court finds probable cause and holds the defendant without bail. The preliminary hearing will be Friday. Be prepared, I don't like continuances."

"Your Honor, may I approach?"

He beckoned me forward. "What is it, Counselor?"

"The thing is, Judge, I'm afraid this is not a good time for me to be taking on a felony-one assignment. I've got two burglary trials scheduled later this month and just picked up a complicated drug case. On the other hand, I couldn't help notice there is another court-appointed attorney in the courtroom." I nodded toward the newbie. "I don't know the young man's name, but as Your Honor can see he appears eager to lend his services. Perhaps the court could –"

"Nonsense, Roman," Bearmond said, grinning. "You've read the Gerstein. The government has a police officer witness and they found what appears to be the murder weapon at the defendant's side. Last thing the poor fellow needs is a hot young lawyer itching to prove himself with a trial. This case needs an experienced attorney. One with your particular skills, I might add. It's got plea deal written all over it."

I ignored his sarcastic look. "Just the same, I would prefer if the Court would –"

"The appointment stands." Bearmond leaned forward. "Do you think a forensic is in order?"

I thought about Bushill looking past me with that thousand-yard stare. The ludicrous image of a silent ninja, stalking the tunnel like a deadly mime, popped into my head.

"No, Your Honor."

Bearmond dismissed me with a wave of his hand and turned to Bushill. "The defendant is held without bail and will be remanded to the District of Columbia Jail. I don't know if you are guilty, sir, but woe betide you if you are."

No kidding. If Bushill was being held without bail, then of course he'd be remanded to the jail. The fact Bearmond felt the need to reiterate something like that was what turned me off about the man.

And woe betide you? I hated it when he said that.

As I turned to leave, the newbie flashed a thumbs

up and a goofy grin as if I had championed the day, as if he hadn't been sitting there when Bearmond agreed with Shelly and ordered my client to languish in jail.

Adding insult to injury, it occurred to me that Shelly hadn't uttered a word.

CHAPTER FOUR

Turned out, Shaniqua was right. The courthouse sidewalk teemed with media, at least two camera crews and what looked like the press. Staring through the windows of the courthouse lobby, I plotted my escape. The media jackals would undoubtedly have had a spotter in the courtroom who would tip them off I was Bushill's attorney the instant I stepped through the door.

"Excellent argument back there, Mr. O'Brian," a deep voice sounded from behind. "Mind if I speak with you?"

I spun and was face-to-face with the newbie from the courtroom.

"I know you?"

"Boston Stewart." He held out a card. "Just need a moment."

I'll be damned. The way he had been clamoring for Bearmond's attention had been a dead ringer for a novice attorney looking for a case. Pretty crafty, but there was no doubt about it. He was the spotter.

The jerk had media jackal written all over his face.

"Sorry. I have another appointment."

I turned and side-stepped onto the escalator. The embarrassing thing was, I had stepped onto the up-stairs which had me peddling my feet twenty miles-per-hour just to go down at a snail's pace. The jackal had been savvy enough to take the correct stairs and was having no trouble pacing me by just standing still.

"Mr. O'Brian." He extended his card over the handrail. "I was hoping to speak with you about –"

I wove around a judge in a billowing black robe. "Afternoon, Your Honor."

"Mr. O'Brian! What are you doing on the –"

I leapt off at the John Marshal level with the jackal in hot pursuit, and squeezed into an elevator just as it hissed shut in his face. When the elevator chimed open at the basement level I made my play for the back door, but could see through the glass it was the same as the front. The sidewalk swarmed with media scum set to pounce on me for a quote.

I resigned myself to riding it out in the men's room until they got tired and called it a day. I was definitely going to miss happy hour.

"Mr. O'Brian!" The Jackal said, bursting through the stairwell, out of breath.

"Give it a rest, Jackal!"

"Jackal?"

"I've got nothing to say to the press."

"I'm not with the press." He held up his card so I

could read it. *Boston Stewart, Esquire. If you've got a pulse, you've got a lawyer.*

Nice slogan. I had clearly misjudged the man.

"Graduated from Howard last spring," he said. "But wanted to do something meaningful, you know? So I signed up to take court-appointed cases."

"That a fact."

A break in the media swarm was forming on the left. If timed right, I could be through the hole, around the corner and up the street before they knew it. I positioned myself against the door.

"The thing is," Boston was saying. "When they told me you were going to be my mentor I couldn't believe it."

"Mentor?" I spat the word out. "I don't know what they told you at the clerk's office. I'm not anyone's –"

He reached in his jacket and handed me a flyer that read, *Superior Court of the District of Columbia – Attorney Buddy Program* and looked as if it had been printed by some yahoo bureaucrat.

"Attorney buddy program? What the hell is . . . Damn!"

The media hole closed tight.

"It's where older, I mean experienced attorneys like yourself mentor new ones. Dan Jones in the clerk's office assigned me to you. I can't tell you what an honor this is. He said you have an excellent reputation."

Double Down Dan.

It figured.

I owed him four hundred from last week's Texas hold 'em. He took my college ring as collateral, pawned it, then claimed I still owed him two. The guy was a shark.

Outside, the jackals noticed us and were drifting closer to the courthouse door.

"Tell you what, Camden."

"Boston."

"You want a piece of this case?"

"The Bushill case?" His eyes lit up. "I was just looking for a little guidance, but . . . Wow! I won't let you down, Mr. O'Brian. To be honest, though, I haven't had much experience with –"

"You'll do just fine," I assured him, and pushed through the door.

They were on us like suburban housewives at a yard sale, pushing and shoving their microphones in my face yelling, "Mr. O'Brian! Did your client do it? Mr. O'Brian! Can we get a statement? Mr. O'Brian . . ."

"Attention! My colleague, Baltimore Stewart, will be joining the Bushill defense team. He's prepared to answer your questions!"

Shoving me aside, they descended upon him. "Mr. Stewart! Is Bushill planning to go to trial?"

"Baltimore! What's the defense?"

"Ah . . . that's Boston," he said. "B-O-S-T . . . Mr. O'Brian? Mr. O'Brian!"

Smiling, I picked up my pace to a jog.

The thing about happy hour in Washington is, you

have to get there on time. Bartenders in our nation's capital adhere to a strict, six o'clock cut-off when it comes to half-priced drinks.

It was just after five and I had to stop at the office to pick up a file for the next day, so I hustled across Fifth Street toward the shoebox-sized office I worked out of. Truth be told I was lucky to have it.

Most Fifth Streeters worked out of their briefcases.

CHAPTER FIVE

The District of Columbia legal community is a caste system. K Street lawyers from the mega-firms downtown are the elite. Ivy League jerks, they guide the fates of multinational corporations without ever stepping into a courtroom. Boutique lawyers from the smaller firms form the second tier. Solo practitioners, not too proud to do worker's comp and personal injury, occupy an even lower stratum.

None as low as the Fifth Streeter.

The term Fifth Streeter is reserved for attorneys who accept court-appointed criminal cases, seasoned trial lawyers who squeeze out a living defending the indigent for the legal equivalent of minimum wage. The nickname derives from the neighborhood surrounding the Superior Court at Fifth and Indiana where most court-appointed attorneys make their home.

Dilapidated for decades, the area was experiencing something of a revival. Many of the older buildings had been torn down and replaced with high-tech office suites which none of us could afford. Thus far, my building had been spared renovation.

I once took one of those career placement tests, the kind that ask about your current job and try to match you with an alternate profession. The question that stood out was, *What word best describes your current work environment?*

Stains. That's what I wrote.

To get to my office you took an elevator to the third floor, crossed a field of coffee stains, hung a left by a rust-colored watermark, then followed a trail of carpet tears and encrusted gum to the glass door at the end of the hall.

I had mixed feelings about that door. One of my first clients was an art student from the Corcoran who hadn't qualified for a court-appointed attorney, but had no cash to pay. Instead, he agreed to paint a logo on the door for me and my investigator, Vicky Bronco.

Vicky got the best end of the deal. *Bronco Private Investigations* it said, with one of those cool-looking eyeballs. *Law Office of Roman O'Brian* was scribbled below like an afterthought.

"Hey Roman," Vicky cooed, as I stepped through the door.

It was a one-room office with a small reception area Vicky used as a workstation. Vicky wasn't my employee, exactly. She investigated my cases and billed the government just like I did, but acted as my legal assistant in exchange for rent. I got to play it off like I had staff and Vicky got a work station, rent free.

"Whadaya say, Vick? Any calls?"

"Your mom called. Four times. Your wife called twice.

"Ex-wife."

"Whatever, Ro. Why don't you just get it over with and call the woman back?"

"Anyone else?"

"Tito's Grandmom."

"Two-Bit Tito?"

"Fat Tito. He got tagged last night on a shoplifting beef. Pure case of mistaken identity. Planted evidence. A fabricated surveillance video of him stuffing frozen burritos down his sweatpants. The usual."

"Uh huh."

"Grandma wants to know if you'll take it on a payment plan."

"The old biddy ever pony up the six bills she owes from last time?"

"Nope."

"Next."

Vicky eased back in her chair and folded her hands behind her head. "Every newspaper and TV station in town has been calling non-stop for the past half hour. So you picked up a high-profile murder case, huh? Doesn't sound like you."

"No?"

"Nah. Sounds like work."

"You know, I was thinking about handing the investigation over to that Emma Barnes girl, the new investigator with the cherry-blond hair? You know the kid, the *young* one?"

Since turning thirty, Vicky had become sensitive about her age. She looked great, though. Sexy and thin, she had a dark complexion and a poofy afro she liked to tie down with a bandanna.

My clients loved her.

"Give it up, Ro. You know I'm your woman on this one. We go back a *long* way."

I dropped the charging documents on her desk. Court-appointed attorneys can choose their investigator, but there was never a question I would hand the Bushill case to Vicky. An old-school investigator, she relished chasing down witnesses and was eager to hit the streets when I picked up a new case.

"Dig it," she said.

But she talked like she watched too many '70s detective shows.

She snatched up the paperwork and read through it, scrunching her face when she got to the Gerstein. "Far out! How'd you pick up this nightmare?"

"Poor guy came through in a wheelchair. An old man, shot in the leg. Pockets was representing him at first, but –"

"Pockets? For real?"

"Go figure. The judge vacated his appointment and the only other attorney in the courtroom was this sorry looking kid with one foot out of law school. I couldn't just sit there and let the judge dump the poor old man on a newbie like that, so I –"

"Uh huh. Who's the judge?"

"The Bearrrr . . ."

Vicky flashed me one of her looks. "Bearmond appointed you to a murder? That's suspect."

"Why?" I asked, but I knew why.

I had a case with Bearmond six years earlier that had gotten a little weird. It started out usual enough with my client sticking a gun in the face of a hot dog vendor and demanding cash. The genius was arrested four blocks from the scene, sitting on a curb with the gun poking out of his jacket, counting out three hundred and forty-two dollars. The exact amount stolen.

We caught a break when the vendor testified my client wasn't the stick-up man despite having identified him in a line-up. The jury acquitted him of armed robbery, but convicted him of carrying a pistol without a license.

At his sentencing, he started strong by expressing remorse for carrying the pistol, then sent a shockwave through the courtroom by apologizing for bribing the vendor to say he couldn't recognize him.

Dealing with incredible acts of stupidity is a huge part of the job description.

The U.S. Attorney's Office promptly charged him with obstruction of justice and Bearmond went ballistic. He appointed another lawyer to the case and referred the matter to Bar Counsel to investigate whether I'd known about the payoff. Bar Counsel cleared me, but only after the most harrowing three months of my career. Since then, Bearmond always treated me like I'd gotten away with something.

"I'm sure His Honor has forgotten about that."

Vicky laughed. "If you say so. What do you want me to do?"

"Print out discovery requests for Shelly Jarvis."

"Discovery? You know the rule. There's no way Shelly is giving up discovery until after indictment." Her face soured. "The skinny little prude hasn't given up anything since high school."

"That aside," I said, not wanting to get drawn into another Shelly-bashing session. "I need you to hit the crime scene right away."

I ducked into my office and began the frantic search for tomorrow's file. With forty-five minutes left on the happy-hour clock, I could still make it to Madam's Organ, but I'd have to hurry.

"It's some kind of abandoned railway tunnel next to the Fourteenth Street Bridge," I told her. "Take lots of photos. Attach them to a motion asking that the crime scene be preserved as it is. Have you seen the Melendez file?"

"Are you for real? A motion to preserve a railway tunnel? The Bear is going to –"

"Deny it, of course, but not until after Shelly has gone to the trouble of filing a response. Give it a few days, then file one of my standard motions to dismiss. After Shelly responds to that, go ahead and file, lemme see . . . I'm thinking something novel under Rule 16, maybe a request for –"

"Solid. I'm starting to get the picture here, Ro."

"Just keep up the pressure. You know the deal. The bigger the pressure . . ."

"The better the *plea*," Vicky sighed.

I spied the Melendez file under the remains of my lunch. A few mustard stains, but no harm done.

"And get Hatch over here," I added, making for the door. "I want those discovery requests hand-delivered tonight."

"Hatch?" Vicky jumped up, blocking my way.

"Make nice, Vick."

"You make nice. I'll print the discovery requests, but you can sit here and wait for that turkey yourself."

"Suck it up. I've got research to do."

"Uh huh." She glanced at the clock. "There's forty-five minutes until *research* hour is over at Madam's. Grab a seat."

I conceded the point, dropped in my chair and kicked my feet up on the desk.

"I'll never understand why you use that guy, Ro."

"He works cheap."

"Free, and you get what you pay for." She hunched her shoulders, shuddering as she went back to her work station to call Hatch. "The little creep freaks me out."

Hatch was a dying breed, a bicycle messenger who still managed a living in an age when electronic court filing and email attachments were making deliveries obsolete. He worked as a freelancer and earned pretty good coin, but dropped most of it on exotic marijuana and a fiendish comic book habit. He hired me several years earlier to represent him on a weed charge. When his check bounced, I gave him a choice. Find another lawyer, or work it off. Three arrests later I was still representing him and he was still working off my fees.

K Street lawyers have the resources to pay for luxuries like messenger service.

Fifth Streeters have to live by their wits.

I grabbed a handful of darts from the drawer. The first shot went wide and struck the board in the outer zone labeled, *Turn State's Evidence,* which was no help at all. A half-crazed alcoholic like Bushill wouldn't have information to trade.

Vicky pecked at her computer, expressing her displeasure at having to call Hatch by cranking her music up loud. It was classic R&B at first, a little Otis Redding, some Al Green, then a song I'd never heard before, a soulful female vocalist crooning, *Drop your skivvies, baby . . .*

"Title and artist," she called out from her desk.

"Ahhh . . . Drop Your Skivvies."

"That's brilliant. Artist?"

Vicky was always doing that to me.

"Nina Simone," I guessed. "What's the ETA on your buddy Hatch?"

I launched another dart and cringed when it looked like it might actually strike center, in the red circle marked *Trial*, but at the last instant it arced down and scored a hit in the *Plea Deal* zone.

Now we were talking.

"Get real. You might as well have said Aretha." Vicky threw the discovery requests onto my lap. "It's contemporary. Sara Slick and the Refunds. Damn!"

"What?"

"The creep is here."

I checked my watch. Hatch had gotten there quickly, but since Madam's was several metro stops away, there was no way I was going to make it. If I wanted to catch happy hour, I would be forced to walk around the corner to the F.O.P.

Straight into the deep, dank, belly of the Beast.

On the other hand, the F.O.P. was a great place to obtain discovery, which I desperately needed.

Vicky was right. Shelly would undoubtedly toss my discovery requests in the back of her file to be answered at her leisure when Bushill was indicted. Putting the squeeze on a prosecutor by filing frivolous motions was all well and good, part of the game, but the best way to generate a good offer was to poke a few holes in the government's case. Problem was, I didn't even know the star witness's name.

If I was to have any hope of engineering a decent deal I would need discovery right away and, like it or not, there was no better place to acquire it than the F.O.P.

Hatch swung through the door in a *Silver Surfer*

tee, wearing a pair of spandex bicycle pants so tight you could see the outline of his jock strap. He was the skinniest person I had ever seen outside of a hospital, concentration camp thin, in his late thirties with long frizzy hair and a patch of brillo-like stubble on his chin.

And always with a strange odor, a sickly blend of fresh sweat and stale pot.

"*Wassssup,* Vick," he said, in a voice that came out like escaping steam.

I figured it'd be a good idea to run interference. I stepped out to where Vicky was hurriedly packing her things. The good thing about Hatch was, he worked more-or-less for free. Bad thing was, he liked Vicky.

A lot.

"Gotta book, Ro," Vicky said, backing as far around Hatch as was possible.

"Call me from the crime scene tomorrow," I told her. "I'll meet you."

"You're coming?" She stopped halfway through the door. "To a crime scene?"

"Why not?

"Suit yourself," she snickered. "Thought you had the Melendez trial."

"Got a feeling it's going to resolve early," I told her with a smile.

"Dig it. Good luck with that. And Ro?"

"Yeah?"

"Call your ex."

"What's up, Chief?" Hatch asked, straining to eye Vicky as she disappeared down the hall.

I rapped him across the chest with the discovery package. "I need this hand delivered to Shelly Jarvis at the U.S. Attorney's Office."

"Mmmm, Shelly." He flashed a smile, then turned serious. "So how's my case going? You're still takin' care of me, right, Ro?"

"How many times have I represented you, Hatch?"

"Uh, three?"

"And how many times have you gone to jail?"

"Dude, you the Man!"

CHAPTER SIX

The F.O.P. – the Fraternal Order of Police Lodge – is a union hall for the Metropolitan Police Department. They operate a small bar on the second floor. There is nothing more cheerless, more depressing or bleak to a criminal defense attorney, than a bar packed with off-duty cops and prosecutors celebrating fresh victories at court.

I dreaded the place.

Then again, chatty cops and tipsy prosecutors were an excellent source of inside information, they carried Yuengling on tap, and the Buffalo wings weren't bad. It was a private club for cops only, but since they waived the rule for prosecutors I could usually slip through the ranks without trouble. Most cops were gracious about it, giving me a hard time about the trials we'd had together or sniggering "defense counsel in the house!" when I walked in.

When I stepped through the double-glass doors at the top of the stairs I got my first hint that the mood was going to be less than collegial. The line at the bar was two cops deep, all of them transfixed on the TV where a reporter held out a microphone and Boston Stewart's baby face filled the screen.

"Yes," Boston said. "I mean, no. What I mean to say is . . . it would be inappropriate to comment on a defense strategy at this time."

I smiled. The kid was a natural.

"Surely you can tell us why Mr. Bushill pleaded not guilty," the reporter said. "Is he claiming mistaken identity?"

"I'll need to speak to attorney O'Brian about –"

"Self defense?"

"A possibility, I suppose, but I really must –"

"Will the defense team be taking this case to trial?"

"Of course," declared Boston, suddenly confident. "Attorney O'Brian will be defending Mr. Bushill to the fullest extent of the law."

The camera swung back to the reporter. "Roman O'Brian could not be reached for comment."

I stood, open mouthed, while the reporter wrapped up. "And there you have it. A police officer brutally killed in the line of duty. A homeless man charged with the crime. The whole matter headed to trial and *justice* hanging in the balance. Channel Seven will follow this story as it develops. Douglass Withers, reporting from the Superior Court of the District of Columbia."

Damn it to hell.

Angry eyes focused on me as I tried to make a nonchalant approach to the bar. I squeezed in between a young street-cop, whose name I'd forgotten, and Shawn Harlow, a middle-aged detective who'd given me hell on the witness stand more than I cared to remember.

"Whadaya say, Shawn?"

Harlow turned his back.

"A little crowded in here," I observed to the young cop, who grabbed his beer and walked away.

"What's new, Ro?" the bartender asked. "What'll it be?"

It was Stan Roth, a retired patrolman who'd traded his badge for a bartender's apron long before I came on the scene. Short and squat, he had salt-and-pepper hair and the grizzled face of a battle-worn street cop. Stan was never stuck for a friendly word, apparently even for the likes of me.

"Jack-n-Coke," I said, then tried to maintain a low profile by focusing on the television, where a reporter stood in front of a building downtown.

"The District's most infamous vandal has struck again," the reporter was saying.

The reporter stepped aside and the camera focused on the graffiti mural behind him. It was as tall as the reporter, twelve-feet wide, and emblazoned with the name "REPO." Underneath the REPO graffiti was scribbled the words:

This building has been REPOssessed
for the dispossessed.

I'd heard of the guy.

The press called him "Repo Man." The previous winter, REPO graffiti started to appear all over the city. Repo Man reached icon status among the bohemian, twenty-something crowd for vandalizing the *Welcome to Washington, D.C.* sign above the Key Bridge with a REPO mural featuring the phrase, *Yuppie Free Zone*.

You had to admire his nerve.

"Eighteenth and K, Northwest," the reporter said. "The heart of the business district and where Repo Man has struck again. During the day this area is bustling with downtown workers, with everything from hot dog vendors to high-powered lobbyists. But as you can see, after-hours the streets and sidewalks are deserted."

The camera panned the intersection, then settled on the graffiti.

The reporter put on a serious face. "Nevertheless, it is hard to imagine how this culprit could have executed this large emblem undetected. It appeared between one and four this morning. A contact at the Metropolitan Police Department, familiar with urban graffiti, has informed Channel Seven that it would have taken at least an hour to complete. The MPD has offered no explanation as to how this could have been accomplished unnoticed by passing patrol cars."

The screen switched to a montage of Repo's prior accomplishments: *REPO HATES URBAN RENUAL* painted across the entire span of the 14ᵗʰ Street Bridge, MAKE LOVE NOT CONDOS on the stone columns of Union Station, and *REPO SAYS GENTRIFICATION*

SUCKS across the top floor of a new condominium building in Southwest.

"Some call him a vandal, others a graffiti artist. What's *not* in dispute is that he has been a thorn in the side of District property owners for almost a year. For this installment, Channel Seven takes to the streets to elicit the reaction of Washingtonians."

The screen flashed to a shriveled old man in front of a liquor store on Rhode Island Avenue. He spoke in an Eastern European accent while shaking an angry finger at the camera. "He's a criminal, pure and simple. It cost three-hundred and seventy-two dollars to have his garbage sandblasted off my establishment. There should be laws. There should be —"

"Art for the people!" proclaimed a young man with long stringy hair, clenching a fist in the air in front of the 9:30 Club on V Street. "The bourgeoisie value property over culture. The media demonizes Repo because he uses the city for his canvas. He's a modern artist. A genius. Go Repo Man, go!"

It went on like that for a while, some hailing Repo as a performance artist, others expressing outrage.

I turned to Detective Harlow. "Bet you wish you could get your hands on that punk, eh Shawn?"

Harlow threw back the rest of his beer and tossed a few dollars on the bar. "Keep the change, Stan," he said, pushing away.

Stan tossed me a look. *Come on, Ro. You're bad for business tonight.*

I took the hint, ordered two more half-priced Jack-n-Cokes and retired to a table in the corner.

Halfway through my second drink, Shelly Jarvis strolled in with a man I recognized. Tomlinson was his name. Husky. Bald. A narcotics detective who somehow managed a year-round tan.

Muffled applause went up as the cops cleared a space at the bar. Several of the older detectives started speaking with Tomlinson in hushed tones while others conferenced with Shelly. Someone sprung for a round of drinks and they both settled in.

Things quieted as I watched a report on the latest Redskins debacle which had the cops in an even fouler mood than before. I was about to call it a night when Stan tapped Shelly on the shoulder and pointed me out.

"What's up, Shells?" I said, as Shelly slid her slim legs off the barstool and sashayed my way, barefoot now, having left her flats at the foot of the bar.

"You're what's up, Roman. You're a big star." She sat down without an invitation, not that Shelly needed one. "Caught that news report, by the way. Where your little sidekick announced Bushill is going to trial? Kid looks green."

"Boston is in training. I'll be handling the strategic decisions. He's just along for the –"

"And I received the discovery requests from that messenger of yours as I was leaving the office tonight. Interesting character. Tell me, where do you *find* these people?"

I could see Shelly was in confrontation mode, so I played along. "You just come over to harp on me, Shells? Cause if that's the case, take a number."

"Good point." She flitted her eyes around the bar. "Not sure I'd be in a cop bar if I were you. In fact, way I figure it, the only reason you'd show your face tonight would be to fish around for a little discovery. Sound about right?"

"Or," I said, shooting her a grin. "When I saw you in the courthouse earlier, it reminded me I'm in love with you and I just stopped by to chat you up."

"Or," she said. "Those discovery requests were a ruse and what you're really looking for is a plea deal, despite what your minion said on the news. Yeah, that's it. Figured you'd land one of those sweetheart deals you're famous for finagling?"

"Or," I raised a finger. "Maybe I'm just here to –"

"Because if it's a plea offer you're after, I can make one right now. Gotta tell you though, it ain't gonna be pretty."

"I'm just here for the beer," I told her. "But since you're feeling generous, mind telling me what evidence you have?"

"You know the rule. You'll get discovery after he's indicted. Besides, you have the Gerstein. There's a police officer witness, a positive ID and a handgun at your client's side. Firearms is still working the gun, but rest assured, won't be long before it comes back a match. You don't need discovery to figure out this one."

"Maybe, but if I could tell whether a man is guilty without looking at evidence, hell, I'd have landed a job at the U.S. Attorney's Office myself."

"Same old Roman," she chortled.

Her playful smile and the vodka twinkle in her eyes caught me off guard. In court, Shelly was all business.

"Go on," she said. "Huff and puff to the media. Milk it for all it's worth. You and I both know this case isn't going to trial. It's going to plea. And the smart money says, do it early. Once Bushill is indicted, it'll be hard for me to get you any kind of deal at all."

"What makes you think I'm looking for –"

"You're a good lawyer, Roman, but I know you've never done a murder. Let me clue you in. It ain't like Felony Two."

"No biggie," I said. "Way I hear it, a murder is no different than a simple assault, except there's one less witness."

Her smile evaporated. She leaned in close. "You really think this is the place for jokes like that?"

It felt good to hit a nerve. "Sorry. Forgot where I was."

She eased back. "Speaking of witnesses, I have one and you don't, except for your deranged client. Trust me, if this slam dunk ever reaches a jury, it's pretty simple math which one they'll believe."

"Probably right, Shells. Your witness sounds like a stand-up guy. Who is it? The Gerstein doesn't say."

"You'll find out at the preliminary hearing on Friday. He's going to testify. Suffice it to say, he's a veteran detective who's itching to send your guy deep for killing a brother cop. Tell you what. I might be able to swing a twenty-five-year stretch if Bushill cops an early plea. What is he, in his fifties? With time off for good behavior, he might even survive it and get a little street-time before he croaks."

"Again with the generosity. I'm tempted to plead him out right now."

She rolled her eyes. "Just so you know, the longer this drags on, the worse it'll get. Christ sake, Roman, this isn't one of the knucklehead stick-up artists you normally represent. We're talking about a cop killer. Look around. The MPD wants a crucifixion and my supervisors will do anything to pacify them. All I'm saying is, you'd do well to bail out of this one early."

"Thanks. I'll take it under advisement."

"And while I'm on the subject of bailing out," she said, standing. "Every badge in this place is looking at you sideways, and they're not even drunk yet. Might be a good idea to hit the road before they get their party on."

Her smug attitude had gotten under my skin, so I paid her back by forcing myself to look the other way as she made her way back to the bar. It was a tough give up. Shelly had the best legs in the U.S. Attorney's Office. Bar none.

I decided to call it quits. It didn't look like I was

going to squeeze information out of anyone at the F.O.P. and I had the Melendez trial in the morning. It was just a simple assault, a petty misdemeanor, but I was anticipating it would end in a dwip, which meant I had to be in the courtroom first thing.

In the entire Fifth Streeter universe there is nothing finer than the dwip. To get one, however, you have to strike early.

I stopped by the bar on my way out, directly behind Shelly so I could see Detective Tomlinson's face in the bar mirror.

"Tell me one thing, Shells. When they came for Bushill, he have a rope tied to his leg?"

She glanced at Tomlinson, who was nodding yes.

"Sorry, Roman," she said. "Don't know. You'll get discovery soon as he's indicted."

I kept a poker face until I cleared the double doors, then smiled bounding down the stairs. Tomlinson had to be the other detective in the tunnel. The government's star witness. And Bushill was right about someone else being in the tunnel and tying his leg with a rope.

Sure, I knew the rule, but there was more than one way to get discovery.

CHAPTER SEVEN

The Dismissal for Want of Prosecution – the *dwip* – represents all that is holy to the criminal defense attorney. It's what judges do when they get annoyed at the prosecution for not being ready for trial. The ritual plays out every morning in courtrooms across the country with the defense announcing ready for trial, the prosecution unable to determine if its witnesses have checked in, and with the judge, frustrated at the delay, dismissing the case.

A dwip is a gift from God in heaven, unearned and undeserved, but to be worthy of the blessing the defense has to have its case called early enough to take full advantage of the chaos and confusion of the morning trial call.

I awoke a half hour earlier than usual because I had a domestic violence trial that had dwip written all over it. The client, Ruffio Melendez, was charged with leaving threatening messages on his ex-wife's cell. The calls went on for so long the wife started saving them, which had the prosecutor salivating about going to trial with a recording of the defendant committing the crime.

But in order for the recordings to be admitted into evidence, the wife would have to show up at trial and identify Ruffio's voice. Knowing this, Ruffio had sent flowers to the woman on a weekly basis and was pretty confident that, come trial time, she wouldn't show.

It sure sounded like a dwip to me.

I rummaged through my closet for suitable attire, settling on a grey pinstriped suit, a green shirt and my yellow tie. The one I always wore to domestic violence court. The one with the little kangaroos on it.

Two duffel bags of clothes and a plastic trash bag bulging with toiletries was all I brought with me when I first moved into that tiny room at the Sergeant Hotel. I rented the efficiency when things started to sour with my wife, Brenda, expecting to stay a few nights. Just until we worked things out.

That was a year ago.

Since then I'd acquired a small cache of personal items. An afghan from the Middle-East Bazaar draped across the loveseat in my room, hiding a tear, but more important, reminding me of the afghan in our bedroom back home. The generic lamp on my night table came with the place, but its lampshade I bought at Versailles Furniture, a boutique Brenda favored.

My most prized possession was the rock. Perched in a place of honor on the windowsill was a souvenir from our Adirondacks getaway the previous fall, a river stone we picked up in a gift shop and had engraved. *Roman & Brenda*, with a heart around it.

Brenda dropped the divorce bomb the day we came home from that trip. Hostile from the beginning, she demanded the house, the car, the furniture and the dog. Put up a hell of a fight about everything. But in the end, the joke was on her.

I got the rock.

I took the elevator to the lobby, which was a monument to the Sergeant Hotel's illustrious past. A pretentious row of columns surrounded a marble floor, faded yellow from decades of neglect. The row of mail slots behind the concierge desk looked quaint, but the desk itself went largely unattended. And the Victorian mirror by the entrance may have been an antique, but was cracked in two places and in need of cleaning.

The Sergeant was in the center of the Adams Morgan nightclub district, four blocks of raunchy bars that turned the area into Mardi Gras every night. The neighborhood was rife with crime.

And it had a serious drinking problem.

I stopped in Tryst before catching a cab to court. The new-age coffee shop was a tad bohemian for my taste, but the only place in the neighborhood carrying the Post on a regular. I wasn't keen on speaking to the press, but was curious about the coverage.

The Bushill article was buried on the third page of the Metro Section. It started with a tribute to Detective Alberto Knox, the man Bushill was accused of killing.

A fifteen-year veteran of the MPD and father of four, Knox's funeral would be on Saturday. The rest of the article was the usual drivel and concluded with a quote from Shelly, who predicted Bushill would "never see daylight."

The Metro Section cover-story is what caught my eye: *Repo Man on a Rampage.*

Turned out, the graffiti tag from last night's news report had been only the tip of the iceberg. The punk had vandalized several buildings in Foggy Bottom and scored another tag on the Key Bridge. There was a photo montage of REPO murals throughout the city. According to the article, there was a ten-thousand-dollar reward for information leading to the capture of D.C.'s most celebrated villain.

When I arrived at court, the first indication that Ruffio's case might not dwip as easily as I'd thought was when I saw his wife waiting outside the courtroom. The second was when Ruffio walked up and wagged an angry finger in her face.

"Mr. Roman! This woman is lying!"

Barely five feet tall, Ruffio compensated with a high pompadour and platform cowboy boots. Colorful tattoos started at his neck, and as far as I could tell, went all the way down. The man looked like an inked-up, Salvadoran Elvis.

The wife was scrawny, a recovering methamphetamine addict from the backwoods of West Virginia, with stringy blond hair and *Ruffio* tattooed above her left breast.

The perfect couple.

"Take it easy, big fella." I lowered his hand and pointed him to a neutral corner.

The wife laughed at my poke at his height, loud enough for Ruffio to hear as he sulked away. Good, a sense of humor. She might be willing to work with me.

"Mrs. Melendez, what a pleasant surprise. Didn't expect to see you today."

A furious look washed over her face. I'd obviously miscalculated the sense of humor. Before she could let loose, a prosecutor stepped between us. One look told me she was a *special*, a government attorney from some bureaucratic back-water, temporarily assigned to the criminal division for trial experience. Specials have a cocky air about them.

It offsets the fear in their eyes.

"Your client can't stop," the special said. "Mrs. Melendez received another threatening voice message last night."

"That's a lie!" Ruffio shouted from across the hall. "I have a witness."

I raised a hand to Ruffio, then peered around the special at Mrs. Melendez, whose smug look told me everything I needed to know.

"I'm sure we can work this out," I said. "Why don't we agree to a continuance, so this new development can be investigated." I flipped open my calendar. "Lemme see, I'm available . . ."

"Investigated? It's a voice message, counsel. Either he left it, or he didn't. I'm giving notice right now. We're introducing it to establish his threatening pattern of behavior. See you inside."

The special disappeared into the courtroom. Mrs. Melendez stormed to the witness room. Ruffio walked up saying, "Mr. Roman! That woman is lying. I have —"

"A witness," I finished. "I heard you, Ruff. Listen, what I told you before about getting the case called early? Not such a good idea all of a sudden. Plan B. We wait a bit. Show up fashionably late. With any luck the judge will have scheduled so many trials, he'll have to continue yours to another day. Maybe next time your wife won't show."

"Ju mean come back? I don't want to come back!" He pushed through the courtroom door. "That woman is lying."

Assuming Mrs. Melendez would be a no-show, I'd arranged for Ruffio's case to be called as soon as I stepped through the door. I did favors for the courtroom clerks and could usually count on them to call a case first, or last, as the situation required.

"United States versus Ruffio Melendez!" the clerk said, smiling in my direction.

I smiled back graciously as Ruffio and I stepped up to the defense table.

Damn it to hell.

"Mr. O'Brian!" Judge Alvarez boomed. "Been a while since we've seen you in here."

"Morning, Your Honor."

"This early," Alverez qualified. "Let me guess, the government is not ready for trial?"

"Oh, the government is ready," the special said. "In fact, Mr. O'Brian and I were just discussing a recent threatening message the defendant left on his wife's phone, which the government will be introducing at trial."

Ruffio nudged me. "Lying!"

"Your Honor, this is preposterous," I said. "The defense hasn't had an opportunity to listen to this voice message and will need a continuance to investigate the matter. For all we know, the message is not threatening at all."

The special held a cell phone up and Ruffio's voice filled the courtroom. "Ju beeeetch! I gonna kill ju! Ju damn beeeetch! I gonna make ju wish ju was never . . . Ahhhhhh . . . I sorry, baaaaaaby! I love juuuuuuu!"

She finished by clicking off the cell and smiling triumphantly. Ruffio reacted by shrugging his shoulders and looking sheepishly up at the judge. Judge Alverez responded by staring at me blankly and allowing the hush which had descended on the courtroom to speak for itself.

"A pass, Your Honor," I begged. "To confer with my client?"

"Does the government have a witness who will identify the voice?"

"Oh, yes, Your Honor," the special beamed. "The

government most certainly does."

"Trial will begin in five minutes. Defense counsel may utilize that time to speak with his client."

"Thank you, Your Honor."

"You're welcome, Roman." Alverez smiled. "The least I can do."

Outside the courtroom, Ruffio started again with his innocent routine. "Mr. Roman. I have a witness!"

"Really? A witness, you say?"

Ruffio didn't know it, but a witness was the last thing he needed. With his wife eager to testify, what he needed was a plea offer and a chance at probation. If he maintained his innocence, worse yet claimed he had a witness, Judge Alverez would never allow a plea.

A defendant has to admit guilt in order to take advantage of a plea offer. When a defendant claims he has a witness who will prove his innocence, a judge can't accept a plea. The options are to continue the case until the witness can be located, or force it to trial. Since Alverez had already denied my request for a continuance, I was pretty sure which option His Honor would choose.

"It's my mother. Ju need to subpoena her. She can testify my wife is a liar. She knows! She knows she lies all the time! She can testify –"

"Tell me. Does your mother know what your voice sounds like?"

"Sure. Sure she knows."

"Then she won't be much help, will she?"

"But she can –"

"Ruffio."

"She can testify!"

The rules of professional conduct required that I explain the situation to Ruffio, that claiming he had a witness who would prove his innocence would blow any chance of a plea deal out of the water and that, with his criminal record, a plea deal was his only hope of staying out of jail. But rational discussions about the law aren't possible with anyone facing jail time. The phenomenon crosses all educational and socioeconomic lines. When faced with prison, a Harvard educated PhD will devolve to incoherent blubbering before your eyes.

"Wait here," I told him, then ducked in the witness room to speak with his wife. If I could get her consent to a probation deal, it would carry a lot of weight with the special, not to mention the judge.

"May I speak with you, Mrs. Melendez?" I asked, expecting a blast of profanity in return.

She was in the corner, crying into her subpoena. The document had been wrung so repeatedly it looked like a rag.

"Is Ruff really going to jail?" she asked.

"Doesn't look good. With you here to identify his voice, the judge will have no choice but to convict him. It's pretty simple math, I'm afraid."

"Ruffio's a jerk," she said, but with more affection than malice.

"The guy's a knucklehead, all right. He's sure in

love with you, though. Tell me, has he ever made good on any of those threats?"

"*Pthhht*," she sputtered. "He's a pussy cat."

"So what's this all about?"

"He threatened me."

"And?"

She lowered her head, but raised her eyes. "And I don't get enough child support. A hundred dollars every two weeks. We have two girls. It's not enough and he won't pay more."

Bingo.

Plan C.

"I'll be back," I told her, and stepped out to the hallway to work on the knucklehead.

"Mr. Roman! I have another witness. My cousin. I want you to –"

"You have ten seconds to answer a question," I told Ruffio, before he started in with his next wacked-out theory of defense. "And if you give the *wrong* answer you're going to jail."

"What question?"

I had his attention.

"Can you part with an extra fifty dollars out of your paycheck?"

"Que?" His face wrinkled. "She talking about child support? Again?"

"An extra fifty dollars every paycheck. You can do that, I can keep you out of jail. Clock's tickin'. What's it going to be?"

"I... I don't care, Mr. Roman," he said, defeated. "I don't care what I pay. I just can't do no jail."

The little tough guy looked like he might cry.

"Wait here."

I slipped back in the witness room to close the deal. "Mrs. Melendez, Ruffio apologizes for the calls and agrees to pay one hundred and *fifty* dollars every two weeks."

"Well . . ."

"I'm not asking that you not testify," I added, quickly. "That would be unethical. Ruffio agrees to the hundred and fifty either way. If he is convicted and sent to jail, then he'll just have to owe you the money. Of course, if you want, you can always tell the prosecutor you invoke the marital privilege. In this jurisdiction, a wife can't be forced to testify against her husband."

She looked like she was considering it.

"But that's your decision," I assured her. "And if Ruffio doesn't go to jail, then you and I can take him out back and whoop his little butt."

She grinned, a disorganized mass of crooked teeth. The special came back, saying she needed to have a conference with her witness. I stepped out, but could hear them arguing from in the hallway. Couldn't make out what was said, but I could imagine.

When Judge Alvarez recalled the case the special announced that the government was not ready for trial. It seemed they didn't have a witness who could identify Ruffio's voice after all.

"Mark it as a dwip on the record, Madam Clerk." Judge Alverez shook his head. "Case dismissed."

The special shot me a look of disdain as Ruffio left the courtroom. The woman had no appreciation for the subtleties of my profession. Out in the hall, my phone started blasting the theme to *Shaft*.

Vicky's ring.

"Ro, I'm at the Bushill crime scene. Where you at? This place is a trip."

"On my way. Guess what? Ruffio walked."

"Melendez? Guy with the recorded threats? You're jivin' me."

"Watching him head for the door right now."

Ruffio strolled down the hall with an arm slung around his wife's waist and her head dipped on his shoulder.

Sometimes, it was like doing God's work.

"Far out, Ro. Do me a solid."

"What's that?"

"Don't ever tell me how you did it."

"See you in a few."

"Bring a flashlight," Vicky ordered. "And some measuring tape."

Vicky was hell when it came to investigating. No surprise, given her sordid background. But she could also be a bossy pain in the ass.

"And, Ro?"

"Yeah?"

"Bring me a chai."

CHAPTER EIGHT

I met Vicky my first year as a Fifth Streeter. She walked straight up to me in the courthouse and thrust out a card like she was serving a subpoena. I hadn't retained an investigator yet and figured one that looked like Vicky would be a bonus.

The early days were a blast. Vicky loved digging up dirt on government witnesses, investigating the bar fights and petty thefts.

Had a real flair for the drug trade, too.

In a previous life, Vicky had been girlfriend to a mid-level cocaine supplier, Terrell Winston, who ended up convicted of attempted murder and obstruction of justice for having a government witness stabbed in the neck.

According to Vicky, she had no idea the guy was in the game until they subpoenaed her to the grand jury where they made her listen to a wiretap of Winston ordering the murder of witnesses, and of Vicky too, if it ever turned out she'd been subpoenaed by the Feds.

Vicky always maintained she thought Winston was a rap music promoter and that his posse of thugs were just his clients, played it off like she had no idea he was behind one of the city's most notorious drug crews. But she had *Gangsta Gurl* tattooed on her left shoulder and a ragged scar across her abdomen she never talked about. I was pretty sure I hadn't gotten the full story on the Terrell Winston chapter of her life.

When they started appointing us to narcotics cases, Vicky came into her own. She could speak the lingo and knew all the angles.

Take the Briscoe case.

Donovan Briscoe had been spotted by an undercover officer slinging crack on Montello Avenue. From the wad of cash he pulled out during each sale, they figured he was more than a casual player. But when they busted him, all they found was cash. No cocaine. Briscoe had been going back and forth to an abandoned car between sales. They tossed the car and found sixty-six zips of crack cocaine.

Briscoe's stash.

It looked pretty bad until Vicky rounded up three crack dealers from that very neighborhood willing to testify the stash belonged to a rival drug crew down the block and not to Briscoe. How she found them, she never said.

And I never asked.

They were convicted felons whose testimony would not have carried much weight with a jury. Nevertheless, just having them on board was enough to convince the prosecutor we could put on a defense and Briscoe was given a decent deal.

Vicky was the best.

It was a pleasant walk from the courthouse to the Starbucks on Seventh Street. Fall had been kind to Washington, the cool air a welcome break after a brutal summer. The young woman behind the counter smirked as I placed the order.

"Large coffee and a small chai latte with cinnamon sprinkles, please."

I hated ordering that frilly crap.

"Venti coffee and a tall chai?"

"Yeah."

I also hated how they made you use their screwed-up lingo.

I hopped in a cab and spent five minutes trying to explain where I was going. The abandoned rail tunnel on 14th Street was not a well-known tourist attraction. It was finally agreed I would direct. After ten minutes of *turn here – turn there*, he let me out in a parking lot by the Fourteenth Street Bridge.

A tunnel ran below an abandoned warehouse at the far end of the lot, its exterior littered with liquor bottles and refuse of every conceivable kind. Layers of graffiti camouflaged its entrance.

Three tracks led into the tunnel. The debris on the center track indicated that it had been unused for some time. The Gerstein described the tunnel as abandoned, but the rails on the outer tracks were clear and shiny.

Live rail lines.

There was a flashlight moving deep in the tunnel along the center track and I headed for it, figuring it was Vicky.

A graffiti museum would be the most accurate description. The tracks were separated by retainer walls covered in graffiti, everything from simple names to elaborate airbrushed murals. The murals were complex, as if painted by artists, not thugs. Breaks in the walls every ten yards allowed passage to the adjacent tracks and a view of the artwork within.

Makeshift shelters lined the center track, some constructed from cardboard boxes, others from material salvaged from construction sites. One had a plywood floor, vinyl siding walls, and a roof made of sheet rock. A hand-painted sign in front warned, *Private – Keep Out!*

I fell in love with the place.

The light dimmed as I stumbled along, balancing both drinks in a cardboard tray with the flashlight ahead as my beacon. I couldn't see her face in the darkness, but could tell it was Vicky by the silhouette of her hippy afro, bellbottom jeans, and leather jacket with its collar flipped, real cool.

"Groovy crime scene," I said, staring at her getup.

"You're a dork, Ro. I see you forgot the flashlight. You remember the measuring tape?"

I handed her the chai latte.

"Glad to see you have your priorities straight." She took a sip. "And yeah, this place is awesome. Check it out."

She swung her flashlight in a circle. The makeshift shelters from the tunnel's entrance had given way to crusty mattresses. Empty bottles lay scattered on the ground, lodged between the rotted trestles.

Yet even here, in the darkness of the tunnel's center, the walls were covered with graffiti. Mostly they were unintelligible names scribbled in fields of colorful design, but some I could make out like *EXIST*, *SPACE*, *WARP* and *IRAN*. The ceiling above had been violated as well, years ago from the look of it, with the faded name *COOL DISCO DAN*.

A few of the images were more sophisticated. In one mural, a business man walked a poodle down a dark street toward a gang of monstrous thugs who were crouched in the shadows, waiting to spring. The title read, *JUSTICE FOR YUPPIE SCUM*.

The flashlight settled on the crime scene.

"That's it right there," she said. "C'mon."

A section of the abandoned track had been roped off with yellow crime-scene tape, indicating the area searched for evidence. In the center was a mattress. Scattered around it were crime scene markers, numbered placards indicating where each piece of evidence had been found. Half the markers still stood upright. The rest had been knocked over by rats, or by the homeless who lived in the tunnel.

Vicki positioned her flashlight on the retainer wall to illuminate the mattress. The thing was foul, a Jackson Pollack of stains made from God knows what, including a brownish patch that looked like dried blood.

"Bushill was obviously shot here." She pointed to evidence marker seven, atop the mattress.

"Numbers one through six?" She indicated the markers next to the mattress. "Probably the clothing the paramedics cut off Bushill while treating his wound."

"Eight and nine?" She pointed to the corresponding markers on the ground. "My guess is, eight is the gun found next to Bushill and nine is the cartridge casing that ejected when Bushill, I mean *whoever . . .*" she said, rolling her eyes, ". . . shot that cop."

"That's assuming the gun was a semi-auto," I said. "A revolver wouldn't have ejected a casing."

"Guess we'll know for sure when you get us the crime scene evidence report," Vicky said, perturbed at being thrown off stride. "Any luck shaking discovery out of Shelly?"

"You know the rule."

"Right on. So until we know different, we'll go with my theory. Which brings us to the corpus delicti." She led the way down the tracks toward an evidence marker sitting amid a field of medical debris.

The Hollywood depiction of a murder scene with a body chalked on the ground could not be further from reality. The primary way a crime scene is documented is with photography and evidence markers. A list of the evidence corresponding to each marker is contained in the Crime Scene Evidence Report.

But as Vicky pointed out, that's discovery.

"Roman O'Brian?" Vicky swept her arm at tag number ten. "Meet Detective Alberto Knox."

"Did you know him?"

"Nah," she whispered.

We stared at the spot where Detective Knox had drawn his last breath. There was the sound of dripping water and the hum of a transformer down the tracks.

"That leaves the casing left by the government's star witness," she said. "The detective who shot Bushill. C'mon."

We stumbled a few feet to another marker, number eleven.

"His name is Tomlinson," I announced.

Vicky looked at me, impressed. "White guy? Bald? Kind of looks like Mr. Clean?"

"You've had the pleasure?"

"Investigated a distribution case for Jacobson last month. Tomlinson was the lead detective. It dwipped."

"Dwipped?"

Vicky raised an eyebrow. "Dismissed on the day of trial."

I raised an eyebrow myself. Misdemeanors like Ruffio's little domestic violence case dwipped all the time, but it was unusual the government wasn't ready to roll in a felony. When it did happen, it was typically because a crucial piece of evidence couldn't be found.

Money taken from drug dealers, for example, had a habit of disappearing from the evidence locker before trial.

Occasionally, a felony case would dwip because a police officer witness was under investigation. Internal Affairs investigations of police witnesses have to be revealed to the defense. Every once in a great while, the government would allow a felony to be dismissed rather than compromise the investigation of a cop by revealing it to defense counsel.

There was virtually no chance it would happen in a murder case, but if Tomlinson was under investigation, we could use that fact to impeach his credibility at trial. Better yet, as a bargaining chip during plea negotiations.

"Could be Mr. Clean isn't so clean," I suggested.

"Dork, Ro."

"Snoop around the Narcotics Branch," I told her. "See what you can find out."

"I'm on it."

I pointed to marker eleven at Vicky's feet. "This is where Tomlinson was standing when he shot Bushill?"

"Not quite." She tugged on her collar, heightening the funky, bad-ass detective look she worked so hard to project. "This is where his cartridge casing landed."

"So where *was* Tomlinson standing?"

"Can't figure it out?" She tossed me a look. "MPD standard issue is a Glock nine millimeter, correct?"

"I guess."

"Which, assuming Tomlinson stuck to his training

and held his weapon straight up-and-down, would have ejected its cartridge casing approximately nine feet."

"Okay."

"Nine feet to the right, to be specific." She paced off nine baby steps, which had her through the opening in the retainer wall and on the next track. "That places Tomlinson just about here when he got off that shot at Bushill. Notice anything strange?"

I waited, figuring she would tell me soon enough.

"What's at tag number seven?" she asked.

"Uh . . . Bushill's mattress."

"Brilliant, Ro. Go stand there."

I fumbled across the tracks to Bushill's mattress and when I turned back around it hit me right away. Vicky was hidden from view behind the retainer wall. There was no way Tomlinson could have shot Bushill from where Vicky was standing.

"Sweet!"

"Of course," Vicky said, reappearing through the opening and walking my way. "That's assuming Tomlinson held the weapon straight, assuming the evidence tag hasn't been moved, and assuming Bushill was exactly where his mattress is now when he was shot."

"Details," I scoffed. "Either way, we can use the apparent discrepancy to ramp up the pressure on Shelly. If she thinks there's a chance we can convince a jury Tomlinson's story doesn't make sense, she'll shave five years off the plea offer. The bigger the pressure, the better the –"

"Right, Ro. There's more."

She retrieved the flashlight and beckoned me to follow. We ducked under the police tape and walked thirty yards up the tracks, away from the crime scene. She stopped at a final evidence marker.

Number twelve.

"What the hell is that?" I asked.

"Was hoping you could tell me."

"Got me," I confessed. "I like it, though, whatever it is. Crime Scene officers typically only search the area roped off by the tape. If they found evidence this far out, we can argue the search area should have been expanded, that the investigation was sloppy and missed important evidence. Sure it's from this investigation?"

"One through eleven back there and twelve here? Damn right it's from this investigation. You've got to get that evidence report."

"What I've got to get, is Bushill's permission to negotiate. The discrepancy about where Tomlinson was standing is huge. And now there's an evidence marker outside the crime scene? None of it fits with the facts in the Gerstein. Good work, Vick. Just the sort of discrepancies I was hoping to . . . What?"

Vicky turned the flashlight on herself so I could see the look of exaggerated disappointment on her face. "Seriously, Ro. You're talkin' plea? Already?"

"Dig it." I ticked off the reasons with my fingers. "One, Crime Scene found a handgun at Bushill's side.

Two, Tomlinson is going to testify that Bushill shot Knox in a drunken rage and that Tomlinson returned fire. But three, my superfly investigator uncovered an apparent discrepancy in Tomlinson's story. Judging from where his casing landed, it's doubtful Tomlinson could have shot Bushill from where would have been standing. And four, evidence marker twelve is hell and gone from the crime scene. Which, five, gives us a few cards to play despite the fact that we have no defense, no witnesses, and only a day or two before Firearms comes back with a match on the gun and blows the whole deal out of the water. So, yeah. I'm talkin' plea."

"You're not even going to check out his story?"

"Whose story?"

"Your client's!"

I laughed. "You know what his story is?"

Vicky cocked a hand on her hip.

"A ninja did it," I said, matter-of-factly.

"That's suspect, Ro."

"Ya think? Well, to be accurate, he doesn't blame the ninja. Not directly. What he says is, he doesn't know who shot him, or who shot Knox. He has no idea what happened, except that . . ." I crooked my elbows and waved my arms, doing Bushill. "When it was all over, a ninja stepped out of the shadows and tied a rope around his leg to stop the bleeding." I let my arms down with a flap. "The guy is as loony as . . . What?"

The light was on her face again, this time twisted into a smug grin.

"You mean like this rope?" She lifted a piece of yellow nylon rope from inside her jacket. It had been tied into a loop about the size of a man's thigh, but the loop had been cut and it was crusted with dried blood. "Found it lying next to the mattress. Didn't know what to make of it, until you told me that ninja story."

"I'll be damned."

"So I've always said."

"Whatever. The paramedics probably used it to –"

"An unsanitary piece of rope like this? Get real. They probably cut it off him. According to the Gerstein, Tomlinson had to exit the tunnel to call for assistance because he couldn't get a signal. Whoever tied this rope to Bushill's leg must have done so in between when Tomlinson split and the medical team arrived. Which means that we have –"

"Noooo," I said, trying to stop her from saying it.

"A witness," she finished. "And you can't even think of pleading out this case just yet."

It was like Ruffio all over again. If Bushill couldn't remember what happened, and there was a witness who might prove his innocence, there was no way Judge Bearmond would sign off on a plea.

I composed myself. "We don't have a witness. What we have is a rope. Which was tied to our client's leg by who?" I let Vicky ponder the question before answering it myself. "A ninja. Thank you."

"Roman –"

"All I'm saying is ... Dammit. What?"

She was serving me the intolerant look she reserved for when she knew something I didn't. "I know who tied the rope to his leg. The witness. The ninja. C'mon."

She led the way across the last set of tracks to the tunnel wall. It was not totally dark on that side. Strands of daylight leaked in through fissures in the concrete and cast the tracks in a soft eerie glow. I had changed my mind about the place, though. It was starting to give me the creeps.

"Take a close look at that rope." She held it to a thin stream of daylight. "What do you see?"

"What am I looking for?"

"Right here," she said, pointing.

"All right, green paint."

"Not green, teal. Metallic teal." She turned it over so I could see its metallic sheen.

"Okay, metallic teal. So what?"

"So whoever tied that rope to Bushill's leg had metallic teal paint all over their hands."

"Got it. We scour the city for a teal ninja. Brilliant, Vick. Unadulterated genius."

"When you get to the jail, tell your client we have a lead on a witness."

"What witness?" I said, annoyed with the game.

She shined her flashlight on a graffiti mural next to us on the wall. The mural was unfinished, but the name complete. In metallic teal paint it said:

REPO.

CHAPTER NINE

In colonial times, jails were not used as punishment, merely to house defendants awaiting trial. Convicted criminals were fined, sentenced to the stocks, beaten or killed.

It was the Quakers who came up with the idea of the penitentiary. The thinking was that corporal punishment did little to reform the wayward, but that forcing them to spend time in quiet solitude, pondering the error of their ways, would offer the promise of rehabilitation.

Not one of those Quaker bastards had envisioned the modern American penal system.

The cabbie let me out by a sign that read, *Department of Corrections, Central Detention Facility.*

D.C. Jail.

I walked past the entrance, a concrete facade with narrow inset windows which gave the place the look of a community college, then headed toward the lawyers' entrance in the rear of the complex where I was greeted by more ominous architecture. Barbed wire and a guard tower straight from a maximum security prison. The jail was the tallest building in that depressed quadrant of the city and towered above it like a monolithic warning.

I glanced at the time on my cell. I didn't wear a watch, and since cell phones had to be turned over at the check-in station, it would be difficult to gauge the passage of time once inside. There were no windows or clocks in any of the holding cells or visiting halls. In jail, time isn't measured by the arc of the sun, but by the Count, the inventory of inmates performed every eight hours.

"Empty your pockets! Walk through the metal detector. Spread your arms and legs!"

She was a bruiser in a plus-size uniform. I assumed the position and braced for a pat-down. She mauled my shoulders, barking questions as she worked her way south.

"Weapons?"

"No."

"Drugs?"

"No."

"Cell phone?"

"Yeah," I said, handing it over.

As if on cue, the phone sounded an urgent *Beeeep! Beeeep! Beeeep!* like the all-hands-on-deck alarm of an aircraft carrier.

Mom's ring.

"Your wife?" she asked.

"Not currently attached. Why? You lookin'?"

"Pick up the phone at the end of your visit," she

snapped, then turned toward the next victim in line. "Empty your pockets! Walk through the metal detector! Spread your arms and legs!"

I put in a request for a legal visit with Bushill and was escorted to the second-floor visiting hall. The large space was filled with tightly packed seats and a panel of stalls, each with a window and telephone. A guard sat in a security bubble in the center of the room directing traffic. Like the rest of the jail, the visiting hall was coated in thick layers of dingy white paint which put a gloppy rounded surface on every bar and bolt in the place.

And it was mobbed.

Some of my colleagues scheduled visits in the late hours when the throngs of visiting family members and baby's mamas subsided. I tried late-night visits a few times. Just couldn't do it. The place was depressing enough in the daytime.

Visitors had only fifteen minutes to speak with inmates through two-inch plexiglass. Fifteen minutes, no exceptions. The sign posted on the security bubble warned of the one thing visitors absolutely could not do. *Do NOT linger when your time is up or you will be BARRED.* To be fair, the sign also contained a trove of advice as to what visitors *could* do:

Control your children or you will be BARRED.

Refrain from touching the glass or you will be BARRED.

*Follow ALL orders of the corrections officers or
you will be . . .*

Inmates lived for visitation. They solicited visits
from family and friends, sometimes from people they
hardly associated with on the streets, and pressured
their visitors to obey the rules to avoid being barred. I
sat with young women and gaggles of kids, crowded
into that stuffy room for hours, who behaved as if they
were at Sunday service.

Lawyers didn't have to use the phone banks and
met clients face-to-face in plexiglass enclosed rooms. A
lieutenant led me to an interview room where Bushill
waited at a table in an orange jumpsuit, his leg encased
in a rickety brace, a testament to the top-notch medical
treatment he was surely receiving at the D.C. Jail.

Go Quakers.

Vicky wanted me to inform Bushill about the
possibility that Repo was a witness, but as far as I was
concerned a paint-can wielding punk who would likely
confirm Bushill's guilt didn't change the game plan.
Negotiate a plea.

Vicky was right about one thing, though. It was my
job to tell him about Repo. The problem was, mystery
witnesses created the type of false hope to which clients
clung like life boats. And as harsh as it sounds, it was
also my job to take leaky boats of false hope and smash
them against the rocks of reality.

"Good evening, Mr. Bushill. Remember me?"

"Frenchie."

His jumpsuit was an improvement over the ratty hospital gown, his hair had been washed and the deadpan stare was gone from his eyes. He looked like a completely different man.

I waited until the lieutenant stepped out, then winked at Bushill and said "Officer!" into the intercom on the wall. No reaction from the security bubble. The guard wasn't listening. The intercom was supposed to be for the lawyer's protection, but I'd heard rumors about guards eavesdropping.

It paid to be careful.

Bushill cleared his throat. "I wish to apologize for my behavior yesterday. I was a little out of it, but I'm feeling much better."

"No need to apologize, Mr. Bushill." I took the seat across from him. "I see they've got you out of that wheelchair. How's the leg?"

"Fine, thank you."

"Getting your meds? If not, I can put in a medical alert so that –"

"If it's not too much trouble, can you tell me when I'm getting out?"

I tried not to sigh too conspicuously. The question was always top of the list. The trick was to give a quick answer, just not to the question.

"Your preliminary hearing is Friday," I told him.

"So I'm getting out Friday?"

"That's not what I meant."

Sometimes the strategy didn't work.

"Hmmmm . . ." He stroked his chin and eyed me suspiciously.

I had to lay down the facts as bluntly as possible, but wanted to keep the warm and fuzzy feeling going, which meant I had to spend some time convincing him I was on his side before bringing down the hammer of reality.

"Listen here." I tapped a finger on the table. "At the hearing this Friday? I'm going to ask the judge to rule that the government doesn't have enough evidence against you."

"I see."

"Demand that you be released."

"Excellent."

"That your case be dismissed. Sound good?"

"Mm hmm."

"I have to say, though, a dismissal isn't likely."

"Yes, of course . . . Huh?"

"It's going to be a lot like yesterday, except the government has to put on a witness. They have to establish what we call probable cause, which is not a high standard. Nothing like proof beyond a reasonable doubt. All they have to do is flash a few cards, give the judge a reason to believe you committed the crime. If they can't, the case will be dismissed and you'll go free. If they can, the case will go forward."

"When will I get my trial?"

"About a year from now. And with a cop witness and all the physical evidence, it's a safe bet the judge will find probable cause and hold you in jail until then."

Bushill's look of complete astonishment melted into a sly smile. "Right . . ." He struggled to the intercom and winked. "Sounds like they really got the goods on me, eh, Frenchie?"

"I'm afraid it's going to be tough. On the other hand, we may be on to something. My assistant and I did a little investigating and it appears there are a few holes in the government's case. Holes we can exploit to get you a good deal."

"By all means," Bushill said into the intercom. "Tell them I'm willing to cooperate completely."

His paranoid behavior was a little off-putting, but I was getting used to it.

"In fact," I told him. "I'm fairly confident we can get the prosecutor to knock significant time off the standard plea."

Bushill gave me a thumbs up, then leaned in so close I could smell the tuna he'd had for dinner. "You find the ninja?"

Damn it to hell.

"Not exactly. About that –"

"A plea offer!" Bushill announced, springing back to the intercom. "How magnanimous of them. We must consider it, of course."

"Mr. Bushill . . ."

"We'll have to come clean, I suppose. Tell them everything we know. Full disclosure!"

I beckoned him from the intercom and he leaned

my way. "We found some evidence linked to the person who tied the rope to your leg."

"The ninja?"

"Right. But we don't have much to go on. It seems he's a graffiti artist the police have been looking for since –"

"Gotcha," Bushill said, with a finger to pursed lips. He leaned toward the intercom again. "You go right ahead and tell them I'll cooperate unfailingly. Oh, the stories I could tell about that tunnel. The crimes. The malfeasance!"

"Alex, no kidding. It's time to consider a plea."

Bushill's head whipped my way. "I'm not pleading guilty to a crime that I didn't . . . I didn't . . . You're my lawyer. You're supposed to find *out* what I did!" He cringed at the volume of his voice and looked at the intercom.

"Don't think that thing is working," I told him.

"Funny. Just thinking the same about you!"

"Back to the witness."

"The ninja."

"Right. All we have is a nickname on a wall. And since you don't remember what happened, and since the government has all this evidence against you, I'm pretty sure we don't want to find him. We'd be looking for a government witness."

"You have to find him."

"We discovered some real inconsistencies. The cop who shot you? He got mixed up about where he was standing."

"You *have* to find him."

"There's an evidence tag in the wrong place, at least thirty yards outside the crime scene. We can use those things to negotiate for –"

"No!" He banged a fist on the table. In an instant his crazed look from the day before was back. He snatched me by the lapels and slammed me against the plexiglass. I couldn't help wonder if those wild eyes were the last thing Detective Knox had seen before he died.

"You're my lawyer!" he screamed, backhanding me. "I need to know what the ninja knows. Find out the truth!"

"The truth?" I spit out the word with a wad of blood that dribbled down my shirt. "That's not really what I do."

"Stand down!" The lieutenant burst in the room. He wrestled Bushill onto the table, twisted his arm behind his back, then unclipped his radio and spoke into it matter-of-factly, "Code seventeen. Conference room five. North Two." He turned to me. "You all right?"

"Yeah," I said, dabbing blood from my lip with my sleeve. "Don't hurt him."

"Right," he laughed. "You're welcome, counselor. This interview is over. Go sign out."

Bushill's anger converted to despair. "Please," he mumbled, one cheek pressed against the table. "I need to know. Promise me you'll find him."

I signaled to the guard in the security bubble to open the gate. It was late, my crazy client wanted the truth, and it was about time for my evening appointment with Bart, which I never missed.

"I promise," I said, as the lieutenant led Bushill away.

Clients were always asking me to promise. To get them out of jail. To get them off the hook. Whatever. And I never hesitated to parrot back the two words they needed to hear.

I promise.

CHAPTER TEN

It was dark by the time I hit the street. There was no way I was going to score a cab in that part of Southeast, so I hoofed it to the Metro, caught a train to Woodley Park and walked over the Duke Ellington Bridge toward Adams Morgan.

The Ellington Bridge is an early twentieth-century, limestone monstrosity spanning the park separating Adams Morgan from the more civilized neighborhoods in Northwest. The Duke may have gotten his start in the jazz houses that used to line U Street, but these days the strip on Eighteenth was the heart of the neighborhood's live music scene.

At Eighteenth and Columbia I passed Asylum, one of the neighborhood's rock-n-roll bars. The motorcycle crowd was just showing up, revving engines and getting dirty glares from patrons at Bukom where a reggae band and a dreadlocked crowd were going full tilt.

A guitar riff floated up from Madam's Organ, a blues bar with a flair for tacky. Madam's was an assault on the eyes. A portrait of an aging madam was painted across the building like an advertisement for a Cajun bordello. Written in red across the cleavage of the madam's sagging breasts were the bar's name and its infamous slogan: *Where the Beautiful People Go to Get UGLY.*

The portrait had been the subject of a decades-long lawsuit. The city claimed it was a commercial billboard subject to tax as an advertisement. The bar claimed the droopy-breasted madam was exempt as fine art.

In the neighborhood, opinions varied.

Music always flowed out of the joint and spilled into the street. On Saturdays it was rhythm and blues. Tuesdays were bluegrass. It was Wednesday, tour band night, which according to the banner above the door, meant the Johnny Hammond Band.

And what would be so terribly wrong, I thought, with a little nightcap?

"Yo Ro!" Bart yelled from behind the bar. Bart was skinny, six feet tall, with long dreads swooping down his back like a cape. Although he didn't look it, Bart was the best drink-slinger on the strip. Belgium Bombs. Chattanooga Chasers. Rare drinks from any corner of the globe.

You just couldn't stump the guy.

I helped him with legal trouble a few years back which ended in probation for him and half-priced drinks for me.

"Whadaya say, Bart?" I pointed to his Madam's Tee. "New uniforms?"

"Yeah, mon." He spun so I could see the Madam portrait on the back of his shirt. *Tip, You Bastards* was printed above it. "Ya here ta meet Vick?"

"Vicky's here?"

I scanned the place. The first floor was a carcass menagerie. Buffalo heads and an assortment of stuffed mammals adorned the walls between oil paintings of nineteenth-century prostitutes. A neon sign above the bar flashed, *Big Daddy's Love Lounge and Pick-Up Joint.*

Two stools down sat a woman in her mid-thirties with dirty-blond hair and a dynamite body stuffed into a tight party dress, wearing the overdone makeup and desperate look of a seasoned barfly. From her chipped nails I figured her for an office drone.

I watched as a young guy walked over and treated her to his best line. "Can I buy a lovely lady a drink?" She soaked him for an apple martini, then pretended to answer her cell, dropping her purse on the empty stool between us when he made his move to sit down.

"Nicely played," I said, as the kid wandered off with his tail between his legs.

She scowled, and started on her martini.

Bart smacked a draft Yuengling down on the bar and pointed toward the stage. "Over there, Ro. You know how it is. If Johnny be here, so do Vick."

Vicky was at a table by the stage with a tie-dyed bandanna strapped across her fro, wearing tattered blue jeans and a denim jacket old enough to have been to

Woodstock. She was nursing her usual tonic water with a lemon twist. I had never seen Vicky take a drink, the only thing I didn't like about her.

Johnny Hammond was onstage preparing for his big finish, introducing the band members and reminding everyone to take care of their wait staff and bartenders. I was pretty sure Vicky had a thing for Johnny. She played it off like the relationship was casual since Johnny came through town only a few times a month, but she never missed a performance.

Johnny carried himself with a charm developed during a decade playing blues houses like Madam's. With his dark skin, black sunglasses and pinstripe suit, he cut the figure of a corporate executive of rhythm and blues. Women liked Johnny. I wanted to tell Vicky the guy probably had girls up and down the coast, but Vicky wasn't big on taking advice.

I folded a napkin into an airplane and launched it.

"Vick!"

She plucked the projectile from her hair and walked to the empty stool between me and the barfly, glowering with a hand on her hip until the barfly lifted her purse and dropped it on the bar. Vicky took a seat and brushed the barfly's purse aside as if it were filled with toxic waste.

"Damn, Ro. You can't gimme one night off?"

"Not stalking you, kiddo. Just stopped for a beer. You and Johnny got a hot date?"

"It's not a date."

"Yeah? In that case, why don't we blow this joint. Catch a movie. Whadaya say?"

"Get off my ass." She turned toward the stage, bopping her head to the blues riff Johnny was laying down, a funked up version of a Marvin Gaye number I'd heard him play a hundred times. "Call it."

"Marvin Gaye," I said without thinking. "Make Me Wanna Holler."

Vicky looked begrudgingly impressed. "It's Gaye alright, but *Inner City Blues*, final track from *What's Going On*. You're slippin', Ro."

"I spoke with Bushill."

"I see." She snatched a napkin off the bar and handed it to me. "Looks like it went well. Let me guess, he wants a new lawyer?"

I dabbed a spot of blood from my lip. "I wish."

"You tell him about the witness?"

"Yep."

"What'd he say?"

"Said he wants us to find out the truth."

She tossed back her head and let out a laugh that had the barfly scowling. "That's a new one."

"Crazy, eh?"

"No. It's brilliant. The truth. A completely novel legal strategy. Why didn't we ever think of that?"

I drained my beer and jiggled it in the air. Bart topped another and slid it my way.

I was in the middle of a healthy swig when Vicky announced, "Guess that means we have to find this

Repo guy."

I almost spit out the beer. "Why? So he can testify Bushill shot a cop?"

"What if Shelly gets to him first?"

"Fat chance. The guy's off the grid. The rope is the only thing linking him to the crime scene and the cops left it behind like trash. They don't know he exists."

"Unless he comes in on his own."

"Right. Like this street rat, probably from a project in Southeast, is going to just –"

"How do *you* know where he's from?"

"He does graffiti. I mean, I just assumed . . ."

"That he's a black kid from the projects?" Vicky shot me a look, then let it slide. "I just think we should talk to him. Whoever he is. What's the matter? You got a problem with the truth?"

I pointed to her glass. "You sure that's just tonic water?"

Vicky rolled her eyes.

"And yeah," I added. "Got a big problem with the truth when it isn't good for my client. Besides, how are we supposed to find him? Put up wanted posters? Knock on doors asking for Repo Man?"

"Way I see it, as long as our client is on a quest for the truth, we don't have a choice." She pulled a sheet of paper from her jacket and slapped it on the bar. "Meet me there tomorrow night. Six o'clock. We'll take a stab at turning you into a real lawyer again."

I lifted the paper off the bar. It was a printout from

a website for Wuma, a fancy art gallery in Georgetown. According to the web page, the curator was a man named Adrian Wallace and the gallery specialized in *Urban Wall Art and Hip-Hop Design.*

"What's this?"

"Graffiti gallery."

"You're kidding."

"Did a little research today." She rubbed her hands together. "Seems that some of these graffiti types have artistic aspirations. There's even a niche market for the stuff. Ever hear of Basquiat?"

"Yeah, the Haitian kid. Started out as a homeless graffiti artist. Ended up making millions selling his crap to rich idiots."

"Not quite," Vicky corrected. "He ended up dead of a heroin overdose on his way to making millions. According to the Wuma website, Adrian Wallace is the patron saint of graffiti artists in the D.C. area. Gives them shows. Sells their art. I called the gallery and Wallace agreed to meet us. Figure it's as good a place to start as any."

Georgetown, with its trendy shops and restaurants was hardly my idea of a thrilling night out, but Vicky seemed pumped.

"Fine," I sighed. "I'll be there. Good work, kiddo."

"Thanks. And so you know, I absolutely live for compliments like that. In fact, sometimes . . ." She slung an arm on my shoulder. "I lie in bed at night thinking, what can I do to make Roman happy?"

"All right, Vick."

"Then it dawns on me. Find him a woman. It's been some time since he's had a decent –"

"You done?"

No one could lay it on like Vicky.

"Roman!" Johnny stepped off the stage and slapped a hand on my back. "Not tryin' to mack on my girl, are ya?"

"Might be, Johnny. You know, Vicky and I are a couple during the day."

"Nighttime, Ro. She's all mine."

Johnny switched his affections to Vicky, wrapping both arms around her and kissing her neck. Her face lit up and she turned the other way.

You couldn't fake a smile like that. Kid had it bad.

Johnny put on a serious look. "Listen, Ro. I got a friend who plays the Circuit. Picked up a drunk driving beef last time he was in town. Think you can do something for him?"

"Sure thing, Johnny. Just tell him to call my *girl* here. She'll set something up."

I wanted to get Vicky back for that "find me a woman" crack. Dangerous messing with her, though. In the end, she'd have the last word.

"Go easy," Vicky scolded, tapping my beer. "You have the Bradley trial tomorrow. Ready, Johnny?"

"You two kids have fun," I called out, as Johnny led her toward the door.

Bart waved goodbye to Vicky, then tossed me a

glance.

"Hit me again, Bartholomew," I told him.

He slapped down another Yuengling.

"So what's the deal with Johnny?" I asked. "He make a living doing places like this?"

Bart raised an eyebrow. "You worried about Vick? She a big girl, mon."

"Curious, is all."

"Johnny just play da Circuit to get his name out there. His real cheesecake is corporate gigs, law firm parties downtown. Stuff like dat."

Made sense. There was good money to be made doing blues shows for uptight professionals, for people who fooled themselves into thinking they patronized the arts, but would never set foot in a place like Madam's, or in a neighborhood like Adams Morgan.

"Fancy parties at downtown law firms, eh?" I smiled. "Guess you'd never get that crowd in a swanky joint like this."

"Yeah, but da Morgan is changing, mon. Won't be dat long before those bastards own dis neighborhood. Bunch of pasty-faced posers. No offense to you, Ro."

"No worries."

It was my fault. If you wound Bart up on the subject of yuppies, you got what you deserved.

"Use ta be nothin' but jazz and blues bars up-n-down da strip. Now we got Starbucks, yoga studios and tanning salons. Tanning salons, Ro, in da Morgan! Da place is startin' ta look like Georgetown."

Washington has always had white enclaves like Georgetown, but until the early '90s its population had been eighty percent black. Since then, upper-middle-class whites had trickled back into the city and were disturbing the order of things. Changing the landscape. Like everywhere else, trendy coffee shops and upscale boutiques were sprouting up in Adams Morgan.

"Won't be dat long," Bart called out as he headed to lubricate another patron. "Georgetown, Ro!"

An alert went off and I fished out my phone, assuming it was Vicky texting me her sarcastic last word. There were two messages, one from my ex-wife and one from Mom.

I glanced down the bar and weighed my options. Spend the next hour taking a run at a surly barfly, having a depressing walk down memory lane with my ex-wife, or listening to Mom drone on about Dad losing his focus. I opted for none-of-the-above and hunkered down another beer.

Repo.

We had squat to go on. No name. No address. No description, other than a ninja. All we knew was his graffiti name and that the MPD had been looking for him for almost a year. What chance did we have to find him?

More important, why would we want to?

I made a pit stop on my way out. The restrooms at Madam's had some of the best bathroom graffiti in the city. Drawn on the wall above the urinal was a beautiful bombshell leaning against a bar next to a geeky-looking fellow with horn-rimmed glasses who was trying to pick her up. The bombshell was ignoring him. The caption read, *What matters to God is that you TRY.*

I straightened my tie, headed back to the bar and hopped on the stool next to the barfly.

"Right on time," she said, holding up her empty.

"Apple martini, Bart" I said. "And another beer."

I loved that neighborhood.

CHAPTER ELEVEN

Thursday morning and I was out of Café Bustelo, the thick South American espresso which had gotten me through law school. There was a tea bag behind a pack of ramen noodles in the cupboard. I dropped it in a mug, added a shot of hot water from the sink, and stirred in an aspirin. A poor substitute for the Café Bustelo, but it took the edge off.

I sat on the bed watching the outline of the barfly's breasts rising and falling under the sheets and for the first time noticed the tattoo on her shoulder, a heart with a circle and a line through it. Her makeup had smeared, but even so, she was far from the worst-looking woman I'd woken up with since Brenda and I split.

My cell blasted *Shaft*. I whisked it up and took it to the bathroom, so as to not wake sleeping beauty. I had the Bradley trial that morning and was supposed to rendezvous with Vicky in Georgetown later that night. Playing let's-get-to-know-each-other with a groggy barfly wasn't on the schedule.

The plan was to leave a note saying she looked so peaceful I just couldn't bring myself to disturb her. I considered suggesting she leave her phone number for appearance sake, but was fairly confident she wouldn't, and absolutely certain I'd toss it.

"Hello?"

"Ro . . . Damn, you sound rough. Just waking up? Don't you have the Bradley –"

"Helloooo . . ." the barfly called from the other room. "The fuck?"

I cupped a hand around the phone. "I'm a little tied up right now, Vick."

"Who's that?" Vicky laughed. "You and your wife get back to –"

"No."

"The geeky chick from the seminar last week?"

"I'll call *you* back."

"Then it's gotta be the martini ho from Madam's."

"Helloooo . . ." said the barfly, standing at the bathroom door, wrapped in my sheet. "Got coffee in this rat hole?"

"Be with you in a second, sugar." I swung the door shut.

"Sugar?" Vicky cackled. "You're a class act, Ro."

"Gotta go."

"Wait. Two things. First, you squeeze the crime scene evidence report out of Shelly yet?"

"Workin' on it."

"I need that evidence report."

"Number two?"

"Did you tell some newbie named Boston Stewart that he's co-counsel? On Bushill?"

"Why?"

"Youngblood called this morning and demanded to know how my investigation is going. He wants to come with us to Georgetown tonight."

I could hear the barfly rummaging through the cupboards.

"Boston was assigned to me," I said, "under the Attorney Buddy Program."

"Attorney Buddy what?"

"I may have insinuated that he could, you know, play a role. The kid's a legal wiz. Could be helpful."

"I don't work with newbies, Ro."

A knock sounded at the front door.

"Hang on." I walked past the kitchenette where the barfly was staring into the fridge with disgust.

"Don't eat anything you find in there," I told her, as I yanked open the door.

"Darling!" my mother said, standing next to Dad in the hallway. "You didn't get my messages? Your father and I are here for a visit!"

Damn it to hell.

"Far out, Ro!" Vicky screeched. "Please tell me that's your mom. Oh my God, I wish I was there!"

"Is that Victoria?" Mom reached for the phone. "Hello Victoria!"

"Hello, Mrs. O'Brian . . ."

I hung up on Vicky.

"Ma! Thought you guys were in Fort Lauderdale."

Mom was sixty-nine, short and thin, with a thick mane of brown hair dyed to match her eyes. Her magenta lipstick, I noticed with alarm, was the same shade as the barfly's.

Dad weighed in at two-eighty-five, had the crewcut he'd been sporting since his Marine Corps days, and was wearing a Hawaiian shirt, open in front to expose his magnificent potbelly.

Were they not my parents, they would have struck me as a darling pair.

"Don't even get me started about Fort Lauderdale," Mom said. "Hank, were you born in a barn?"

Dad kicked the door shut and dropped his luggage. "Good to see you, son. We really appreciate this."

"It's just for a few days," Mom added, giving me a hug. "Uncle Sal has us lined up for a two-week stay at a lovely time-share in Massanutten. Don't you think that place looks wonderful, Hank?"

"Gorgeous," announced Dad. "Cathedral ceilings and a mountain view. You're gonna love it, sugar."

"But someone got his dates mixed up and we don't check in until Monday."

"That was Sal, sugar."

"Um-hum. So we figured, why not drop in on our favorite munchkin? Oh! It's so good to see you!" Mom put a hand on my cheek. "Are you okay? Your lip is swollen."

"It's okay, Mom. Just a little –"

"Hello there!" Mom made a beeline for the barfly, her arms spread. "This is Hank and I'm Amelda." She gave the barfly a squeeze, then held her by the arms and announced, "I'm Roman's mother!"

The barfly stared back, stunned.

"Well," said Dad. "Aren't you going to introduce us, son?"

"Ummmm . . ." I tossed a look of apology at the barfly. "This is . . ."

"Brenda," said the barfly, with a sham smile. "Glad to finally meet you. Roman has told me so much about you."

Mom said, "Brenda? Strange coincidence. Same as Roman's wife."

"Ex-wife, Ma."

"Yes, of course. No matter. We're thrilled you're with our Roman. The poor dear has had such a rough time, what with the divor –"

"Suuuuugar," Dad interjected.

"I'm just saying," Mom finished.

"Mom," Brenda said, looking like a hung-over version of the Statue of Liberty, still wrapped in the sheet with her hair frizzed and a mug held in the air. "I've been searching for months, but can't seem to find where that darn son of yours hides his coffee."

"Tsk, tsk. Shame on you, Roman." Mom took the mug. "You get yourself situated, dear. I'll fix a nice cup for you."

"Thanks, Mom, and you too Dad. It's a pleasure to finally meet you."

The barfly, Brenda apparently, shot me a nasty look as she gathered her clothes and headed for the bathroom, dragging the sheet behind her.

"She's lovely, darling," Mom whispered. "But where did you find –"

"Suuuugar..." Dad said. "She's swell, Roman."

"On second thought," I said, throwing on a fresh shirt and yesterday's rumpled suit. "I think I'll take Brenda out for that coffee. Meeting you guys like this? Probably a big shock for her."

"Anything you say, Munchkin."

"Sure," added Dad. "It'll give us a chance to get unpacked."

The toilet flushed and Brenda emerged in her party dress, her hair tied back in a ponytail. She flashed another sham smile as she struggled to balance while putting on her pumps.

"You know what, sweetheart?" I said. "Why don't we go to Tryst for that coffee?"

Brenda snatched up her purse. "Anything you say, *honeybunch.*"

The waitress behind the counter at Tryst gave me the eye as she poured our coffee, then walked off and whispered to another customer while nodding my way, not even pretending she wasn't talking about me.

As it happened, Vicky had been right about the

geeky chick from the seminar. She ended up at my place and we had coffee the next morning at the same counter with the same nosey waitress.

"What the fuck was all that back there?" Brenda asked. "I didn't sign up for Parents Day."

"Thanks for playing along."

"What are they? One of those retired couples you see on the Travel Channel, driving around the country in an R.V.?"

"Close. My parents are sort of grifters.

"Drifters?"

"That too. They're resort hoppers. They live in resorts."

"Which ones?"

"All of them."

"So they're rich."

I laughed. "Their portfolio went belly up years ago. They re-mortgaged the house to make ends meet. When the cash ran out, they fell in with the O.H.G."

"Oh H who?"

"The Over the Hill Gang," I chuckled. "That's what my Uncle Sal calls it. There's a whole underclass of seniors out there whose retirement funds went up in smoke after the S&L Crisis and a slew of financial scandals you never heard about.

"So your parents are destitute."

"Technically not true. Mom and Dad, Uncle Sal, and about a dozen others got together and figured a way to live the high-life for free. They all own houses that are mortgaged to the hilt and none of them have income except social security, so they rent out their homes to make the mortgage payments."

"And they're homeless."

"Technically that *is* true, except for Uncle Sal. They pitch in to rent him an apartment in Fort Lauderdale where he spends his time arranging for the others to take buyers' tours of time-share resorts."

"How could they afford –"

"They don't buy, just take the tours. Time-shares farm out sales to brokers who hand out vacations as perks to qualified prospective buyers. The buyers spend a day touring the resort and listening to the pitch. In return, they get a free week or two."

"Right. If these geezers, no offense, are flat-ass broke, how could they qualify for something like that?"

"Technically, they still own their homes – big, took-fifty-years-to-buy-them houses. The brokers don't go to the trouble of an extensive credit check. When it comes to seniors, they just verify they own a home and look up the value. They never see the second and third mortgages. Don't realize the places are in hock, rented out, and that the O.H.G. are basically homeless."

Brenda nodded and smiled, not the fake smile she had given my parents, an ear-to-ear grin that lit up her face. She had washed off her makeup and underneath had smooth skin. Cute freckles. Soft blue eyes. She looked nothing like the painted barfly from the night before.

"Grifters, eh?" She let off a laugh. "Scamming vacations. Cute."

"It's more than vacations. They do it year round. Florida. The Outer Banks. Tahoe and Vegas. Wherever there are time-shares, which is everywhere. Every once in a while they get caught without a reservation and have to bite the bullet and rent a motel room for a few days, crash with Uncle Sal, or –"

"Barge in on you."

"Yeah," I said, grinning. "Whadaya gonna do?"

"That's . . . actually decent of you." She looked me up and down. "To be honest, I had you pegged as a self-centered prick."

"I have my moments."

Brenda finished her coffee and pushed the cup forward. "Guess that's it. Thanks." She picked up her purse, but hesitated before leaving.

I honestly don't know what came over me.

"Why don't you give me a call?" I handed her my card. "We'll go on a proper date."

"Fuck," she said, staring at the card. "You're *that* Roman? Roman O'Brian the scumbag lawyer? The one representing that cop killer?"

"Ahhhh, yeah. You may have seen some crap on the news about that, but I'm just trying to get the guy a fair –"

"I don't watch the news."

"Me either. So what are you, then?" I laughed. "A cop?"

She rummaged through her purse, dug out a card and handed it to me. *Detective Brenda Bowles, Third District, Washington Metropolitan Police Department.*

"No way," I said.

She flashed her badge. "Way."

I ran a hand through my hair. "All right, but we didn't know. It was a fluke. Hell, you didn't even know my name until this morning. I don't see any reason –"

"And I don't see any reason why anyone needs to know. You?"

I thought about the rough time the cops had given me at the F.O.P., and about the raw harassment she would endure if we were even seen together.

"Gotcha."

"My friggin' luck. Just when I was starting to not be totally offended by the sight of you." She slung her purse over a shoulder, flicked my business card back, and headed for the door. "Have a nice life, counselor. Worst of luck with your case."

The waitress slapped down the check, smirking as she watched Brenda exit. I placed four dollars and two quarters on the four-fifty check and wrote, *What matters to God is that you TRY* in the tip column.

There's a tip for you.

I had bigger problems that morning than a prying waitress. Thursday was Junk Day in Judge Roscoe's courtroom, but by calling in a favor with his law clerk I managed to schedule the Bradley case for trial. And if there was one thing Roscoe hated, it was a scheming attorney who finagled a trial on Junk Day.

CHAPTER TWELVE

I t's good to be the judge.

The corridor in front of Roscoe's courtroom was packed with lawyers, which meant his courtroom would be standing-room only. Friday was Junk Day for most judges, the day they heard the annoying motions that would clog up their calendar on a regular trial day. Roscoe set Junk Day on Thursdays so he wouldn't have to compete with the other judges and could command the presence of every defense attorney not in trial. His clerk issued numbered tickets to the attorneys, and the fools had to hang around all morning like patrons at the world's slowest delicatessen.

It was a pretty good system, for Roscoe at least, so long as no sneaky son-of-a-bitch scheduled a trial.

"Morning, Mr. O'Brian." Boston Stewart strode up and matched my pace, wearing a double-breasted suit, a starched white shirt and his trademark bowtie. "What have you got today?"

"Trial. Buy-bust."

Boston whipped out his legal pad. "What are the

facts?"

"Undercover cop *buys* weed from the defendant. Undercover cop *busts* the defendant. Buy-bust, get it?"

"Um-hum," said Boston, scribbling furiously.

"Whole thing is caught on video. They found the marked money in the idiot's pocket. Three ounces of weed in his shorts."

"Interesting. What's the defense?"

"Defenses are for suckers, Boss."

Boston wrote that down. "Mind if I tag along?"

"Suit yourself." I parted the lawyers waiting outside Roscoe's courtroom and stepped into the madness of Junk Day.

The jury box was filled with attorneys, the center aisle lined with defendants, and every seat in the audience taken with the overflow standing against the walls. The marshals led a man in shackles before the court.

Pockets turned in his ticket to the clerk and stepped up to represent him. He looked good that morning. His comb-over had been recently washed and the pouches of his jacket were empty.

The day was young.

"Emerson Rathbone for the defendant, Yah Honor, who demands his *immeeeediate* release!"

Judge Roscoe buried his face in his hands. "What are we doing today, Mr. Rathbone?" Only nine thirty-five in the morning, but Junk Day had already gotten the best of Roscoe.

"Setting my client free, Yah Honor."

"Really? And why would we do that?"

"My client is held on a five-hundred-dollar bond. He's tried, Yah Honor, but can't raise the money. The bond is therefore oppressive and constitutes an impermissible hold."

Pockets waved a hand in the air, as if the matter were settled.

"Government?" Roscoe muttered.

"Judge," said the prosecutor. "Had Mr. Rathbone bothered to check before filing this frivolous motion, he would have learned that his client is serving a sentence in an unrelated case. Therefore, even if Your Honor does release the defendant –"

"He ain't goin' nowhere," Roscoe finished. "Mr. Rathbone, were you aware of this?"

My guess was, Pockets would have concocted some sort of response, might even have made it sound like he knew what he was doing, had he been paying attention, but at that moment he was turned toward me, mouthing the words, "Need to speak with yah, Roman."

Roscoe snatched his gavel and raised it high, but lost grip and it smacked the wall behind him. "Mr. Rathbone!" he said, scrambling for the gavel. "I have thirty-two motions to hear this morning, many filed by attorneys actually familiar with their own cases."

Pockets spun to face the judge. "How's that, Yah Honor?"

On his knees behind the bench, Roscoe found his

gavel and wielded it. "Motion denied!"

Clack!

I nodded at the clerk, Margaret Bellows, a single mom whose son I'd represented a few times in juvie court. Pro bono, of course. She nodded back and called my case.

"On Your Honor's trial calendar. United States versus Arthur Bradley!"

Tickets are for newbies.

Arthur Bradley sauntered in right on cue and met me at the defense table. The man hadn't returned a call in six months, but waltzed into court in the nick of time, sporting long greasy hair and a Ramones concert tee over tattered jeans, looking every bit the weed dealer he undoubtedly was.

"How's the case going, my man?"

"Going great, Arthur." I wanted to tell him that he was going to need a toothbrush. "Really think we got 'em on the run."

"Cool."

"This case is here for trial?" asked Roscoe. "On Junk Day? How'd that happen, Mr. O'Brian?"

"It's a mystery to me, Your Honor."

Roscoe's face dropped back in his hands. "Is the government even ready for trial?"

"The government is ready," said the prosecutor.

Roscoe sighed and scanned the file. "Mr. O'Brian, you filed a motion to dismiss this case for discovery violations? Two days ago?"

"The motion was filed on time," I assured him.

As a rule, motions have to be filed at least a month before trial, but motions alleging discovery violations -- those claiming the government failed to turn over evidence -- can be filed up to two days before trial.

Roscoe frowned. "Has the government received a copy?"

"Uhhhhh . . . yes," said the prosecutor, pulling an envelope from a stack of mail. "The government has received a copy."

"And the government's response?"

"Court's indulgence," he said, tearing open the envelope.

Had it been possible to feel sorry for a prosecutor, I would have. On a typical Junk Day in Roscoe's court there was a mountain of files on the government table and two prosecutors to work them. This young man was flying solo with what looked like twice the normal number of files. Papers were falling out of some, mixing with the others.

He was in for a brutal day.

I knew he'd received a copy of the motion because Hatch hand-delivered it two days earlier. Inexperienced attorneys will email motions to the government. It's simple, doesn't require messenger service, and can be accomplished with a click.

Problem is, email is fast.

When serving discovery motions, hand-delivery two days before trial is the way to go. It takes a full day for the motion to wind its way through the mailroom at the U.S. Attorney's Office and another full day for it to be carted upstairs to the floor on which the assigned prosecutor works. If timed correctly, it ends up in the prosecutor's mail slot on the morning of trial, giving the overworked bastard just enough time to grab it and bring it to court, unread.

Email is also for newbies.

The prosecutor said, "The defense is asking that the case be dismissed because the government failed to provide the radio run? In a buy-bust case?"

"Exactly," I said. "The government hasn't turned over the police radio recordings, an essential component of the defense in this case."

"As Your Honor knows," said the prosecutor. "The defendant sold a bag of marijuana to an undercover officer and was immediately arrested. The arresting officer would have used his radio to request transport of the prisoner, nothing more. A recording of the police radio communications will not be relevant in any way to the actual sale of –"

"When did the government receive this motion?"

"Ummm . . ." The prosecutor checked the date on the envelope. "Two days ago, Your Honor."

I could see the wheels turning in Roscoe's head as he surveyed the lawyers waiting to be heard.

"Has the government ordered the recording?"

"I just read the motion this moment and haven't actually checked to see when the recording was . . . The point is, Your Honor, the relevance of the recording is questionable at best and the timing of the motion makes me wonder if this isn't a ploy by Mr. O'Brian to –"

"May I be heard on that issue?" I asked.

"No you may not," snapped Roscoe. "Although the timing of Mr. O'Brian's motion is suspiciously familiar, the court finds that the government has failed to provide the requested discovery in time for trial. This case is dismissed without prejudice. The government is free to re-file the charges once the radio run is obtained. Next case, Mrs. Bellows."

"Your Honor," the prosecutor blubbered as I ushered my client past him. "The government requests a brief continuance to see if the recording can be –"

"It's Junk Day, counsel."

Clack!

Good to be the judge.

In the lobby, Boston and I watched Bradley burst through the courthouse doors and strut down Fifth Street, swinging his arms defiantly as if immune from prosecution.

King of the World.

"Nicely played, Roman," Pockets said, stepping between us. "But you know, of course, he'll be back."

"No doubt." I laughed.

I wasn't worried the government would go to the trouble of re-charging Bradley with the case he'd just beat. With a hundred new cases each day, they could barely keep up. Still, it wouldn't be long before Bradley was back on a new charge. A flake like that couldn't help it.

"So what's so important, Mr. Rathbone?"

Pockets removed his glasses and used them as a mirror while adjusting his comb-over. "Tomlinson. Familiar with the name?"

"Of course. He's the star witness in the case you gave me."

"*Haaaardly* say I gave it to yah, Roman. Be that as it may, yah might want to make a Lewis request for information on Tomlinson. Had a case last week where he was the arresting officer. Just a little distribution charge, but mah client had a rap sheet long as mah arm. They dropped it cold, soon as I made a Lewis request." Pockets left his comb-over be and stroked his goatee. "Word is that Internal Affairs got a humdinger of an investigation goin' on Tomlinson."

"Thanks for the tip."

"Any time."

"I'm curious. How'd you find out the witness is Tomlinson?"

"Been around a long time," he said, grinning.

Impressive. Pockets had been on the case less than ten minutes, and the newspapers hadn't mentioned Tomlinson's name.

"Hope you don't mind if I ask you something personal, Mr. Rathbone. Why don't you work serious cases anymore?"

Pockets' smile evaporated, then returned in full

force. "We'll see what you're like after four decades of guns, drugs, murder and mayhem. Good luck with the case, young fella."

Pockets strolled away.

I gained some respect for Pockets. He was way past burned out, but still kept an ear to the ground. Besides, anyone who called me 'young fella' was all right, I figured.

I also figured it was time to call Shelly Jarvis and check it out.

"Jarvis speaking," Shelly answered.

"Shells! We don't see enough of each other. Let's get together. Whadaya say?"

"Roman . . ." Shelly sighed, as if sorry to hear from me.

Deep down, I suspected she liked me just fine.

"We need a face-to-face."

"Come on, Roman. What's this about? You know I can't fork over discovery until after indictment, no matter how much I like you."

"Knew it."

"Knew what?"

"Nothing, Shells. Not important. I'm not looking for discovery. I'm looking for Lewis, any information you have about your preliminary hearing witness being investigated by Internal Affairs."

Shelly took it in stride. "Oh, yeah? What witness is that?"

"Tomlinson."

There was quiet, then she said, "I've got witness conferences all afternoon, but if you can get over here right away, I guess I can give you five minutes."

"I appreciate the five minutes. What I was hoping for was the Lewis."

"See you in a few."

The phone went dead.

"You might want to tag along," I suggested to Boston. "This will be an education for you."

"Where to?"

"The heart of darkness, Boss. The Triple Nickel."

CHAPTER THIRTEEN

It takes a certain type of person to be a prosecutor, a cross between a bookworm and Dirty Harry. Shelly Jarvis fit the bill.

According to her bio on the U.S. Attorney's Office website, Shelly graduated valedictorian from Kettering High School in Detroit, *summa cum laude* from Temple University in Philly, and top of her class at Fordham Law.

She had a reputation for being a "blue believer," a prosecutor who regarded every word out of a police officer's mouth as Gospel truth. Shelly was tough, and would always gun for the harshest sentence.

Despite that, Shelly could be counted on to follow the rules. She would hem and haw, of course, refusing to hand over discovery prior to indictment, but in the end would place her cards on the table face up.

We'd crossed swords a few times, back when we were newbies. There had been this one case where my client was charged with assaulting a neighbor.

According to my client, the neighbor made up the

assault allegation because he was angry at my client for parking his spot. The client knocked on the neighbor's door in response to a nasty note left on his car. A few words were exchanged. That was it.

A case of pure fabrication.

The neighbor claimed my client pounded on his door to discuss the note, then burst inside while the neighbor was dressing and kicked him square in the rear-end.

Photographs of the welt on his ass corroborated the neighbor's version.

When reviewing documents seized from my client during his arrest, Shelly came across a printout from a website: *SpankMeBaby.com*. Curious, she went to the site where she found photographs of the neighbor in a pink thong, hogtied over a couch, being whipped by another man with a strap. A tantalizing discovery like that calls into play a rule called Brady, which requires a prosecutor to turn over evidence potentially helpful to the defense. Since the welt could have been attributed to the neighbor's extra-curricular activities, as opposed to the alleged assault, the bondage pics were arguably Brady. The connection was tenuous, but rather than skirt the rule, Shelly forwarded the pics to me.

At trial, I changed the defense from fabrication to consent. I introduced the neighbor's bondage pics and argued that the neighbor invited my client into his house and begged my client to whack his rear, that my client had indeed whacked the man, and that they were both into that sort of thing. Why the relationship had soured, and why the neighbor was claiming assault, was anyone's guess.

These things happen.

My client was furious. Turned out, his wife was in the audience. In my defense, had I known the little woman was present I would have dialed it down a notch. That issue aside, it all worked out. My client was found guilty, but received probation and a referral from me to Ralph Gelmont, a colleague who did low-cost divorce.

Whether the guy was a maniac who would kick a man with his pants down, or a bondage enthusiast on the down-low who'd fallen out with his gay lover, isn't the point. Point is, there were plenty of prosecutors who would have turned a blind eye to evidence like that.

Shelly wasn't one of them.

They call it the "Triple Nickel," the United States Attorney's Office at five-five-five Fourth Street, just around the corner from the courthouse.

There are prisons easier to enter.

Boston and I surrendered our ID, ran everything we had through an x-ray machine, submitted to an intrusive search and posed for photos. After ten minutes we were cleared to take the elevator to the ninth floor.

Major Crimes.

Sharing the elevator was Carmine Torino, a Fifth Streeter nearly as ancient as Pockets, but who dressed like a K Street lawyer. His ensemble that day consisted of a Valentino three-piece over a royal blue shirt with a matching silk tie.

"Roman," Torino said, without looking up from his phone.

"Whadaya say, Carmine?"

"Who's your friend?"

"Boston Stewart." I waved a hand of introduction. "Meet Carmine Torino, snitch lawyer extraordinaire."

"Hardy har har . . ." said Torino, still engrossed in his phone.

"You gonna triple-nickel someone today? Thought you only did that on Tuesdays."

"Screw you, O'Brian." Torino stepped off at the seventh.

"Who's that?" asked Boston.

"Snitch lawyer. It's a niche practice. Torino doesn't represent honest criminals. He makes his living representing informants."

"Is he . . . one of us?"

"Not quite. Snitch lawyers work both sides of the fence. It's dangerous for prosecutors to meet informants at the jail. Snitches get stitches, know what I mean? So they're brought to the Triple Nickel on the sly where snakes like Torino get them sweet deals for testifying against their friends."

"You ever triple-nickel anyone?"

I didn't know the kid well enough to answer a question like that. For the record, hell yeah I'd done it.

We all did it on occasion.

But there are rules.

Courtesies.

Conventions to be followed.

A fellow defense attorney will stab you from time to time, no doubt about it, but usually in the front. After flipping a defendant to testify against someone else's client the expected thing, the honorable thing, is to give the guy's attorney a heads-up. A phone call. A voice message. A text or an email. No need to go into detail or to violate attorney-client confidentiality. Everyone knows what, *Bob, I don't think you should go to trial in the Johnson case*, means. It means plead it out, Bob. I'm getting ready to triple-nickel your client's ass.

It's just common courtesy.

A snitch lawyer will stab you in the back. They'll triple-nickel your client after breakfast, then grin at you over lunch in the cafeteria. Most times you won't see it coming until the smiling prick steps into the courtroom during your trial, probably wearing a Valentino three-piece over a royal blue shirt with a matching silk tie, just as his fink client takes the stand.

There are standards, even in this business. In a world characterized by deception and chicanery, snitch lawyers like Torino are pariah.

"Just promise me one thing, Boss."

"What's that?"

"You ever triple-nickel any of my clients? You do me a solid and let me know before the squeal hits the stand."

I smiled. Boston wrote it down.

The elevator chimed open on the ninth. I've always suspected Marriott Corporation designed the Triple Nickel. The same pastel colored wallpaper and bargain-basement impressionist prints can be found in any cheap hotel in America. The décor reminded me that I needed a vacation.

We stepped into the reception area where all two-hundred-and-eighty pounds of Yolanda Harding was manning the desk. Yolanda's hair was in a tall beehive, wrapped by tight braids. She had one massive paw wrapped around a compact mirror and was applying a thick coat of red lipstick with the other, making wet smacking sounds as she evened them out.

"Yolanda, darling." I leaned on her desk. "When are you going to marry me?"

"Soon as you hit the lotto, O'Brian." She looked up. "Well, well, well . . . Who *is* your friend?"

"Boston Stewart," I said, with a hand on Boston's shoulder. "Meet the lovely Yolanda Harding."

Yolanda lowered the mirror and leaned forward. "And what can I do for you, Mr. Stewart? May I call you Boston?"

"I'm fine for the moment, thank you."

"We're just here to pick up a package from Shelly Jarvis," I told her. "The crime scene evidence report in the Bushill case."

"A package?" She sifted through the documents on

her desk. "I don't see any package."

"Shelly must have forgotten to leave it. You know how busy the poor dear is. How about you print me a copy?"

"A crime scene evidence report? I'm not sure I'm allowed to –"

The intercom let out a *buzz* and Shelly's voice cut the air. "Yolanda, Mr. O'Brian will be here shortly. Let me know the instant he arrives. Don't talk to him. Don't show him anything. Don't –"

"Whadaya say, Shells?" I said.

Shelly's office door swung open.

"Roman," she said, waving me in.

I winked at Yolanda and headed for Shelly's office. Boston followed, with Yolanda's eyes burning a hole in his rear.

"Tell you what, Boss." I stopped short. "Why don't you hang out here for a while? Keep Yolanda company. Ms. Jarvis and I won't be a minute."

He gave his bowtie a tug, then took a seat on the couch opposite Yolanda.

Yolanda pursed her lips at Boston. "You take your time, Mr. O'Brian."

Shelly's office could not have been more different than mine. Her files were lined neatly on shelves. Her desktop clear. It was hard to believe she practiced law in the place. Typical Shelly, she started right in.

"You're a bigger pain in the ass than I'd have given you credit for, Roman."

"So the witness *is* Tomlinson."

"He's going to testify at the hearing. You'd have found out tomorrow anyway."

"And he *is* under investigation."

Shelly had this habit of twirling her cornrows when hiding something. Good people are bad liars. Shelly was definitely good people.

"The U.S. Attorneys' Office will neither confirm nor deny –"

"You giving me the company line? Shall I take it up with the Bear?"

"Yeah," Shelly laughed. "We all know how much Bearmond loves you."

"It's pure Lewis. He'll order you to give it up. Have to."

Shelly kicked back, motioned for me to take a seat, and folded her arms behind her head. She was wearing a tight blouse. The view from my side of the desk was spectacular.

"David has been under investigation for eighteen months," she said.

"David?"

"Detective Tomlinson."

"David, eh? Cozy."

"I can't give details, except to say it's a standard Internal Affairs Division inquiry."

"Right. Nothing IAD does is standard. Just so you know, I intend to cross-examine your boy, David, on that issue."

"Just so *you* know." She sat up and folded her hands, businesslike. "I intend on asking the Bear to preclude any questions regarding details of the investigation."

"On what basis?"

"Relevance. Privilege. Whatever else I can come up with between now and tomorrow morning. My concern is that Mod-Squad investigator of yours. She showed up at the Narcotics Branch this morning, asking questions about an internal investigation that none of them knew existed. Now Tomlinson is tipped off and every detective in the Branch is spooked. Some of them actually think she's working for us."

God bless you, Vick.

"She's just doing her job," I said.

"Understood, but I want to make sure we don't compromise an investigation without reason. Look, I've seen Bushill's record. Maybe he's not the Devil, but I've also seen the discovery. And when you get to see it, I think you'll agree. For reasons that only made sense in his tortured mind, he killed a cop. The fact that Tomlinson may be the subject of an Internal Affairs investigation is Lewis, I'll grant you that, but the details are irrelevant."

I almost told her to save it for the Bear, but Shelly had been straight with me.

"Tell you what. I'd be willing to drop the whole thing, forgo questions about this Tomlinson unpleasantness in exchange for a preview."

"Of what?"

"The crime scene evidence report."

"You trying to bribe me, Roman?"

"Course not." I smiled. "That would be unethical."

"Tell *you* what." She pushed a paper across the desk. "How about a look at the plea offer instead?"

I glanced at it, then shoved it back.

"Warned you it would be ugly," she said.

"You're joking, right? Straight up Murder One?"

"With a thirty-year cap," she corrected. "Without it, he's looking at life."

"Thirty years *is* life for someone Bushill's age. I can't sell it. What incentive would he possibly have?"

Shelly slid the offer forward and tapped a finger on the last paragraph. "A recommendation that he do his time at Butner, North Carolina. Medium security. In-house medical facilities and a modern library. A step up from the tunnel he's been squatting in."

"Sounds like the Hilton. Bullshit, Shells." I slid it back. "You'll have to do better."

"Not up to me, and it's not going to get better. One thing you've always had going for you, Roman, is street sense. You don't need me to tell you what time it is. The MPD is hot for your guy and the U.S. Attorney's Office can't function without them. Case like this? My supervisors will do what it takes to satisfy the boys in blue and this is the offer that makes them smile. Just be glad the District abolished the death penalty or we'd be having a completely different discussion."

"Look, bottom line is –"

"This," she said, shoving the paper back so hard it slid in my lap. "Your client accepts the offer and retires to Butner where he spends his days in relative comfort, reading books in the prison library and not getting his butt reamed at a maximum security in Jersey."

"Or, he rejects it," I said. "Sets it for trial and I cause so much trouble for you that your supervisors authorize a more reasonable offer."

"Or, they don't. The offer gets revoked. You get your ass handed to you at trial and the Bear sends your guy deep. Without a recommendation from us, he'll be shipped to the darkest dungeon in the system."

"Or, I win the trial. Bushill goes back to his tunnel. Vicky and I have the victory party at the F.O.P."

I dropped the offer in my briefcase and headed for the door.

"Got a sick sense of humor, know that?" She sat back, smirking. "Think about it. A guy like Bushill at a max facility for the first time in his life? Too old to join a gang, too crazy to make friends? He'll end up in the food chain. Trust me, there are plenty of worse places than Butner."

"See you at the hearing."

"One more thing," Shelly called out. "I wouldn't make too much of this Tomlinson *unpleasantness*. Lots of narcotics detectives are under investigation. That's how vice goes. Nine times out of ten, the investigation goes nowhere. Friend to friend? Don't put your eggs in this basket, Roman."

It killed me to walk out with Shelly having the last word, but no snappy comeback came to mind. Besides, I knew she was right. By the time Bushill's case went to trial, the Tomlinson investigation would be a thin folder marked "closed."

Yolanda had abandoned her post and was on the couch snuggled up to Boston, who had a death grip on the briefcase in his lap and dread in his eyes. He sprang to his feet, the briefcase still pressed to his crotch.

"We done?"

"For now," I said.

Boston headed for the elevators and I followed, giving Yolanda the "call me" symbol while gesturing at Boston. Her face registered delight.

She winked as the elevator slid shut.

"Awkward," Boston said.

"Get any information out of her?"

"Didn't know I was supposed to. Spent the whole time guarding my jewels."

"Come on, Boss," I chuckled. "Yolanda's a good kid. Lovely personality. You're not gonna give her a shot?"

He gave me a deadpan look. "You're meeting with your investigator tonight, right?"

"Six o'clock. Some art gallery in Georgetown."

"She said I could come along. What's her deal, anyway?"

"Vicky? Don't worry about her. She's all right."

"Sounded hostile."

"Lovely personality."

"She's worried the gallery owner will be reluctant to give up information. Said to tell you we have to go sweet, or something like that."

"Sweet-n-sour?"

"Yeah, that's it."

Damn. I hated the sweet-n-sour routine.

CHAPTER FOURTEEN

My favorite routine was Texas Oil Man.

The biggest hurdle Vicky and I faced when investigating cases was getting witnesses to cooperate. Some situations were easier than others. When serving a subpoena, all we needed a witness to do was open the door. Problem was, if they peeked out and saw a white man and a black woman they'd figure us for cops, or at the very least Jehovah Witnesses.

So I had this suit that once belonged to my Uncle Sal. He wore it at my parents' wedding, my christening and my high school graduation. Far as I know, it was the only item of formal wear the man ever owned. When I squeaked by my first year of college and needed to interview for summer jobs, Uncle Sal passed the cherished garment down to me.

The thing was hideous, a cross between cream and canary yellow. Wide lapels. Hunter green trim and fake stitched pockets. If Roy Rogers had ever worn a leisure suit, this would have been it.

I also had an old cowboy hat, a pair of second-hand Durango boots and a thick belt, one of those woven leather jobs with an oversized buckle. My Texas drawl is weak, but the scam didn't require much in the way of conversation.

When witnesses looked out to see a thrift-store Texas Oil Man with a black woman dolled up like an extra from *Superfly,* it was too bizarre a sight for them to be thinking Jehovah Witnesses, let alone cops. We were downright irresistible. Most would open the door just to find out what manner of freaks had come calling.

And yippee-ki-yay, another witness was served.

Getting a witness to actually talk to us required a more sophisticated method. Folks in the neighborhoods Vicky and I worked knew the score. If you gave up information, you got a subpoena and had to go to court. The smart money was on keeping your mouth shut.

To combat the problem, Vicky concocted a litany of ruses. There was the Washington Post Reporter scam, the Auditioning for *Cops* routine and Vicky's favorite: Sweet-n-Sour.

Vicky opted for Sweet-n-Sour whenever there was a male witness who might not be willing to talk. The scam would start with her hanging all over me like a lovesick teenager while I fired condescending questions at the witness. Vicky would then switch her affection to the witness, flirting and going all sweet over the guy as if she were offended by my rudeness. The witness would flirt right back and within minutes was putty in her hands.

Sweet-n-Sour capitalized on the American male's natural desire to steal the woman of an opponent and, if executed properly, could get the most reluctant of them to give up the goods. Of course, if the witness was gay, a slight modification was required.

One I was hoping to avoid.

After Boston and I parted ways, I went back to the office, turned off the lights and stretched out on the floor for a twenty-minute nap. My night with Detective Barfly had taken its toll. I woke hours later with my face pressed against berber carpet and *Shaft* blaring in my ear.

"Hello?"

"Roman, I'm outside the Gallery, waiting on you."

"Time is it?" I croaked.

"Five forty-five. Jesus, you sleeping?"

"Nah. Right around the corner."

"Our meeting with Wallace at the Wuma Gallery is in fifteen minutes, and I'm supposed to meet Johnny at seven. You gonna make it on . . . Damn!"

"What?" I asked, dragging myself to the door.

"Youngblood just stepped off a bus. I'm not baby-sitting a newbie all night, so get your ass . . . Chrissake, Roman, is that a bowtie he's wearing?"

"That's our boy."

"Dynamite. This might work out after all. Second thought, we're goin' in."

I tried to tell her I'd be late, but she was gone.

144

Finding a cab wouldn't be a problem. The District had an unusual system where cabbies charged by the zone instead of by the mile. A trip within a single zone cost nine dollars, even if just a few blocks. Raising your arm for a cab downtown was like tossing bread in the air at the beach. Cabbies dive-bombed like seagulls looking for that single-zone, nine-dollar fare.

The hard part would be convincing the cabbie to take me to Georgetown. Trips to neighboring zones added only a dollar or two to the fare, making them highly undesirable during rush hour.

A Hilltop Cab screeched to a halt, blocking all traffic behind it. "'Ello, where you going?"

I grabbed the door and tugged. Locked.

"New York and Fifth. Bout' five blocks."

The lock popped open.

I got in and let him go half a block before telling him, "On second thought, I need to go to Georgetown, Wisconsin and M."

Roller coasters don't stop that fast.

"Sorry," he said, holding up his hands as if I were robbing him. "Not going to Georgetown today. Please take the next one. No charge. Have a nice day."

I dropped my briefcase to the floor, making it clear I wasn't going to budge, and pointed to the *Passenger's Rights* sticker on back of the sun visor. *Passengers have the right to be taken to ANY zone on the grid*, it said. I sat there with my arms folded until the angry horn blasts convinced him to put it in gear.

If there's one thing cabbies fear short of armed robbery, it's Georgetown at rush hour. I drove a cab one summer during college and felt bad for lying to the guy, but getting a cabbie to fight downtown traffic only to be bogged down in the narrow streets of Georgetown absolutely requires subterfuge.

We ran into gridlock at the Latham Hotel on M Street where a platoon of taxis were double parked under a banner: *Welcome, American Association of French Literature Critics!* Taking pity on the cabbie, I bailed out and walked the remaining four blocks past an assortment of exclusive restaurants, ritzy boutiques and designer shops. Culturally, Georgetown is hell and gone from Adams Morgan.

It's the Anti-Morgan.

Occupying a storefront on Wisconsin Avenue was the Wuma Gallery, one of those small businesses that never seem to have any customers. It was hard to imagine how the place could stay in business with the exorbitant rent, unless it was a tax shelter for some local mover-and-shaker.

Or a front for the mob, I thought, as I spied the curator, Adrian Wallace, through the window. He was a swarthy fellow in his mid-thirties with slicked-back hair and a muscular build, wearing a tight turtleneck under an expensive suit. He looked like a hit man, like he would have no problem breaking someone's arm for two hundred bucks.

Vicky hadn't waited. She was inside talking to

Wallace with an arm draped around Boston, her hip pressed close to his side, doing sweet-n-sour.

I walked through the door like a patron.

"I see how it is," Boston was saying. "That what you do here, Mr. Wallace? Sell artwork for *vandals*?"

Wallace blew out a sigh. "As I've explained, Mr. Stewart, they refer to themselves as graffiti writers, or just writers for short. Our mission here at the gallery is to . . . Excuse me for a moment."

Wallace took a few steps in my direction, his arms spread like he was welcoming me to the Ritz Carlton. "Welcome to Wuma," he said. Are you looking for something in particular?"

"Actually, I'm with . . ." I trailed off. Vicky was shaking her head behind Wallace. "The convention. The American Association of French Literature Critics? Your gallery looked interesting. Thought I'd stop by and –"

"Oh, parfait! Si ce n'est pas indiscret, que pensez-vous de Houellebecq?"

"Ahhhh, *oui*," I told him, and left it at that.

"I see . . ." Wallace stared, perplexed. "Well, if you have questions, I'll be right over there."

"Mercy bo koo," I answered, stealing a glance at Vicky, who seemed less than impressed.

I busied myself looking around while Boston fired more questions at Wallace, each more ill-mannered than the last. *What makes it art, the fact that someone scribbled it on a wall? Do you get your artists from the police lock-up lists? Did you have to go to college to get this job?* He was coming off like a magnificent asshole and I really had to hand it to Vicky.

She'd coached him well.

Boston was close to getting tossed out on his ear, yet Vicky was still holding back. Instead of going sweet on Wallace, she remained nuzzled up to Boston with an arm hung low around his waist. Not that I was jealous, but it struck me as excessive, particularly since Wallace couldn't even see the hand she had planted on Boston's ass.

"Bottom line," said Boston. "We're looking for a particular vandal."

"Writer."

"Goes by the name, Repo Man."

"I see where this is going," Wallace said. "As I've already explained to the police, I have no idea who Repo Man is, nor would I be in a position to discuss the matter if I did. Now, if you will pardon me, I have another guest to attend."

Vicky put a hand on Wallace's arm and made her move. "Please excuse my associate, Mr. Wallace. He's barely housebroken."

"True. But the fact of the matter is, Ms. Bronco –"

"Vicky.".

"The fact of the matter is, Vicky, I've had no contact with Repo Man. But if you locate him, please tell him to give me a ring. Publicity like the Repo tag has received is priceless, whether or not he has skill as a legitimate artist." Wallace tossed back his head and raised an eyebrow. "Wouldn't mind signing him for a show."

"I bet," scoffed Boston. "Come on, Ms. Bronco. Let's go."

"Would it be too much trouble," Vicky interjected, her hand slipping down Wallace's arm, "to ask for a tour?"

Wallace considered her for a moment, then shifted his eyes toward Boston.

"Why don't you fetch the car," Vicky told Boston. "Mr. Wallace and I won't be long."

Boston raised a hand to object, but Vicky turned to Wallace. "Would you mind terribly, Mr. Wallace?"

"Adrian," he said. "Right this way."

Boston made a production of huffing and puffing as he made his exit. It was a little over the top in my view, but seemed to have the intended effect. Wallace was all smiles as he extended an arm for Vicky to take.

He led Vicky to the canvasses on the back wall, a collection of abstracts incorporating the name *EXIST*.

"We are proud to be showing two artists this week. Exist has done quite well. This piece sold yesterday."

I moved closer and peered over Wallace's shoulder. The painting was balanced, I supposed, but the colors clashed, just a swirl of gaudy brushstrokes. The name *EXIST* started at the top and curved down, left to right.

That was it.

"Remarkable," said Vicky.

Wallace handed Vicky a brochure, photographs of EXIST graffiti. "We provide clients with proof that the artist is a legitimate writer. It's a unique clientele, mostly from Georgetown, Upper Northwest, and the burbs," Wallace rolled his eyes, "who want art that springs from the urban jungle."

Vicky smiled. "I take it Exist didn't spring from an urban jungle?"

Wallace returned the brochure to its rack. "Truth be told, the idea that all graffiti writers are poor youths from economically depressed areas is incorrect. Many hail from middle-class families and live far from the areas where their graffiti can be found. Exist grew up a few blocks from here."

Vicky stole a look my way. I pretended to study the canvasses while her eyes burned a hole in the side of my head.

"So graffiti writers aren't necessarily from . . . the projects, let's say?

"We don't misrepresent our artists," said Wallace. "We take pains to ensure that the people who create the canvasses are the same people responsible for the corresponding graffiti, thus the brochure. But we do withhold personal information for obvious legal reasons and our clients . . ." Wallace draped an arm over her shoulder as he ushered her to the next exhibit. "Our clients draw their *own* conclusions. Now, this series is most interesting."

"Oh yes, these are fascinating," Vicky cooed.

More of the same. Three canvasses with random brushstrokes and blotches of paint, each featuring the name *WARP*. I snatched a WARP brochure from the rack as Wallace explained the exhibit. According to the brochure, the artist boasted over two hundred tags in the D.C. area. The centerpiece of the photo spread was a WARP mural inside a rail tunnel.

Bushill's tunnel.

"Excuse me." I stuck my head between them and handed Wallace the brochure. "Can you tell me where this photograph was taken?"

"Do you mind?" Vicky snapped.

"That photograph was taken in the Hall of Fame," Wallace answered. "I'm with another client. Be with you momentarily."

I took a step back.

Vicky pressed against Wallace. "The *French*," she whispered.

"This painting," continued Wallace, "is reminiscent of —"

"What a coincidence." Vicky pointed to the photo of the tunnel in Wallace's hand. "We found the Repo graffiti right there. That's amazing."

"Not at all." Wallace reached to a display case on the gallery floor and handed Vicky a book titled, *Art Under Pressure*. On its cover was a picture of the same tunnel. "That tunnel is a museum of sorts for graffiti writers. They call it the Hall of Fame."

"They have their own museum?"

Wallace folded his hands in front of him. "Not in the traditional sense, of course. It's more of a meeting place for the writer community."

"Community?"

"Writer underground, if you prefer, but make no mistake, it *is* a community. Writers hang out, meet up and swap war stories much the way skateboarders or golfers do. Sometimes they work in pairs, one writing while the other acts as lookout. They even form graffiti teams, called *crews*. The Hall of Fame is a favorite haunt. You've seen it. Acres of wall space. Secluded. It's perfect for them."

I glanced over Vicky's shoulder as she thumbed through the book, page after page of photos from inside the tunnel.

"Incredible," Vicky fawned. "But why paint such beautiful images where no one will see them?"

"To the contrary, other writers see them, and that's who they're trying to impress. As with any group of young people, respect from peers is what fuels graffiti writing. In order to gain respect, a writer must get an *up* in the Hall of Fame."

"And an up is a graffiti tag?"

"Correct. An up can be anything from a quickly scrawled name, called a *throw up*, to an airbrushed mural, a technique called *piecing*." Wallace took a breath. "It breaks down like this. Writers gain respect by getting ups. An up in a conspicuous location, a wall facing a busy intersection, for example, is most revered.

Bombing, doing multiple tags on a single building, is also prized. The bottom line is, getting ups in high traffic areas is how writers establish themselves."

"On the other hand," Wallace leaned against Vicky as he flipped through the book. "The Hall of Fame is an exception. Its isolated location gives writers the opportunity to do complex pieces that would be risky to execute on a public street. That tunnel is simultaneously a meeting place and a showroom for a writer's best work."

"Do writers hang out anywhere else?"

"Most definitely." Wallace ushered Vicky toward the door with me following. "These days, writers hang out at punk clubs, or associate with the anarchist bunch. You know the crowd, young folks in their late teens or early twenties, wearing lots of black with anarchist symbols or punk band patches sewn to their clothing. And they sometimes squat in abandoned buildings." Wallace smiled. "Playing poor."

"Any reason a writer might wear a black mask?"

"That's common. Writers do their thing at night and often wear black, including black ski masks, to avoid being seen."

"Adrian." Vicky looked at him sweetly. "Is there any way you could provide a list of places writers hang out? I'm especially interested in the vacant buildings you mentioned."

Wallace stopped by the reception desk. "I'm afraid that's out of the question. The artists who supply my inventory depend on discretion. If any them were to find out I divulged –"

"I would never reveal where I got the information and it would really help, I can tell you that."

Wallace smiled, reached to the desk, scrawled a few names on a pad, tore off the sheet and gave it up.

Yippie-ki-yay.

"There you go," he said. "See that last item?"

"The Kafka House?"

"Used to be a bohemian coffee house, but it's been closed for years. Just an abandoned building now. It would absolutely destroy my reputation if it got out I told you this, Ms. Bronco."

"Vicky."

"I can count on discretion from your associate as well?"

"Absolutely."

"The Kafka House is a squat for young anarchists and graffiti writers, a fact not known to the police. It's quite the popular hangout."

Vicky squinted. "Is it possible Repo lives –"

"A long shot. But chances are excellent someone there knows him. It's boarded up, but you can access the second-floor using the fire escape in the rear."

"Sounds like you've been there."

"By invitation," he said, proudly. "One of my first artists squatted there. The kid had a studio on the top floor, canvases on the walls, and a jury-rigged light system." Wallace laughed. "He tried to list the place as his business address, but I insisted he give me his parent's address. Income tax purposes, you understand."

Vicky extended her hand. "I appreciate your help, Adrian."

"The pleasure was mine." He cupped Vicky's hand in his own. "I'd hate to get your hopes up, though. I doubt this will help in your quest to find Repo."

"Why?"

"Writers won't speak with you. They're a secretive bunch. Your best chance was to catch Repo doing that piece in the Hall of Fame."

"The Repo piece in the tunnel wasn't finished. Do you think –"

"Why didn't you tell me that before!" He released Vicky's hand. "There's no way he would leave a mural in the Hall of Fame unfinished. It's unthinkable. He'll be back. All you have to do is wait. Evening is your best bet, of course."

Vicky winked at me as she handed the art book to Wallace.

Dammit.

"Please keep the book with my compliments," said Wallace. "And give me a ring, Ms. Bronco . . . ah, Vicky . . . if I can be of further assistance."

"One last thing, Adrian. Mind telling me how you got into this line of work?"

"Got involved in a little graff myself before I went to art school." He grinned, slyly. "Still get an up or two when the fancy strikes." Wallace pointed to a painting behind the desk, incorporating the name *COOL DISCO DAN*. "I began by collecting pieces from fellow writers. One thing led to another. Ended up here."

"What does something like that go for?"

"That," said Wallace, "is not for sale."

Vicky pushed out the door, but Wallace lingered, watching her walk away. He made a point of ignoring me, which was fine. I had heard enough about graffiti.

I made my way toward the door. It was still early enough that I could hit the jail and meet with Bushill to discuss a new strategy. Nothing Wallace said changed my view of the case. Finding Repo would be a waste of time, taking the case to trial would be a disaster, and the plea offer was laughable.

In other words, the case was prime for a McAllister.

There was one hitch. I had to catch up with Vicky and let her in on the new scheme. She had been fired up to find Repo, even before meeting Wallace, and the inside information he'd given her could only have fanned those flames. It would be wrong to douse them behind her back, especially with the ice cold water of a McAllister.

"Now," Wallace said, turning to me. "Comment puis-je être d'aide?"

CHAPTER FIFTEEN

Elroy McAllister was a legend, his exploits as a Fifth Streeter retold as parables to every newbie in the courthouse. He won his first murder trial by convincing a jury the government hadn't proven the victim was dead, simply because the man's name was misspelled in the autopsy report. Rumor had it, he'd once gotten a prostitution case dismissed by mailing the prosecutor a picture of the prosecutor having sex with the very same prostitute. The tryst had been arranged, so the story goes, by McAllister who was aware of the man's proclivity for utilizing escort services when his wife was out of town.

Unethical perhaps, but not without a certain ironic charm.

McAllister was most known for developing the plea-bargaining strategy that bore his name. Discrepancies in the government's evidence drive plea offers. The more discrepancies a defense attorney can uncover in the government's case, the better the offer. Some defense attorneys don't disclose the discrepancies they uncover, preferring to sandbag the prosecutor with them at trial. Others drop them on the prosecutor all at once in the hope of generating a quick deal: a strategy I had planned to use in Bushill's case.

McAllister took a midline approach.

When faced with a tough case, McAllister would demand an immediate plea offer. But instead of saving the discrepancies he discovered during his investigation for trial, or dropping them all at once on the prosecutor, he would dole them out slowly, using each to get the offer reduced an appropriate amount. After whittling the offer to his target number, the case resolved.

The McAllister was a useful strategy in cases like Bushill's where going to trial wasn't an option, but where the plea offer was so harsh the defendant had no incentive to accept. The prosecutors were hip to the scam and welcomed it. Plea offers had to be approved by supervisors who didn't try cases and had no cause to be reasonable. Front-line prosecutors, on the other hand, were overworked and actively looking for reasons to convince their supervisors to sweeten deals so their cases would plea and they'd be saddled with fewer trials.

Despite McAllister's reputation for engineering stunning deals, he was unable to secure one for himself. Ten years into his career it was discovered he had no license to practice law. He was a paralegal who had simply strolled into Superior Court one day in the early eighties and signed up as a court-appointed attorney using his father's bar number. Dad was a real-estate attorney, dead for years.

The U.S. Attorney's Office prosecuted McAllister for unlicensed practice and pushed for the max. He ended up doing an eight-year bid at Lorton Penitentiary where he was beaten to death by another inmate for cheating at craps.

A plaque to the man still hung in the courthouse defense attorneys' lounge.

Georgetown at night is a cabbie's dream, crawling with drunken suburbanites willing to pay whatever it takes to haul their candy-asses back to the burbs. I caught up with Vicky and Boston on M Street as they flagged one down.

"Adams Morgan," I told the driver. We scrunched in the back. "Got to admit, you were pretty good in there, Vick."

"Pretty good? Had him wrapped around my finger, you mean." She stuck out her chest and stared me down.

I knew what she wanted to hear.

"You da woman, Vick."

"Dig it." She settled back, throwing an arm across Boston's shoulder. "And you, Mr. Stewart, are a stone natural."

They recounted every moment scamming Wallace, laughing uncontrollably when they got to the part where Wallace had addressed me in French.

"The American Organization of French Literature Critics?" Vicky asked. "Where the hell did that come from?"

"American *Association* of French Literature Critics. Shows what you know."

"Que pensez-vous de Houellebecq?" Boston asked, doing a fair Wallace impersonation.

"You speak French," Vicky observed.

"He was asking what you thought of Houellebecq," Boston explained. "The French writer?"

"Yeah," said Vicky. "And you said . . . oui."

They cackled like schoolgirls, until Boston leaned forward suddenly, pointing to a CD on the dashboard. "Excuse me, sir. Is that Hambone?"

"Coming right up." The cabbie snatched a fedora off the front seat, cocked it on his head, slipped on a pair of dark sunglasses and slid the CD in the slot.

A *ba ba ba boom* baseline filled the cab.

"And a blues aficionado too," said Vicky. "You're a man of hidden talents, Mr. Stewart."

"Please." Boston batted his eyes like Vicky had done at Wallace. "Call me . . . Boston."

"No, call me Vicky."

"No, call *me* Vicky," Boston shot back.

"No, call me . . ."

I thought I might puke.

The cabbie navigated through Georgetown in what had to be darkness, feeling his way through the winding streets with Hambone Jones, *Bell Tower Blues*, blaring from the speakers, and the two idiots next to me beating out a rhythm on the roof. When we pulled up in front of Madam's, Vicky and I exited the cab. Boston stayed behind.

"Hate to bust up the party, Vick," I said. "But we need to talk about the case before you and Johnny do a disappearing act."

"Not even you can bring me down tonight, Ro. Just a sec." She stuck her head in the cab. "Join us, Boss. I'll introduce you to my friend, Johnny Hammond. He's a blues guy. You'll love him."

"Not much for nightclubs. Thanks anyway."

"Next time, maybe."

"Bonne nuit, mon cheri!" Boston called as the cab pulled off.

"Ahhhh . . . Oui!" Vicky hollered. "Know what, Ro? I was wrong about that guy. Youngblood's okay."

"I need a beer." I swung open the door to Madam's.

"Ro!" Bart had a draft Yuengling on the bar by the time we sat down and was already starting on Vicky's tonic and lemon. "What you doin' here, Vick? Johnny canceled. Picked up a gig in Baltimore. Supposed ta be back Saturday."

Vicky stiffened. I flashed Bart the evil eye and he scurried away.

"About Johnny . . ."

"Whatever, Ro." She placed *Art Under Pressure* on the bar. "Thought you wanted to talk about the case. This book is amazing, by the way. There's a serious graffiti underground in D.C. Has been for decades. Listen to this."

"In the mid-eighties," she read, "an abandoned building on F Street became a hangout for writers when a disc jockey named Franski started doing Hip-Hop shows in the graffiti-bombed first floor. As the eighties gave way to the nineties, the development of eighteen-and-over clubs gave writers more legitimate social venues. Some gravitated toward Go-Go's."

"Stripper bars?"

"No, Ro. Go-Go is like a mix of funk, R&B and hip-hop. It started in the District, though I don't think it's caught on anywhere else." She looked around the junky bar, then back at me. "Big world. Ought to get out of here every once in a while."

"Each his own." I blew foam off my beer.

"The trend in recent years," Vicky read, "has been toward D.C.'s fledgling punk movement, music halls like DC-9 and the Hells Point Lounge."

"Uh-huh. Listen. I met with Shelly this morning. She made an offer. Thirty years, but I'm sure we can –"

"Here's the kicker." She dropped a hand on my arm and read on, "But despite the social nature of the graffiti community, writers remain secretive, never revealing their true names and referring to each other only by the tags they write. Fiercely suspicious, writers rarely associate with outsiders due to the ever-present fear of informants."

I slapped a hand down on the bar. "Exactly. It's

like Wallace said. We wouldn't last ten seconds in an eighteen-and-over club before every punk in the place figured us for cops."

"I totally agree."

"It was a noble effort, Vick." I placed a hand on her shoulder. "And not a complete waste of time. Way I figure it, after I cross-examine Tomlinson tomorrow with what you discovered in the tunnel, Shelly will realize that Tomlinson couldn't have shot Bushill from where he was apparently standing. Boom, she drops the offer to twenty-five."

"So that just leaves –"

"We give it a week," I said excitedly. "Then we clue her in about evidence marker twelve being outside the crime scene. Depending on what it is, maybe she knocks off another two."

"I was saying, Ro, that leaves –"

"We let her cool her jets for a month, then hit her with the big guns. The bloody rope. The matching paint on the Repo mural. Make her think we might actually have a defense witness." I laughed aloud at the brilliant stupidity of it.

"Really, Ro? A McAllister?"

"Why not? Maybe the offer goes down to twenty. Factoring in time off for good behavior, Bushill is out in seventeen. With any luck, he gets a little street time in his old age and . . ." I held up my mug for a toast. "We get to bill out the case."

"Roman." She stared at me blankly.

"What?"

"Your laziness is exceeded only by your greed. I was saying that leaves the stakeout."

Dammit.

"Nope. No way I'm crawling around a vermin-infested tunnel in the middle of the night looking for a mythic creature named Repo."

I snatched my hand off her shoulder and drained my mug to illustrate the point.

"He's a potential witness, Ro."

"He's a ghost . . . a legend . . . a name scribbled on a wall. And what's wrong with *my* plan?"

"It's like all your plans these days. I don't know what happened to you. Remember the Marcus case, four years ago? You and I scouring the Sursum Corda projects for three weeks looking for a witness we knew only as Inky? When we first started out, we used to *work* these cases, but the past few years . . . I dunno. It's like you'd prefer to scheme your way around a case rather than work it. And it's gotten worse since Brenda dumped you."

I shot her as nasty a look as I knew how.

"Well, I don't know what happened there," Vicky said. "Known each other ten years and you haven't even told me. What I do know is this. You started out a superstar. I used to be proud to tell people I worked for you. And I liked the old Roman." She dropped *Art Under Pressure* in her bag and climbed off the stool. "Haven't seen that guy in years."

"C'mon. Where you goin'?"

"You know where I'm going."

She waved to Bart and headed for the door.

"We lost," I hollered.

"Lost what?"

"The Marcus case. Lost, remember?"

"Yeah, maybe," she said over her shoulder. "But not for lack of tryin'."

I stared in the bar mirror.

Vicky had a point. The split with Brenda had been rough. No doubt. And maybe I had been coasting.

But Repo?

At best we'd find him and he wouldn't talk. At worst he'd corroborate the government's entire case. It would be a masterpiece of foolishness to track down a witness like that.

The better plan would be to inform Shelly that Repo had been there, leaving open the possibility we had him on-board as a witness. As ridiculous as that was, it could be used as part of my McAllister scheme to engineer a decent plea. Bushill's only hope.

She could crawl around that nasty tunnel all night if she wanted.

Bart appeared at my end of the bar. "Trouble wit Vick? Hope I didn't upset her by mentioning Johnny split."

"Nah, nothin' like that. Just a little professional disagreement."

"Dat's good." He grabbed my mug and topped it.

"I really like Vick."

I smiled. So did I.

"She wanted me to stake out an abandoned rail tunnel."

"Yeah?"

"Place is awful." I laughed. "Crawling with rats."

"Really?"

"Spaced-out homeless guys living in there and . . ."

The thought of Vicky in that tunnel alone suddenly lost its humorous appeal.

"Hang on to this for me, will ya, Bart?" I scooped up my briefcase and placed it on the bar. "Guess I'll be taking a rain-check on that beer."

Smiling, he emptied it. "You a good man, Roman."

The cab stopped as we pulled up to the parking lot next to the tunnel, or as Wallace had called it, the Hall of Fame. There was a metal gate drawn across its entrance.

"Nine dollars."

I told him to turn the corner. The tunnel was two blocks long. I was hoping there'd be access on the other side.

It was an industrial looking street. On one side was the wall of the tunnel. On the other, shuttered warehouses. At the halfway point, I spotted a passageway through the wall into the tunnel, a commuter entrance with white tile walls, dimly lit by fluorescent lights, leading to an abandoned train platform.

"Right here," I told him. I hit Vicky's number for the third time, trying to determine whether she was bluffing or had actually gone in there. Way I figured it, she was sitting at home, still too pissed to take my call.

Or in the tunnel unable to get a signal, I reminded myself.

When Vicky didn't answer, I called Hatch and told him to pick up my briefcase from Madam's and deliver it to the office in the morning. It was shaping up to be an all-nighter.

The cabbie cut the engine. "Nine."

"I'm meeting someone," I said.

"Good to have friends. Nine."

"If she's here, I'll come back and cut you loose. If not, I'll be needing a ride to Adams Morgan."

He looked up and down the desolate street, then tapped a finger on the *Driver's Rights* sticker on the back of the seat. *The driver has the right to demand full payment for a partial trip and three dollars per five minutes while waiting.*

I handed over a twenty. "Be back in five."

The engine fired up as soon as I stepped onto the sidewalk, but I didn't turn to look, not even as the cab screeched from the curb and took off down the street.

Friggin' cabbies.

At the entrance of the passageway was a chain-link fence that had been scaled so many times by the local homeless it hung loose on its poles. Attached to it was a sign, *No Trespassing!* I hoisted over the rickety fence, being careful not to cut my face on the dangling barbed wire, and dropped to the dirt-caked floor on the other side.

Just like the entrance on the other side, the passage was littered with wine bottles, drug works, garbage even homeless didn't want. The fluorescent lights softly lit some of the most intricate graffiti I'd ever seen. Illegible names were scrawled everywhere on the once white walls, but underneath it all was a layer of murals. Some adolescent, others sublime.

An airbrushed mural caught my eye, a portrait of a woman with her face bent upward, twisted in agony and screaming in pain at the stars. It made me wonder why Wallace didn't commission his artists to do murals instead of the rubbish he had in his gallery.

A devilish image glared down from the arch at the end of the passage, a menacing face part hidden by the rim of a black hat and a twisted goatee. The tag above it read, *DANTE*. Beneath was written, *Abandon All Hope Who Enter Here*.

The shadow cast by the arch drew a line between the dim light of the passageway and the darkness of the tracks before me. Nothing emerged from that blackness, except the faint glow of a campfire burning somewhere down the tracks and the muffled, drunken ranting of the tunnel's residents.

Damn you, Vick.

I jumped off the platform into the shadows.

CHAPTER SIXTEEN

The first thing that hit me was the smell, rank and musky, that subway stench of rat feces and human urine. Slurred voices bounced off the walls in a jumble that would have been comical were it not for the campfire down the tracks, casting the tunnel in such gloomy shades of red and dull yellow that the laughter seemed maniacal.

Moments like that I reflected on the things they fail to prepare you for in law school. None of my professors thought to mention the hazards associated with rail tunnels. There were no lectures on dodging trains or on breaking the ice with graffiti writers plying their trade.

Many of my classmates went on to work for K Street firms representing the largest corporations in America and some of the richest assholes on the planet. Less than five percent would see the inside of a court-room. Fewer would stake out a tunnel at night.

I received invitations to alumni events from time to time, which went straight into the bin. Guess I never wanted to keep in touch.

My ex-wife, Brenda, was the exception.

First day of law school she cut in front of me in the bookstore and snatched up the last casebook for Contracts, leaving me without a text. I gave her such a hard time about it she agreed to let me study with her. One thing led to another.

There are novels dedicated to the angst of law school. Brenda took to it like a teenager with a new videogame, hammering out lecture notes and producing outlines worthy of publishing. She sought out other talented students and formed study groups for each class. I barely hung in there and had to work nights as a bartender in Capitol Hill to make ends meet.

I wanted to get married, but was hesitant to ask. Brenda finished at the top of our class and landed a gig with Sharden and Epps, the most prestigious legal whorehouse on K Street. I finished in the bottom third, had no prospects and in six months would have to begin repaying student loans.

It was Brenda who popped the question. She said she didn't mind being the primary bread winner, and was supportive of my plan to work for the indigent as a Fifth Streeter. We married a year after graduation.

At first, she invited me to the firm social events where she took delight in introducing me as a fellow lawyer and seemed proud to announce I represented the downtrodden. But the corporate-law world has its own culture. Being called a Fifth Streeter isn't a compliment. After a few years, the invitations tapered off. By the time Brenda made partner her income was four times my own and she was urging me to get a *real* job.

The Adirondack trip was the last time we were together as a couple. When we returned, I learned she had already taken my name off her life insurance and retained a lawyer. She'd been planning to bail on the marriage for a month.

I felt along the retainer wall on the center track, trying to remember whether it was one of the abandoned rails or the live one. I passed a number of makeshift shelters, indicating I was on the right rail. Fifty yards in, a rail-stone whizzed past and smacked the wall.

"Ro!"

She was crouched against a retainer wall, sipping a Starbucks, holding out one for me.

"Yeah," I said. "You knew I'd show."

"Bogus, Ro. Got two for me, but if you don't want it . . ."

"I'll take it. Thanks."

Black. No sugar. Bullshit. She knew I was coming.

Night vision started to kick in. I could make out the REPO mural twenty yards down the tracks.

"All's been quiet?"

"Except for the campers." She jerked a thumb at the homeless guys down the tunnel.

I spread my jacket on the ground and we sat with our backs against the wall. I had expected the tunnel to be frightening at night, but hadn't counted on dim firelight dancing on the graffiti-covered walls making it look like the hip-hop room in Hell.

"Check out that one." She pointed to a mural with two cartoonish characters, a bald black man with a tear streaming down his cheek and a long-haired white man with a friendly arm draped over his shoulder. The white man had a bottle marked, *Old English XXX*. The caption said, *Take this, brother. You gonna need it.*

Some of the murals made less sense. There was a painting of a strange creature with horn rimmed glasses and a cone-head, an anarchist symbol across its chest, holding a sign that read, *I'm a Mofo and Proud.*

I pondered the meaning of that.

"So," Vicky said. "Tell me about Brenda."

"You know her?"

"Your ex-wife? I was at your wedding. How many beers did you have?"

"That Brenda, right. What about her?"

"She catch you stepping out on her?"

"Nothing like that. No big blow outs. She just . . . I dunno . . . had enough, I suppose."

"Of what?"

"Marriage, whadaya think?"

She gave me one of her looks.

"All right," I said. "Had enough of me."

"Dig it, Ro. I'm glad to hear you say that. Shows you've removed your head from your ass since then. Honestly, though, I never really saw her as your type."

"Too respectable?"

"Too uptight."

I laughed, but accepted the compliment. "Quid pro quo. What's the story with Johnny?"

"There's no story."

"You know, I wish I could stare at you the way you stare at me sometimes. I mean it, Vick. Absolutely forces me to stop bullshittin'."

She breathed out exasperation. "We date when he's in town. Wish it was more, I guess, but that's stupid. He's a traveling blues man. What'd I expect?"

"Yeah, figured it was more than just –"

She held up a hand. "Oh, man . . . *bummer*."

There was a low rumbling. The headlight of a train appeared beyond the tunnel entrance. I could see it was on the rail behind us, but when the rumbling exploded into a mechanical shriek as it entered the tunnel it sent us scurrying to the furthest wall.

Trash blew in every direction as the first of three engines lumbered by. It was a freight, long and slow. The campers had a grand time smashing bottles against the cars for five minutes until it passed.

"Your turn," Vicky said, as we retook our position. "Brenda's been calling, saying you don't return her messages."

"I don't like you chatting with Brenda."

"Groovy. Call back. I won't have to."

"Good point. Chat away."

"Seriously, Ro. Suppose the woman wants to get back together, what's wrong with that? You've been a wreck for a year."

"Eleven months. And a half."

"Been living in that ratty flop house –"

"Hotel."

"– with that rock that has your names on it."

"Paperweight."

"Don't even try to tell me you're not still in love."

I silenced her with a shove to the shoulder.

There was a dark figure walking down the tracks. Vicky motioned downward and I rolled over to get in the shadows while Vicky crouched against the retainer wall and peeked through the opening.

At first, it looked like a man walking a dog. Cop maybe. As he got closer, I could see it was a tunnel resident carrying a duffle bag, wearing a baggy coat with the hood flipped. I never got a glimpse of his face.

I joined Vicky and looked through the opening. The man stopped in front of the REPO mural and shed his coat. Underneath he was dressed in black, a black sweat suit, black ski mask and black shoes. He started pulling spray cans from his duffle.

"I'll be damned," Vicky whispered. "He does look like a ninja. Guy should work for the C.I.A."

"Let's go."

"Not yet." She grabbed my arm. "Let him set up. Let the little jerk get comfortable."

We watched Repo prepare his workspace, propping a flashlight on the track to illuminate the mural, and lining up spray cans like surgical instruments.

I laughed. "Takes himself seriously."

"Nothing wrong with taking pride in your work."

I let the jab go.

Repo went to town on the wall with the spray cans. Every once in a while he would pull a paintbrush from his back pocket and add a brush stroke with a sweeping flair as if working on his masterpiece.

"Trippy," Vicky said. "He's an artist."

"Impressive."

"A little dramatic, though."

"Nothing wrong with incorporating a little drama into your work."

"Speaking of drama, who was that hussy shacked up at your place when your mom –"

The sound of footsteps on gravel cut her off. Repo stepped back and was squatting on the tracks admiring his creation, his chin on his fist like The Thinker.

What did she mean, *hussy*?

"Showtime," said Vicky. "Let's keep this simple, a straight-up criminal defense investigation. We identify who we are. Tell him we're not interested in his graffiti activities. Ask him flat out about the murder. Solid?"

"Solid."

"I mean it, Ro. Nothing tricky. I'll do the talking."

"Dig it, Vick. I'm *hip*."

We crept along the opposite side of the retainer wall so he wouldn't see us coming. It was hard to do quietly with the rail stones and broken glass, but I kept an eye on Repo as we passed openings in the wall and he seemed transfixed on the mural.

Vicky stopped at the opening opposite Repo and motioned for me to wait while she positioned herself on the other side. It made me smile. She did it silently, like a marine on patrol.

Repo's flashlight was dim, but bright enough to create a circle of light around him. To the mural he'd added a swirl of olive branches.

Magnificent.

Vicky motioned and we both stepped into the light.

CHAPTER SEVENTEEN

The thing that bothered me about the Adirondack trip was, while I viewed it as a second honeymoon, a chance to get the marriage on track, Brenda viewed it as a last hurrah. We had barely unpacked when she pulled me aside saying, "Listen, Ro. We've got to talk."

Long story short, I was crammed into that room at the Sergeant within a week. At first, I was confident the separation would be temporary and looked forward to a few nights on the town, figuring that, after a couple days she'd be clamoring for me to come home. A week passed without word, then two, then a month. When she finally called it was to tell me she'd filed divorce papers and we had mediation later that week.

Mediation is where they send you to work out a divorce in a civilized fashion. It's the legal equivalent of a cage wrestling match. The attorneys tally up marital possessions, then fight over them like rats over cheese. Brenda laid claim to the bulk of our assets, the house, the Mercedes, the hundred-thousand in our retirement account, and little Marcus.

When we first got the Chihuahua its name was Buster, a name bestowed upon it by Alphonso Marcus, the client who gave it to me as a going-away present. Except it wasn't me who was going away.

It was Alphonso Marcus.

Brenda initially objected, especially to its name which she thought was low-class, so I changed it to "Marcus" in my client's honor.

Why she insisted on keeping the rat-faced brute was a mystery. It spent its waking hours gnawing on the furniture and the rest of its existence sleeping on the persian rug in the foyer.

The "foyer," I learned, was the nook in the living room by the front door where guests were supposed to stop and admire the rug as they entered. What usually happened was, they got leg-humped by Marcus, who in addition to being hornier than a rabbit on Viagra, had laid claim to the foyer as its private boudoir.

I'm not much for domestic squabbling. When her lawyer faxed me the proposed divorce agreement, I signed without reading. A few days later I received my "cut," a box containing a few personal possessions, a framed picture of Marcus, and the rock. At the bottom was a card that read, *Roman, let's be friends.*

I was in no mood for the friend thing.

The years leading up to our breakup had been much the way I described them to Vicky. No domestic brawls. No big fights. Brenda and I simply drifted apart.

A fan of the arts, Brenda dragged me to every

exhibit in town. It wouldn't have been a hurdle had it just been museums, but there was also the National Symphony, the Shakespeare Theater, and the *Baltimore* opera for Christ's sake. Not even our vacations were safe. The one time I convince her to join me in Cancun, thinking we'd have a blast downing margaritas on the beach, she had me spending the week climbing Mayan ruins.

Cultural traveling, she called it.

I tried to stay abreast, brushing up on art trends, reading librettos for the operas we were seeing, and doing my best to hold up my end of the conversation at dinner parties with her artsy friends. In the end, I just couldn't keep up and we went our separate ways.

Pretty close to the way I described it to Vicky, but not exactly.

There was one incident I failed to mention, but I'd be dammed if I was going to provide Vicky with that kind of ammo.

Repo spun to face us as soon as we stepped into his circle of light, his masked face twitching in jerky motions like he was planning to run.

"We're not police," Vicky announced, holding up her palms. "This is Roman O'Brian and I'm Victoria Bronco. We're –"

"With the City Paper," I finished. "We just want an interview."

Vicky flashed angry, but held her tongue as Repo

teetered left, then stood rigid.

"Why do you want to interview me?"

Vicky and I locked eyes in shared astonishment. The voice was unmistakably female.

Repo Man was a *girl*.

"You're big news," I said. "People are interested, curious why you're doing this."

"Yeah right." She collected her cans and tossed them in her duffle. "Just what I need, my name in the paper."

"Let's put it this way. We don't want to know your name. You spend all this time, take all this risk, but the public doesn't really know why. You obviously have a message. You're against all this yuppie gentrification, right? We're offering you an opportunity to get that message out, and not just on a wall. In the City Paper."

Repo slung the duffel over her shoulder. "Get out my message? To who? The condo-fucker scum who read that rag in Georgetown and Adams Morgan, tryin' to pretend their old asses are still cool?"

"Humph," snorted Vicky, with a restrained smile.

The smartass knew I read the City Paper.

"Exactly," I said. "The condo-fucker scum. Isn't that who you're railing against? We can give you the chance to tell them what you think of their wrinkled, yuppie asses."

Through her mask, I could see her smile.

"Fuck off," Repo said. "I don't believe you."

"Look," Vicky told her. "Cards on the table. We're

not with the –"

There was no warning this time. One minute there was relative quiet and the next, the ear-piercing scream of a train bearing down on us, a silver, high-speed commuter. I grabbed Vicky and yanked her backward.

We hit the ground on the center rail a second before the engine blew past. I could see Repo's feet under the train, beating a path down the tunnel on the other side.

"Let's go!" Vicky shouted, yanking me up.

We bolted down the center rail guided by the light of the train and the occasional explosion of sparks. I barreled into a cardboard shelter and landed face down in a pile of beer cans. My knee smacked something hard and I had to lay there wallowing in beer until the pain passed.

When I struggled to my feet, Vicky was fifty yards down the tracks, leaping obstacles like an Olympic hurdler. The last car zoomed past and plunged the tunnel into darkness. I could hear the gravel footsteps of Repo and Vicky up ahead, but there was no way I was going to catch up without breaking my neck, so I gimped along with the odor of sour beer wafting from my jacket.

By the time I got to the platform, Repo was hoisting herself over the top of the chain-link fence at the end of the passageway. Vicky jumped to grab her, but came back with only Repo's duffle in hand. I limped down the passageway and launched at the fence as Repo dropped to the other side.

The fence swayed under my weight. I had to duck to avoid the dangling barbed wire. As I neared the top, Repo reached through a tear in the fence and grabbed one of my shoelaces. I ended up clinging sideways, unable to go up or down, with barbed wire gashing at my face.

"Lemme go, Repo! Front page story, guaranteed!"

Repo laughed. "Not real bright, is he?"

"He has his moments." Vicky said. "But to answer your question, no."

"Toss me the bag." Repo tugged the shoelace. "Or the old man takes a fall."

"Right." Vicky laughed. "What's that, seven feet? Answer one question. I'll toss you the bag."

Repo yanked, illustrating her resolve. The fence swayed. The barbed wire sawed my cheek.

"It's just one question," Vicky said.

"Toss her the bag!" I screamed.

Vicky slipped a pen from her jacket, scribbled her number on Repo's duffle and chucked it over the fence. "You change your mind, give me a call. I'm available anytime."

Repo released the shoelace and caught the bag. I dropped to the ground, mashing my face on the dirty floor. Repo hopped on a bicycle and peddled down the street in a clink of cans.

"Repo's a girl," I announced, climbing to my feet.

"Brilliant, Ro. Yeah, caught that."

Out on the street, an engine fired up. A Crown Vick pulled from the curb and headed after Repo. I caught a glimpse of the driver as it passed. White guy. Bald. Big and burly. A determined look in his eyes.

I turned to Vicky. "Tomlinson?"

"Sure looked like Mr. Clean to me. C'mon, let's get the hell out of . . ." She curled her nose. "What's that *funky* smell?"

CHAPTER EIGHTEEN

Brenda took to calling it "The Incident." In reality, there were two separate events, each contributing to her decision to throw in the towel on the marriage.

The first was fairly insignificant. Three weekends in a row she'd signed up for walking tours of private art galleries in Dupont Circle, an artsy neighborhood in Northwest, D.C. The tours had been arranged by a colleague at Sharden and Epps, Andy Fuentes, a young attorney fond of silk shirts and tight pants. I made the mistake of referring to him as *Andy the Dandy* once, not so much because of his hip huggers, as it was out of suspicion that he and Brenda were developing a closer relationship than was healthy. Brenda chastised me for my lack of tact and let it slide.

Insignificant really, when viewed alone.

It was the second event that started us on the downward spiral toward divorce. The Sharden and Epps holiday party is something to behold: a Georgetown caterer, a string quartet, and a ballroom of jerks with surgically enhanced trophy-wives in tow. It was a magnificent soiree to which I was not invited.

Andy the Dandy, on the other hand, was.

After hinting I was interested in attending, and getting the you'd-be-bored routine from Brenda, I decided to take the matter into my own hands. What I learned in college about modern art would fill a small notebook. What I learned about crashing parties would fill volumes.

I waited until after dinner, when the guests were bellying up to the bar, to make my entrance. Decked out in a rented tux and liquored up on vodka martinis, I blended right in.

K Street lawyers have a penchant for the vodka martini.

Had I to do it over, I would have stopped at the second martini, certainly at the third or fourth. Five put me way out in front of the pack.

The quartet was playing Strauss. A waltz.

Of that I'm certain.

What I know about what happened next comes from foggy memories and reading the police report. I'm pretty sure I saw Brenda and Andy at a corner table, fairly certain she was holding his hand, and absolutely positive I broke his nose. I'll never forget that sound of crunching bone.

Most everything after that's a blur.

According to the police report, Witness-One, *Andy*, was showing a ring to Witness-Two, *Brenda*, that Witness-Three, *Andy's gay lover*, had recently given him. Suspect-One, *Yours Truly*, approached the table and engaged in what they called "unprovoked assaultive conduct." It took five of them to pull me off Andy who was rushed to Washington Hospital Center.

They released me from Central Cellblock the following morning and dismissed the case after Brenda got Andy to drop the charges. She had less luck with her employers, who served me with a restraining order forbidding me to go within 100 yards of Sharden and Epps.

Like I cared.

I called Hatch while Vicky and I waited for a cab and told him to forget about dropping the briefcase at the office and instead to meet me at Madam's. He sounded out of it, even for Hatch, like he had smoked a quarter ounce and washed it down with a pitcher of beer. He agreed to meet me so long as I could get there in a half hour. We got lucky, caught a cab on Fourteenth, and Vicky busted my chops the whole ride.

"The City Paper? Really, Ro?"

"Like your plan would've worked. We're investigating a murder and need you as a witness? She would have cut and run as soon as you spit it out. The truth. *Again* with the truth. Second time this week. This case is getting bizarre."

"Speaking of bizarre. What's that smell?"

"Ran into a little trouble back in the tunnel."

"You smell like my drunk Uncle Roscoe."

"Roscoe?"

The thought of ultra-mod Vicky sharing DNA with anyone named Roscoe struck me as the most peculiar thing I'd heard the entire strange night.

"On my dad's side. From Durham. Tell you what, though. You clinging to that fence like a mentally challenged Spiderman? Priceless!" She dove into her purse and tossed me a pack of alcohol swabs. "Take care of those cuts before you get tetanus. So, you still think Repo's off the radar?"

I tore open a swab and wiped my face. "Of course she is." I looked at the swab, a mix of blood, dirt, and brownish goo from the passageway floor I didn't want to think about.

"So what was Mr. Clean doing back there?" she asked.

"Probably following me . . . or you, more likely. Trying to get a bead on where our defense is going."

"And you don't think he's got a bead?"

Good point. I had assumed Tomlinson was spying on us, but his taking off after Repo was suspicious. "You think he'll –"

"Stop her? Hell yeah he'll stop her. Especially if he thinks we're interested in her. Why wouldn't he?"

"Suppose he does? What'll he get? A surly young woman with a duffle of spray paint. She'll get charged with possession of graffiti implements, a misdemeanor, and be out tomorrow."

"Or . . ." Vicky countered. "He'll take her into an

interrogation room and scare the panties off her till she gives up what she knows about the murder."

"Or . . ." I said. "She'll tell him to fuck off, just like she told me, and he'll beat her ass like I should have done."

"Or . . ." Vicky smiled, holding up a finger. "He'll charge her. She'll be processed tomorrow in Superior Court where I can look up her name and address."

"Knock yourself out." The 'Or Game' was giving me a headache.

The cabbie let us out across from Vicky's building, two blocks from mine.

"Thanks for showing up," Vicky said, surprising me with a hug. "Get some sleep, Roman. Preliminary hearing tomorrow."

"Can't." I shrugged. "Gotta stop by Madam's to get my briefcase. Besides, Bart owes me a beer."

"Hmmm. Maybe I'll join you."

It was obvious she was still hoping to run into Johnny. I considered ribbing her about it, but decided to give the kid a break.

We stepped into Madam's and paid our respects to Bart. He slid me a Yuengling and pointed out Hatch, sitting in a booth reviewing a graphic novel with a fellow bike messenger, both wearing spandex pants and reflective shirts.

"Naw, man," Hatch was saying as we approached. "Watchmen rules over Sandman. The character design? The realism? The classic golden-age color pallet? And check out the artists. Dave Gibbons? John Higgins? An all-star friggin' cast!"

"Sandman's better written."

"Neil Gaiman? Who the hell reads . . . Roman! Grab a seat. My culturally challenged companero was just leaving."

"Whatever," the other messenger said, on his way to the bar.

"*Duuuude* . . ." Hatch studied my face. "You get in a fight with a cat?"

I headed to the bathroom to assess the damage.

Vicky slid in the booth across from Hatch. "Be quick about it, Roman."

"Heyyyyy, Vick," Hatch hissed.

The drawing of the buxom blonde and geeky guy was still above the urinal, but someone had crossed out the word "TRY" on *What matters to God is that you TRY* and written in 'SUCCEED.' A little jaded, even for a toilet, but the point wasn't lost.

It made me think of Brenda. The barfly, not the ex. I suppose I had succeeded, at least with the short-term plans we both had that night. Still, I was surprised how much it bothered me Vicky called her a hussy. She wasn't that bad.

Besides, who was Vicky to talk?

Even more surprising was the damage the barbed wire had done to my face. I was prepared for a scratch or two, but it looked like I had shaved that morning with a serrated blade. The cuts were shallow, but long, and curved downward as if inflicted by a large cat.

A puma maybe.

Worse, the fall had reopened my lip. I wiped my face with the alcohol swabs, sending stinging grief through my brain, and stepped out of the bathroom smelling of stale beer and fresh isopropyl. I slid in the booth next to Hatch, who was ogling Vicky as if she were the last slice of pizza.

"Briefcase," I said.

"Right here, Chief." He lifted the case onto the table and slung an arm over it. "Stopped by Tryst to check my email. Don't have a laptop, so I borrowed yours. Figured you wouldn't mind."

"My compliments."

"You know, you should do a history sweep once in a while."

"How's that?"

"Clear your browsing history. If you don't, anyone using your computer can see what internet sites you, um . . . *browse*."

Vicky stifled a laugh.

"If one has the inclination," he said.

I snatched the case.

"Far out!" Vicky said, staring at her phone. "Mr. Clean never caught Repo."

"Who's Mr. Clean?" asked Hatch.

Vicky held up her phone and showed me the text: *Thnx for having that car follow me, assholes. LOL. Ditched it in Rock Creek Park. BTW . . . FUCK OFF!*

"And who's *Repo*?"

"You don't watch the news?" Vicky asked.

"Yeah, right," said Hatch, sliding out of the booth. "We done, Chief?"

"Yeah," I told him

"Not so fast," said Vicky. "I've got an idea. Hatch, we're going to need your services Saturday night."

"Ah, dude?" Hatch shot me a pleading look.

"We need your help tracking down a witness," Vicky explained. "Saturday night. Nine O'clock. Place called the Kafka House. Ever hear of it?"

"Come on, Vick," I protested.

"I heard of it," said Hatch. "My man Barfo flopped there after his old lady gave him the shove. A righteous squat. Ratty, though."

"Let's talk about this, Vick," I said.

"Bring your wheels," Vicky continued. "If we find her, she might take off on her bike. We'll need you to follow her. See where she goes. Think you can handle that?"

"I dunno, man," Hatch said to me.

"You do this," Vicky assured him. "And you'll be square with Roman. The slate wiped clean. Solid?"

Hatch looked at me excitedly. "Dude?"

I gave him a nod. Hatch grabbed his backpack and made for the door. I shot Vicky the evil eye.

"Before you start," Vicky said. "She's a witness. She's out there on the street. The Fuzz is apparently on to her and –"

"Fuzz?" The term seemed dated, even for her.

"Tomlinson. Mr. Clean. Whatever, Ro."

"What are you saying? We subpoena Repo to the preliminary hearing without knowing what she'll say? And who calls a defense witness at a prelim anyway? It's unheard of."

"What I'm saying is, we find out what she saw, then decide. Who knows? She might be helpful. You've got to ask Bearmond for a continuance so that –"

"Nope. No way I'm bringing up the "C" word, not in front of Bearmond. Remember what happened last time?"

"You can take a little heat from The Bear. Done it before. Besides, won't asking for a continuance to locate a witness play well for your McAllister scheme?"

I blew out a sigh. She was right, of course.

"Exactly," Vicky said. "Tomorrow you get the continuance. Saturday night we get Repo. Nine o'clock. The Kafka House. Thirteenth and U. There's a diner a couple blocks from there."

"Lemme guess, The Florida Avenue Grill?"

She licked her lips. "Meet you there."

Vicky loved The Grill and always wanted to meet there when we had business in the neighborhood. She hustled out of the booth and took one last look around, frowning.

"Johnny's got a gig in Baltimore," I reminded her. "Supposed to be back Saturday, remember?"

"Whatever, Ro." She walked away. "When are you

gonna get me that evidence report?"

I smiled. It was cruel mentioning Johnny, but she had it coming.

I entered my room quietly. Dad was sprawled on the bed, snoring, Mom was on the loveseat reading one of her romance novels.

"My, you're home late this . . . Munchkin!" She rushed over and put a hand to my cheek.

"Got in a fight with a cat."

"A cat?"

"Neighborhood's crawling with the feral bastards. Be careful out there."

"Your lip is still swollen. I think it's getting worse. You should see a doctor!"

"I'm alright, Ma. Tired, though. Think I'll turn in."

"Okay," she said, nervously. "I fixed the couch up for you. Your father has to sleep on the bed. His back, you know. How 'bout a nice cup of tea?"

She's a wonderful mom. At the end of the loveseat she'd stacked two pillows, a sheet, and the comforter Brenda and I picked out at Bed Bath and Beyond.

Brenda the ex.

"Thanks anyway, Ma."

"Whatever you say, Munchkin." She leaned close and whispered, "That woman this morning, how did the two of you –"

"Suuuugar," Dad called out. "Come to bed!"

"Night, Munchkin." She climbed into bed next to

Dad.

I scrunched into the loveseat, curling my legs to fit, and pulled the comforter over my shoulders. I grabbed the rock from the windowsill, rubbed its smooth surface and drifted off reminiscing about the Adirondacks.

CHAPTER NINETEEN

A continuance was the last thing you wanted to request from Bearmond. It didn't matter whether you obfuscated by calling it an *enlargement of time*, or straight out lied by claiming you hadn't been notified of the hearing and needed an *administrative extension*. It was still a "continuance."

Drug dealers, sexual predators and homicidal maniacs Bearmond handled with something close to tolerance, but nothing set The Bear off like an attorney who uttered the "C" word.

It just wasn't done.

Boston got into step alongside as I headed down the corridor toward Bearmond's courtroom. He looked spiffier than usual that morning in a dark blue double-breasted with a high-collared shirt and his trademark bowtie.

He handed me a file. "I researched some case-law for the Bushill hearing and . . . You get in a fight?"

"Should see the other guy." I bounced his file, gauging its weight. "Nice, but this is a preliminary hearing. All the government has to do is –"

"Establish probable cause. Right. But if we win –"

"The only way the defense wins a prelim is if the prosecutor shows up dressed like Groucho and smacks the judge with a pie. Shelly hasn't done that in quite a while."

Boston looked like he was trying to envision that scenario. "Shouldn't we at least –"

"This ain't chess," I explained. "It's poker. A mind game where they try to intimidate us into thinking the case is unwinnable and where we try to bluff them into thinking we have a defense. We flash a few cards. Point out holes in the government's case. Bingo, the plea offer gets sweetened. We actually try to win the thing, she'll figure we have no idea what we're doing and continue to offer Bushill a lifetime of soap-on-a-rope."

"Yeah, but –"

"You ever hear of Elroy McAllister?" I swung open the courtroom door.

"All rise!" Ms. Harrison announced. "Come to order. The Honorable Jeremiah Bearmond presiding. God save the United States and this honorable court!"

The calendar in Bearmond's courtroom was called each morning, with military precision, by Ms. Trudy Harrison, a waifish woman in her twenties who wore men's suits with an ascot for a tie.

Judge Bearmond appeared on cue and nodded for Ms. Harrison to begin the morning charade.

"United States versus Donte Jackson!"

An obese young fellow in a black leather trench shuffled to the defense table with the painful slowness of a man nursing a glorious hangover.

"Have you seen your lawyer today, Mr. Jackson?"

"Naw, Yah Honor. Ain't seen her."

Bearmond feigned surprise. "Have a seat until your attorney sees fit to make an appearance."

It was known as the Ghost Docket: cases where the attorneys had not yet arrived. Bearmond insisted they be announced first so he could later chastise the lawyers for not being present when their cases were called. The lawyers who'd arrived on time had to sit through the Ghost Docket until Ms. Harrison got around to the matters actually ready to roll. There were lawyers who gamed the system by waiting in the ante-room so their cases would be called early, then stepping in as soon as they were. I tried it once, but Bearmond got wise and passed my case to the end of the docket.

"Mr. O'Brian." Someone tapped me from behind.

I turned around. "How ya doing, Willie?"

"Ummmm . . . fine. I'm covering the Alexander Bushill case and was wondering if I could ask you a few questions."

William Benton, the Washington Post's courtroom correspondent, had a permanent frown plastered to his face, smallish brown eyes set close, and pockmarked skin. The guy looked like a ferret.

"We know what the police are claiming," he said. "What we don't know is Bushill's version. Case in point, is Mr. Bushill going to claim –"

"Sorry, Willie. You're ferreting up the wrong tree."

"Ummmm . . . Huh?"

"I don't represent anyone by that name."

"I was told that . . . You're Roman O'Brian, aren't you?"

"Most definitely, but I don't have that client. He must be represented by some *other* Roman O'Brian."

"Ummmm . . ."

"Turning to Your Honor's preliminary hearing calendar," Ms. Harrison announced, "United States versus Alexander Bushill!"

"Pardon me, Willie." I headed to the defense table where the marshals were depositing Bushill into a chair. "Roman O'Brian for the defendant, Your Honor."

"Mr. O'Brian," said Bearmond, staring at my face. "Were you mugged?"

"Gardening mishap."

"But you're all right? Ready to proceed?"

"I'm fine, Your Honor, but the defense will be requesting –"

"Shelly Jarvis for the government," Shelly said, stepping to the table.

Boston joined me and cleared his throat.

"Oh, and this is Boston Stewart," I said. "He'll be entering his appearance as co-counsel."

"Leading youth astray, Mr. O'Brian?"

"Doing my best, Your Honor."

"Are you ready to proceed?"

"Actually, Your Honor, the defense is requesting a continuance."

The marshals spun as if I'd threatened His Honor with bodily harm. The attorneys in the peanut gallery froze mid-sentence.

"Denied. This is only a preliminary hearing. Are you telling me you need more time to review the Gerstein? I read it myself in ten minutes."

"The defense needs time to secure the presence of a potential witness." I tossed a look at Shelly. "An eye witness."

"Defense witness?" said Bearmond. "At a prelim?"

"I recognize it's unusual, but the defendant has a right to –"

"And what do you mean *potential?*"

"Well, in terms of being subpoenaed, the witness isn't actually –"

"Who is this witness?"

As a general rule, defendants don't call witnesses at preliminary hearings despite having a right to do so. Since all the government has to do at a preliminary is to establish probable cause, it's not likely even a favorable witness can win the day. And not knowing what Repo would say, I had no reason to think she'd be any help. In all likelihood her testimony would be devastating, in which case I would have provided the government with a witness against my own client. I needed time to find out what Repo knew before I even thought about identifying her to Shelly as a witness.

"I will need to approach the bench to explain. *Ex parte*," I added, with a side glance at Shelly.

"Ex parte? I think the government has a right to hear the reason for the continuance." Bearmond turned to Shelly. "Is the government ready to proceed?"

"Most definitely, Your Honor."

"Then let's have it, Mr. O'Brian. I see no need for a private conference. What's the big secret?"

I stood my ground. "As Your Honor knows, the defense is not required to reveal witness issues to the government and has a right to be heard *ex parte*."

Bearmond stared me down, then rolled his eyes and waved me forward.

"Good to see you, Roman," he said, when I stepped to the bench. "How's the wife? She still over there at Sharden and Epps?"

The oddest aspect of Bearmond's personality was the difference between his public and private persona. In open court, he had patience for no one. Privately, he was your best chum.

"Far as I know, Your Honor. And yes, I hear she's doing fine."

"Excellent. But seriously, I don't want to delay unnecessarily. What's the problem?"

I chose my words carefully. "We've learned of an individual who may have witnessed the shooting and who has, as I said before, the potential to dispute the government's version of the event."

"I don't see an issue there. Why isn't the witness

under subpoena?"

"We're still trying to determine the identity of the witness."

"I appreciate your position, but you can't expect me to delay a preliminary hearing in a murder case when you don't even know the name of –"

"We do have some information."

"Which is?"

Breathing deep, I put on as serious a look as I could muster. "It's Repo Man."

I had heard of blood draining from a person's face upon hearing shocking news, even read somewhere it's caused by a sudden drop in cranial blood pressure, but had never before seen the phenomenon. Sitting back forcefully, Bearmond pointed to the defense table.

"Return, Mr. O'Brian."

"We just need a few days to –"

"Now."

Shelly stifled a snort. She could not possibly have heard the exchange, but Bearmond's reaction had been enough.

"Request for continuance denied." Bearmond gave his gavel a clack. "Ms. Jarvis, call your witness."

She nodded toward the gallery. "The government calls Detective, David Tomlinson."

Tomlinson strolled toward the witness stand like he owned the courtroom, giving Bushill the same hard glare the cops had given me at the F.O.P. After the clerk swore him in, Shelly led him through the facts from the Gerstein: how he and his partner, Alberto Knox, were in the tunnel for an undercover buy, how Bushill screamed *Get out of my house* and shot Knox, and how Tomlinson returned fire and shot Bushill in the thigh. When he got to the part where he checked on Knox and found him dead, Tomlinson broke down and cried, running a hand across his scalp as if he had hair.

The man would be a tough act to beat at trial.

"Further questions?" Bearmond asked.

"Just a handful, Your Honor." Shelly reached in her briefcase and withdrew a clear plastic evidence bag containing a handgun. She strutted to the witness stand and dropped it in front of Tomlinson. "Exhibit number one. Can you tell us what that is, detective?"

"It's the gun, the one used to shoot my partner."

Shelly looked at me. "You mean the same gun that was found on the ground, two feet from the defendant, loaded, with the safety off?"

"Objection," I said. "Leading the witness."

"I'd be happy to rephrase the question," said Shelly. "Detective, where was the gun found?"

"On the ground," said Tomlinson. "Two feet from the defendant. Loaded. Safety off."

Shelly killed me.

"Did you recover that weapon yourself?"

"Yes."

Still looking my way, she executed a dramatic *check* in her notes. "Did you ensure that chain-of-custody procedures were followed?"

"Of course."

Check!

"Were comparisons done between the bullet found in Detective Knox's body and the weapon?"

"It's the same gun used to shoot Alberto."

Check!

"Any tests performed on the defendant himself?"

"Oh yeah," said Tomlinson. "They tested his hands for gunpowder residue."

"Really?" Shelly dangled the pen above her notes. "And are you privy to the results of that test?"

"Objection," I said. "I've not been given notice of gunpowder residue analysis."

"This is a preliminary, not a trial," said Bearmond. "You'll have the opportunity to cross examine. Ms. Jarvis?"

"Detective?" Shelly beamed.

"The defendant's right-hand tested positive."

"Nothing further." She executed a final flamboyant *check* as she headed back to her table.

"Do I understand," Bearmond said to Tomlinson, "that in addition to witnessing the homicide yourself, the murder weapon was lying next to the defendant and gunpowder residue was found on his hand?"

Tomlinson nodded.

"Your witness, Mr. O'Brian," said Bearmond.

I turned to Bushill. "Gunpowder?"

"Go get em, Frenchie."

CHAPTER TWENTY

Abandoned rail tunnels are not frequented by street-level drug dealers. They are, however, the perfect environment for distributers: people moving weight. Isolated and far from the street, Bushill's tunnel would have provided perfect cover for a big ticket sale.

But why would two MPD detectives conduct an operation of that scale by themselves? Without backup? It didn't make sense.

"Detective," I said, rising to the podium. "Who were you going to meet in the tunnel?"

"Objection," Shelly said, without looking up from her notes. "Details surrounding the undercover drug purchase are not relevant to probable cause."

"Sustained," said Bearmond. "That's discovery, counsel. You know the rule."

"But you did testify you were scheduled to make an undercover drug purchase at that location, correct Detective?"

"That's right," Tomlinson said, flatly.

"And this undercover purchase was your idea?"

"Objection."

"Sustained."

"Your superiors didn't know about it, did they?"

"Objection."

"Sustained."

"Is there any documentation that you were in that tunnel on official police business?"

"Sustained."

"Memorandum?"

"Sustained."

"Email?"

"Sustained."

"Corroboration of any kind that –"

"Sustained, counsel!"

"Your Honor, there's been no objection."

"Objection," Shelly muttered.

"*Sussstained*," hissed Bearmond.

The rest of the hearing was more of the same. The only thing admissible at a prelim is evidence related to probable cause. Since the drug buy had nothing to do with the murder, testimony about it wasn't admissible. Most judges are willing to give the defense leeway.

The Bear was a stickler.

"Tell me, Detective. How long have you been under investigation by Internal Affairs?"

"Objection!"

"Both attorneys, approach the bench."

"It's Lewis," I told Bearmond at the bench. "A classic bias inquiry. If the witness is being investigated for anything, even for something unrelated to the shooting, he has incentive to color his testimony in the government's favor. The defense has a right to ask –"

"I know what Lewis is, Mr. O'Brian. Ms. Jarvis, is this witness under investigation?"

"Yes, Your Honor. But –"

"Does he know he's under investigation?"

"He's learned of it." Shelly threw me a dirty look.

"In that case, questions about the investigation are relevant to determine whether the witness has bias in favor of the government." Bearmond glared. "Within reason, Mr. O'Brian."

He dismissed us with a wave.

I turned to Tomlinson. "I ask again, Detective, are you under investigation by Internal Affairs?"

Tomlinson waited for an objection. When it didn't come he sat there silent, with Bearmond looking at him inquisitively and Shelly tossing me her *get-it-over-with* stare.

"Detective?"

"Yeah," he muttered.

"Yeah, *what*?"

"I'm aware of the investigation."

"And this investigation was ongoing at the time your partner was shot?"

"That's what I'm told."

"In fact, what you've been told is that you and your partner were both under investigation, isn't that right?"

It's called fishing. I had no idea if Knox was a target of the investigation. Tomlinson cast a desperate glance at Shelly, who looked away. She knew better than to object. Even Bearmond would allow it.

"That's what they say," Tomlinson spat out.

"And the reason you and your partner were the subject of an internal investigation is because you were engaged in off-the-record, narcotics transactions."

"There is no proof of that. Internal Affairs will clear me."

"You were dealing drugs, were you not?"

"Objection!" Shelly shot to her feet. "This has gone far beyond bias. Mr. O'Brian is engaging in the worst type of unfounded speculation. In addition, the detective has a Fifth Amendment privilege and cannot be compelled to answer questions about the details of the investigation."

"Mr. O'Brian," Bearmond droned. "The existence of the investigation is one thing, but it's hard to imagine the relevance of the particulars. Are you fishing?"

I'd hit a wall. It was time to get to work on the McAllister.

"Let me ask you something else, Detective."

"Excellent idea," said Bearmond.

Snatching my legal pad, I entered the well of the court. "Your testimony is that you were standing next to your partner, Alberto Knox, and in direct line of sight of the defendant when the fatal shot was fired?"

"That's right."

I tossed a look at Shelly while executing a *check* of my own.

"And you returned fire with your standard issue, Glock nine-millimeter?"

"Yeah."

Check.

"Which, correct me if I'm wrong, typically ejects casings nine feet? To the right?"

"I guess."

Check.

Shelly grabbed what looked like the crime scene diagram from her file and studied it. "Objection. The detective is not qualified to –"

"No further questions, Your Honor." I walked back to the defense table, threw my legal pad on the table and dropped in my seat.

Shelly reached over, lifted the pad and smirked.

Blank, except for the checks.

"Follow-up questions, Ms. Jarvis?"

"No, Your Honor."

"In that case, I think we can dispense with oral argument. The Court finds probable cause to believe that the defendant, Alexander Bushill . . ."

"Take a look at this," Boston said, handing me his legal pad.

"Your Honor," I interrupted, trying to hide my contempt for the man, not for being a pompous ass, but for being a tool of the prosecution. "The defense reiterates its demand for a continuance to locate its witness, and if denied will file . . ." I struggled to read Boston's writing, "an inter-locu-torius –"

"Inter-*locutory*," Bearmond corrected.

"An interlocutory appeal of this court's decision."

Bearmond looked at Shelly, who shrugged. "This court stands in a five-minute recess. The parties will remain where they are."

He exited through the judge's door.

I'd heard of an interlocutory, of course, despite having trouble with the pronunciation. Normally a lawyer has to wait until a case is over to file an appeal and get a ruling on whether the judge's decisions were legal. Interlocutory appeals can be filed immediately, but only in rare circumstances.

I had no idea if this was one of them.

"Where's he going?" Boston asked.

Shelly said, "To check whether an interlocutory is possible would be my guess."

"Yeah," I said. "Or to throw more Transylvanian dirt in his coffin."

Shelly suppressed a grin. "What's this nonsense all about, Roman?"

"Quid pro quo. What's the Tomlinson investigation about?"

She rolled her eyes.

Even good prosecutors, like Shelly, fail to appreciate the unfair advantage the government has in every case. If the government refuses to turn over discovery, for months until the defendant is indicted, it's just doing its job. If the defense tries the same thing, it's being obstructive. I don't mind the double standard when it comes to prosecutors. Like us, they're paid to win.

Judges are supposed to be impartial.

"All rise!"

Bearmond returned with a swagger. "This hearing will resume Monday morning. There will be *no* further continuances."

"Excellent," I said, packing my briefcase.

"Mr. O'Brian, I mean that. You have the weekend to find your witness. Woe betide you if you are not ready. Witness or no witness, we are going forward. Understood?"

"Am I excused, Your Honor?"

Bearmond glared until Ms. Harrison, sensing the tension, called the next case. "United States versus Melvin Thomas!"

Bushill leaned toward me. "You find the ninja?"

"Working on it, Alex."

He shot me a wink as the marshals led him away.

Outside the courtroom, Shelly was waiting for us, her arms folded. "You're getting world-class training," she said to Boston. "No one can piss off a judge like Roman O'Brian."

"Thanks," I said.

She pointed to my face. "Dispute with a client?"

"That would be privileged."

"And that bit about Tomlinson's casing ejecting nine feet? Just so you know, that only works if the weapon is held straight, and doesn't take into account whether the casing rolled when it hit the ground."

"Details."

"Nice touch, though. Let me guess, that would put him –"

"On the next track. Behind a wall."

"I'll have to check that out."

"While you're at it," I said, dropping a hand on Boston's shoulder. "Mr. Stewart and I are working on a few more potential discrepancies. No worries. We won't sandbag you. We'll fill you in as our investigation develops."

"Turn the crime scene upside down, Roman. Go ahead. What's it matter? I could convict your client drunk on cheap cabernet. And watching you poke at The Bear?" Shelly smiled. "A trial could be worth it for the entertainment value alone."

"You know my policy. If my behavior can provide entertainment for friends . . ."

"Just do what's right for your guy."

"Getting to that. With regard to the Tomlinson shell-casing discrepancy, I figure that drops the offer –"

"Let me make this absolutely clear." She stepped up, her green eyes burning a hole in mine. "You can McAllister me from now until trial. The plea offer stands."

Boston and I watched her walk down the hall.

"Boss," I said. "Looks like we're going to have to put in hours on the case tonight. You know Madams?"

"Blues bar. Adams Morgan."

"Meet me there at eight o'clock?"

"Sure, Mr. O'Brian. One thing."

"Yeah?"

"What's a McAllister?"

CHAPTER TWENTY-ONE

I glanced at my cell on the way to the office. Eleven missed calls from the same number. I hit return. "This is attorney Roman O'Brian. Someone trying to reach me from this number?" I knew it was Ruffio, but didn't want him to know I had his number saved; might make him think we were buds, that he could call whenever he felt like venting about his wife, which was all the time.

"Mr. Roman, I need your help. My wife called the cops. Said I threatened her again. She lying."

"You pay the extra child support?"

"How am I supposed to do that and pay my brother rent?"

"Tell you what. Call my investigator, Vicky. She'll talk to your wife. Smooth it over. But you're gonna have to come up with the cash. Trato es un trato, know what I mean?"

"Sí."

"And until we get this thing sorted out?"

"Yeah?"

"I'd keep out of sight."

I clicked off the cell and stepped through the doors of the courthouse. It was a beautiful fall day. The D.C. Superior Court opens onto a hodgepodge of streets: D Street, Fifth Street, and Indiana Avenue, converging at odd angles. If you look west, you can see the Washington Monument in the distance, a reminder of the other Washington. Washington the capital. Mecca for tourist from every crevice of the nation. A city crowded with lawyers and lobbyists seeking influence. And all of it crammed into the Northwest quadrant.

What the tourists never see is what lies beyond Northwest. Like any city, Washington has its troubled areas. In the Northeast quadrant are neighborhoods like Edgewood and Trinidad where drug crews shoot up the streets at night. Southwest may be the smallest quadrant, but what it lacks in size it makes up for in crime. Southeast is home to war-torn Anacostia, the Wild West of Washington, D.C. Anacostia represents Washington the city.

Ruffio's Washington.

I opened my office door to find Vicky fuming.

"Dammit, Roman."

"I take it our amigo called?"

"Why do I have to deal with this?"

"You're good at it. Besides, Ruffio comes back on a new case, first thing they'll do is re-bring the old one, and we've already been paid for that. You want to do two cases for the price of one?"

She sighed and tossed me a tube of Neosporin. "You look like Frankenstein's attorney. What happened at the hearing?"

I flinched, touching a dab to my cheek.

"Second thought," Vicky said. "Maybe you better go to the ER. Get you some antibiotics."

"You want to know about the hearing, or not?"

"Down side first."

Vicky was a bad-news-first kind of girl.

"The handgun came back a match to the murder weapon."

"Expected that."

"And they found gunpowder residue on Bushill's hand."

"Drag."

"Upside is, I scored the continuance. The Bear gave us till Monday morning to find our witness."

"Good work, Ro. I know that wasn't easy."

"Turned white when I told him who it was."

"He *is* white."

"You know what I mean."

"Obviously he doesn't believe you."

"That wasn't it. He never believes me. It was more like shock."

"Then maybe he did believe you and that's what shocked him."

Vicky was in one of her moods.

"Speaking of shock," I said "You should've seen the panic on Tomlinson."

"Yeah?" She grinned eagerly. "What'd you get out of him?"

"Oh, nothing much," I said coolly. "Just that his partner was also under investigation."

"Interesting."

"And he copped to the fact that his gun would've ejected its casing nine feet to the right, just like you said."

"Did Shelly reduce the –"

"She's thinking about it."

Shelly had been adamant that the plea offer wasn't going to budge and I certainly believed her. When Shelly dug her stilettos in, that was it. But I didn't want Vicky to know the McAllister had flopped.

"When it comes to Tomlinson," she said, smiling. "That ain't the half of it."

Vicky loved to do that: drop a hint she'd uncovered something big and make me beg for it. I didn't feel like biting.

"I bet," I said. "I'll be in my office."

She'd be through the door in a few minutes, I figured, chomping at the bit to give up whatever dirt she'd uncovered, especially if it was good.

I left the door open and listened to my voicemail: two messages from William Benton of the Washington Post and three from Brenda, my ex. Vicky was doing stretching exercises at her desk, arms folded behind her head, chest pushed forward, arching her back and bouncing to counts of three.

Nice.

She lasted five minutes before bursting in.

"You want the scoop, or not?"

"Lay it on me, Vick."

"Heard your messages, by the way. Why don't you just call the woman –"

"You were getting ready to tell me something about Tomlinson?"

She frowned. "Hard to be friends with you, know that? Get this. The Tomlinson investigation went way beyond Internal Affairs. Two days ago, they brought in the Feds."

"Wow. What does it take for the MPD to bring in the F.B.I.?"

"Credible information, and I quote," she consulted her notes, "that the subject may be engaged in large-scale narcotics transactions across state boundaries or American borders."

"Where'd you get that?"

"MPD Procedural Orders."

"No, the information about them bringing in the Feds."

"Let's just say I have a friend at the MPD."

"How would your friend know?"

"Cause he's in a position to know stuff like that. Know what I mean?

Vicky didn't tell me about her sources. It was better that way. No wonder the U.S. Attorney's Office dropped Pockets' possession case as soon as he requested Lewis information on Tomlinson. Better to let a small-timer go free than compromise the investigation of a dirty cop. There was no way it would work for Bushill though, not in a murder.

At best we'd be able to use the existence of the investigation to impeach Tomlinson's credibility, like I'd done at the hearing. But the juicy details – details that might cause a jury to question the government's case – would be excluded from trial. As far as I was concerned the plea was still the best bet.

"Good luck getting details," I told her. "Bearmond shut me down as soon as I tried."

"Why not request it as part of discovery? You won't get it right away, but eventually."

"Same problem. Shelly's not turning over anything that good. She'll claim it's not relevant to the murder, which as far as we know, it's not. Besides, Bearmond would never allow us to introduce it at trial."

It's called Catch-22 Evidence. You're not entitled to the details of a witness investigation unless you can show that the details will be relevant at trial, but you can't show they'll be relevant unless you know what they are.

Frustrating as hell.

"What about this?" Vicky said. "It's relevant to our defense because . . . it was a drug deal gone bad."

"How's that?"

All keyed up, Vicky paced back and forth in front of my desk. "Say Tomlinson and his partner are getting ready to do a deal."

"Okay."

"But personal, not undercover. You get me?"

"Yep."

"Big ticket buy. Lots of cash."

"I'm hip. And?"

"And Tomlinson burns his partner. Whacks Knox for the drug money. Bang!"

Vicky froze, her hand cocked like a gun.

We burst out laughing.

"Dammit, Vick, that's genius! Totally unsupported by the facts, but genius."

"Can you sell it?"

Good question. As a defense theory it was beyond ridiculous. The murder weapon was found at Bushill's side and there was powder residue on his hand. But we might be able to use Vicky's outlandish theory to convince Bearmond to let us delve into the details of the Tomlinson investigation at the next hearing, and who knows? It might convince Shelly to soften her position and reduce the plea.

McAllister or not.

"Might work," I said. "We wouldn't actually have to prove it, just throw up enough smoke to make it relevant, but we'll need more than just a theory."

"Solid." Vicky reached for the phone. "I'll call my friend at the MPD. See if he'll meet us. Maybe he can give us more to work with. On the sly, you know?"

"Knock yourself out," I told her. "Cockamamie

defense like that? Truly impressive."

"Guess you're rubbing off on me."

"I'm flattered."

"And Ro," she said, as I headed for the door. "We're still meeting with Hatch to track down Repo tomorrow night, right?"

"Of course."

I felt bad not telling her about the McAllister debacle, and that I was headed to the jail to shove the Butner plea down Bushill's throat, but Vicky would only have tried to talk me out of it.

CHAPTER TWENTY-TWO

The jail visiting hall was nearly empty. In the waiting area was an elderly woman in a frumpy house dress. Someone's mom. A chubby woman in her twenties flirted with an inmate at the phone banks, her hair coifed, her face made up to perfection. There's a class of woman, mostly young, mostly overweight, who date inmates. The inmate gets a regular visitor putting money on his commissary account and the woman gets to know for sure where her man spends his nights.

Nothing radiates desperation like a jail visiting hall.

The lieutenant led me to a conference room where Bushill sat waiting.

"Frenchie," he said, grinning.

"Why the cheer?" I asked. Normally I'd be pleased to see a client in good spirits, but I was getting ready to inform Bushill that his choices were to live out his days at Butner or at a maximum security.

The cheer would be short lived.

"I sure liked the way you handled that judge." He furrowed his eyebrows. "You fall through a window or something?"

"Had a little accident tracking down your witness."

"You found the ninja!"

"Sorry, Alex. She wouldn't talk to us."

His head dropped.

"How you been doing?" I asked.

"Outstanding." He sat back, defeated. "Swelling in the leg went down and they have me doing physical therapy. Took a detail assignment in the library. Been spending time reading. Got behind past couple years."

He seemed clearheaded, not the maniac who had me in a chokehold the other night. Amazing what a little detox can do. It made me wonder what landed him on the streets to begin with.

"Tell me. How'd you go from a substitute teacher to homeless?"

He looked at me blankly. "I know what it says in my record, but I wasn't a substitute teacher."

"No?" I'd seen guys lie to interviewers at court before, thinking a classy job on their bail report would get them released.

"I was pretending to be a teacher. Actually, I was doing undercover work. Investigating teachers involved in high school drug rings."

"No kidding."

"I was on to a pretty extensive ring. High ranking administrators. Guess I ruffled the wrong set of feathers. They burned me. Terminated the assignment. Destroyed all record of my employment with the FBI."

"The FBI? Really?"

"No, you fool!" The Bushill from the other day was back. "Drinking. How the hell you think I ended up on the street? Wife divorced me. Took my two boys. In the beginning, I got to see them twice a month, but when she moved to Jersey, well, nothing seemed to matter. Hit the bottle. Got fired from my job. Stopped paying rent."

"Family?"

"Foster child."

"Surely there must be agencies a person in that situation can –"

"*Surely* there must be agencies," he mocked. "What the hell country you from? Yeah, the marshals gave me a list of shelters when they evicted me. And at the time, with no cash and everything I owned piled on the sidewalk, it didn't seem like a bad idea. Figured I'd start over, you know?"

He saluted. "Straighten up, son! Quit drinking! Get a job, you maggot! Sound goooooood? Yes, sir!" He leaned forward and said softly, "Tell me, Frenchie. Ever been to a shelter?"

"Not to stay."

"Lots of scoundrels. Second night, the rogues beat me up while I was sleeping. Took everything I had, which wasn't much. The streets started to look pretty good."

In all those years representing indigent defendants, many of them homeless, I never asked anyone how they ended up on the street. It was mind boggling to think someone could become a tunnel dweller in such a short period of time.

"You ever panhandle?" he asked.

"No."

"Most folks think it's just begging, but it's a skill."

"I bet."

"I could teach a class on the whole homeless scene. Where the food distribution centers are. The best places to stash your stuff. Practical advice, like staying clear of the police, and if you're smart, the shelters."

"So you really were a teacher?"

"Ran into a former student one time. Kid gave me five bucks. Didn't even recognize me. I remembered him, though. Asshole type." Bushill grinned. "People will surprise you."

I didn't know what to say.

"Just listen to me go on," he said. "Monopolizing the conversation. What about you? Family?"

Normally, I wouldn't discuss my personal life with a client, but Bushill seemed in a better mood and I wanted to keep it that way. I pulled a photo from my wallet and handed it to him. "Name's Marcus."

He squinted at the tattered picture. "That fine specimen of womaninity is named Marcus?"

"The dog is Marcus."

"Scrawny little runt. That your wife next to the dog?"

"Ex-wife."

"Right." His face lit up. "But you still keep her picture in your wallet."

"The picture is of the dog." I snatched back the photo. "She just happens to be in it. I was going to cut her out, but she got the scissors in the divorce."

Bushill laughed and slapped a hand on the table, then looked up embarrassed, realizing the joke didn't warrant it. "Sorry, Frenchie."

"Roman."

"I don't mean to make fun, Roman. Just feels good to laugh again."

"I understand."

"The dog is with your wife?"

"Ex-wife." I stared at the photo, taken the day I brought Marcus home. Brenda had just cut her hair in a bob and was wearing one of her Pierre Delacroix pant suits.

"Miss it, don't you?"

"Sure, that dog was –"

"No." Bushill chuckled. "Being married."

The security speakers crackled, "Visitation on this level will terminate in ten minutes!"

"Better get started." I pulled Shelly's plea offer from my briefcase.

"First, tell me about the ninja."

"Alex, there's no reason to believe she'll –"

"She?"

"Go figure."

"What'd she say?"

"Nothing. She ran. That's all I can tell you. We've got a lead on where she might be staying, or at least hanging out, and we're going there tomorrow night." I placed a hand on his shoulder. "But I wouldn't hold out hope. Even if she witnessed the shooting, that's probably a bad thing."

He shook his head. "I don't care. I need to know what she knows."

"I do have some news," I said, forcing a smile. "I managed to negotiate what I think is a reasonable offer, you know, under the circumstances."

I handed him the plea offer.

He stared at the paper. "Thirty years?"

"At Butner in North Carolina." I pointed to the last paragraph. "Medium security. A modern library. It's better than . . ."

Bushill dropped his head in his hands.

Christ, I sounded like Shelly.

"Look Alex, if there was any other way –"

He launched at me. I caught an elbow to the eye as he knocked me out of the chair and took me to the ground. White light exploded in my head.

Straddling me, he pinned my arms to the floor. "Why didn't you tell me you were making deals behind my back?"

"Why didn't you tell me you fired that gun?"

"I don't remember possessing a gun."

"There were powder burns on your –"

"And possession," he said, releasing one of my

arms and lifting a finger, "is nine-tenths of the law. Should know that, Frenchie."

The security gate buzzed open. "Code Seventeen," the lieutenant said, walking down the corridor to the conference room. "North Two. Conference room five."

I grabbed Bushill's jumpsuit with my free hand and pulled him close. "They're gonna run DNA on the gun. What're they gonna find?"

"They're cops!" His eyes flamed. "They're gonna find what they wanna find. All I know is, I wake up in that tunnel. I'm shot. Handcuffed. Thrown in jail. I need a drink and you're not helping with any of that!"

"Yeah," the lieutenant laughed into his radio as he entered the room. "Same lawyer, too."

"Frenchie . . ." Bushill lowered his face to mine, his voice crackling, a bulbous tear forming. "Maybe I killed a man. And maybe I didn't. I need to know. Understand?"

"I do, Alex."

Really, I didn't.

"I promise," Bushill whispered as the lieutenant grabbed his arms. "If I did it, I'll take the plea, eat the whole thirty, but I need to know."

The lieutenant dragged Bushill away.

I stopped at the infirmary on the way out. The lip had reopened and the eye was swelling. They gave me two aspirin and a band aid.

Go Quakers.

Outside the jail, my cell started singing *Shaft*.

"Roman, where you at?"

"Jail, Vick. Wassup?"

"Coming or going?"

"Definitely going."

"Good. My cop friend wants to meet. Ben's Chili Bowl on U Street. How long will it take you to –"

"Time is it?"

"Eight pm."

"Can't," I said.

"Why not?"

"Got a date at Madam's."

"With who?"

Was that a twinge of jealousy in her voice? It made me smile, then cringe from the pain. "Boston."

"You're going on a date? With Boston Stewart?"

"We're working."

"A work date?"

"Networking."

"A network date?"

"It's not a date."

"Look, Ro. This may be our only chance to get dirt on Tomlinson. You can't put this alternative lifestyle, midlife crisis of yours on hold for one evening?"

"I gotta go."

CHAPTER TWENTY-THREE

I took the metro to Woodley Park and called Yolanda while hiking across the Ellington Bridge towards Madam's. Sure, she was Shelly's legal assistant, and a U.S. Justice Department employee, but the woman had needs.

"Gonna be late," I told her.

"Got me sittin' here in a bar by myself, O'Brian. Decent women don't fly solo. Deal's off."

"Our boy hasn't shown?"

"Respectable woman like me, it's just not . . . Hey, baby," Yolanda said to someone in the bar. "Humph . . . O'Brian. O'Brian!"

"He'll be there," I said.

"Haven't seen hide nor . . . Oh . . . Mr. Stewart. *Yoooo Hoooo*! Mr. Stewart! Right here, darling."

"Excellent," I said. "Be there in a few."

"You take your time."

When I got to Madam's, the house band, *One Night Stand*, was on the stage. Bart was slinging drinks. Yolanda was in a booth next to Boston, nursing a drink, bulging out of her dress like three-hundred pounds of potatoes in a two-hundred pound sack.

I took the seat across from them. "Glad you could make it, Boss."

"Mr. O'Brian," he said, tossing a look at Yolanda. "Thought we were here to . . . Your eye. You all right?"

"Fine," I told him. "Bart! Another round!"

An hour later, the table was littered with glasses. The hookah made a gurgling sound as Yolanda took a drag. She handed the pipe to Boston who stared at it suspiciously.

"The best part is," I said, "The guy I got appointed to represent was none other than Spin Cycle."

"Who's that?" Boston asked, through an alcohol fog.

"Local DJ."

"Oh yeah," said Yolanda. "He used to spin at the Go Go's. Oh, my, my, that boy was fly. Didn't he get busted for –"

"Cocaine distribution."

Boston took a hit on the hookah. His eyes rolled back in his head.

"Remember that guy in the news?" I asked. "About two years ago? Putting rats in mailboxes in Capitol Hill?"

"No!" Yolanda cringed. "You're lying."

"I remember," Boston slurred. "My ex got one. It jumped out and ran up her arm when she went for the mail." He laughed. "Bitch thought it was me."

"Turned out it was Spin Cycle's brother," I said. "So I brought Spin to the Triple Nickel to see if we could work something out."

Yolanda said, "Now I remember. The guy triple-nickeled his own brother!"

"Yeah." I laughed. "Ratted him out, if you'll pardon the pun. They were hot for it too, reduced his case to a misdemeanor in exchange for his cooperation. A sweetheart. It's like I always say, the bigger the pressure . . ." I held a glass for Boston to clink, but he just burped. ". . . the better the plea. Bart!"

The band started in with *Hoochie Coochie Man*.

"Shut up!" Yolanda squealed. "My fave!"

She wedged out of her seat, grabbed Boston's arm and dragged him to the dance floor.

Bart appeared and set an apple martini in front of me. "From that lady over there." He pointed to the bar. "Gotta go. Crazy tonight."

Brenda was at the bar, raising her glass.

The barfly, not the ex.

I signaled for her to join me.

She hopped off her tool and slid in the booth next to me. "Playing chaperone?" She jerked a thumb at the dance floor to where Yolanda was giving Boston the groin-grinding, dirty-dance treatment.

"Awfully cute couple, don't you think?" I touched my martini to hers. "Thanks."

"Christ, you look rough. You know you're getting

a shiner, right? What've you been –"

"Thought you'd be avoiding me. Me being a leper, and all."

"Never said you were a leper."

"Scumbag attorney, then."

"That was it."

She was in jeans and a tee. Her hair in a ponytail. No makeup. She looked great.

"So," I said, giving her the up and down.

"So," she said, staring back.

I beckoned to Yolanda, who hustled back, leaving Boston teetering by himself on the dancefloor.

"We square, darling?"

"We square, all right." She reached under the table, snatched her purse, drew out a manila envelope and dropped it on the table. "Deals a deal. Now, if you'll excuse me." She hip-swiveled back to Boston, her arms out like momma bear.

I opened the envelope, grinned at its contents and slid it in my jacket.

"Do I even want to know what that was all about?" Brenda asked.

"Definitely not."

"Your place?"

"Mom and Dad. Yours?"

"Sure, if you don't mind running into my asshole boyfriend."

"I know a place."

Two hours later, I rolled over on the berber carpet in my office and lifted a bottle of Jack from the desk drawer. Brenda had her clothes back on, more or less, and was sitting with her back propped against the wall using my jacket for a pillow.

I poured a few shots in a mug. "It's three in the morning. Won't he be looking for you?"

"Who?"

I joined her on the floor and looked at her sideways.

"Screw him," she said. "He's a scumbag."

"To scumbags." I lifted the mug, then handed it over.

"So what's your story?" She took a gulp. "Short version."

"Divorced a year. No kids. Wife got the dog along with everything else."

"What was everything else?"

"Bunch of stuff she bought anyway."

"Lemme guess. She's a lawyer?"

"Uh huh."

"My scumbag is a lawyer. Hate friggin' lawyers."

I looked at her.

"You know what I mean," she said. "Real lawyers."

I kept looking.

"Sorry." She touched my arm. "My boyfriend, he's in corporate finance, flies all over the world doing, I dunno . . . stuff. And the self-important prick can't keep his pants on. Been cheating for years. Well, guess I'm doing the same. But the thing is, he knows but doesn't give a shit. What the hell is that about?"

"My ex-wife," I said. "She used to drag me to all these society events."

"Tell me about it. You ever been to the Baltimore Opera?"

"Madam Butterfly."

"Last year?"

"Yeah."

"I was there," she said. "Didn't that –"

"Suck," I finished.

"And then," she said, taking a sip. "The jerk starts bringing home books on French impressionists. Says we're flying to New York for an exhibit at –"

"The Met."

"He wants to brush up for the after-party with his limp-dicked friends. What kind of douchebag studies for a party?"

"Hard to imagine." I took the mug and downed it. "How come you never split up?"

"Got comfortable, I guess."

"Yeah, people do that. My marriage was over years before she asked me to leave."

"Awww." She studied my face. "You still love her. That's cute."

"I don't –"

"Bet you still carry her picture."

"Like I said –"

"Lemme see." She laughed. "I demand to see it

right now!"

I fished the picture out of my wallet and showed it to her.

"Cute Chihuahua."

"Back to you," I said. "You've got a good job. Why not move out?"

"Trust me. I'm going to."

"So . . . what are you doing next –"

She put a finger to my lips. "Roman, this is what's called a one-night stand."

"Gotcha."

"Well, technically," she said, unbuttoning my shirt. "Two-night stand."

She pulled me to the floor.

CHAPTER TWENTY-FOUR

Saturday morning, I awoke on the floor in the dark with Brenda snuggled up next to me, snoring. It was the best thirty seconds I'd ever spent in that office, until the lock clicked and Vicky walked in.

"Whoah!" she screamed.

Brenda shot up, scrambling for her clothes.

"Jesus, Ro." Vicky backed out and closed the door. "I'll be out here when you get it together."

We dressed quickly. Brenda stopped me as I was opening the door.

"Who is that woman?"

"Jealous? My investigator. I'll introduce you."

"No names."

Vicky was kicked back at her desk with her feet up, reading a file. "Morning, boss."

"Vicky, this is . . . my friend."

"Nice to meet you, Roman's friend."

"I can find my way home, Roman." Brenda darted out the door.

I skulked back to my office and dropped in my

chair.

"Sophisticated, Ro." Vicky walked in and clicked the overheads. "She the one who gave you that black eye? Don't even know her name, do you?"

"Brenda Bowles." I winced at the light. "Detective Brenda Bowles. She didn't want me to tell you. Doesn't want anyone to know we were together. Ever."

"Solid. I'll add her name to the list." She dropped a memo on my desk.

I searched my desk drawer for aspirin.

"Read it," she said.

I scanned the memo, an Internal Affairs summary of the investigation on Tomlinson. It was unbelievable. He and his partner had been shaking down dealers for cash instead of busting them, pocketing crack cocaine from the arrests they did make, and selling it to their drug dealing buddies. The investigation went nowhere for two years until they found a witness willing to talk: the grandmother of a dealer they'd been supplying. She was identified only as Witness One.

"Where'd you get this?"

"You should have come with me last night, but I guess you were busy. Networking, was it?"

"The memo is great, but without a witness name –"

Vicky held up a bar napkin. Scrawled across it was the name Janet Randolph and an address in Simple City, a notorious section of Anacostia in Southeast, D.C.

"What did you have to do to get that?"

"Nothing close to what you were doing, trust me."

She slid a file across my desk. "My friend? The one who gave me all this? His little brother got busted last week. Felony assault. You're gonna represent the kid. Pro bono."

"Gotcha."

"Sorry to break up your party this morning, Ro, but it's a good thing you're here. The preliminary hearing is Monday. We've got to hop on this Tomlinson witness right away."

"We?"

"I'm not going alone. Not to Simple City. Not after last time."

The last time I sent her to Simple City, she called from the crime scene. I could hear gunshots in the background and Vicky screaming, "God damn, Ro. They're shootin' motherfuckers down here!" It was the only time I ever heard her curse.

"No choice," I told her. "I've got to find Repo."

I was actually serious. With Bushill demanding to know the truth, Repo had become my top priority.

Find Repo.

Repo confirms Bushill is guilty.

Bushill takes the plea.

Case closed.

"*We* have to find Repo," she said. "And that's not till tonight. Plenty of time to hit Simple City first."

"Fine," I said, too tired to argue.

"Issue number two, the black eye. What were you up to last night?"

I slid Yolanda's envelope from my jacket and slapped it on the desk. "Obtaining the Crime Scene Evidence Report."

"Far out." Her eyes lit up. "What's it say?"

"Haven't read it yet."

She spread the report on the desk.

I found the aspirin, popped six and chewed them like candy.

"Bizarre," she said. "Evidence tag number nine is the cartridge casing from the round Bushill is supposed to have fired at Knox, just like we thought. Evidence tag eleven is the casing from the round Tomlinson fired. Again, like we thought."

"And twelve?" I asked. "The one outside the crime scene?"

"That's the bizarre part." She tapped a finger on the evidence list. "It's a third cartridge casing. There were three shots fired in that tunnel, not two."

"You're kidding."

"Trippy, right?"

"So it wasn't just Bushill and Tomlinson doing the shooting? There was a third shooter?"

"Can't tell." She scanned the papers. "There's no Firearms Report in here. The Firearms Report will tell us whether the casing found near Bushill and the one outside the crime scene were fired from the same gun. If they were, the government will argue there were only two shooters, Bushill and Tomlinson. Bushill got off two shots and Tomlinson miscounted. If they were fired from different guns, then we've got a third-shooter on our hands." She looked up. "We need that Firearms Report."

I laughed at the thought of subjecting Boston to Yolanda again. "Let's assume we can't get the Firearms Report until after indictment. In terms of discrediting Tomlinson at the preliminary hearing, the Evidence Report we have means what?"

"That Tomlinson can't count shots."

"And in terms of an actual defense?"

"Without the Firearms Report . . . I dunno." She shot me a quizzical look. "How'd you get this Evidence Report?"

The landline went off, sending a spasm of pain though my head.

"Law Office of Roman O'Brian," Vicky answered. "Yes, Ms. Jarvis. How are you?"

I couldn't hear what Shelly was saying, but from the way Vicky was holding the phone away from her ear, I could tell she was pissed. I crisscrossed my hands in the air.

"Um, no. It's Saturday, he won't be in the office until . . . Have him call you as soon as possible? Yes, Ms. Jarvis, I'll make sure he . . . I will, Ms. Jarvis . . . Yes. Asap . . . Understood . . . You have a nice day, too."

Vicky hung up. "Don't ever tell me, Ro."

"You got it."

CHAPTER TWENTY-FIVE

Tires screeched as the cab veered across two lanes of traffic on I-395 and took the exit over the bridge toward Anacostia. "And on the other side of the river it was an Indian village," the cabbie said.

"Really?" Vicky scrambled for a seatbelt.

"Yuh-huh. Nacochtank Indians. The settlers named them Anacostans after the Anacostia river. Says so right here." He held up a dog-eared paperback, *Secret History of Washington, DC*. "All this you see was Indian land."

It was hard to imagine the urban blight below us as a Native American village.

"Whites named it Uniontown, Washington's first suburb." Cocking an arm over the front seat, he turned to Vicky. "It was built it to house workers from the Navy Yard in 1854. You see, back then –"

"Yo!" I screamed, as we drifted across the lane marker toward the barrier, then the river presumably.

He spun around and in a squeal of tires we were back on track. "In those days, Washington was just a small town within the District of Columbia, but what people don't realize is, there was *other* towns in the District."

"There a seatbelt back here?"

"Probably tucked under the seat. Yuh-huh, George-town, Uniontown, Washington – they was all separate towns till they got corporated into Washington, D.C. They renamed Uniontown, called it Anacostia after the Indians they stole it from. And Anacostia wasn't always black. Used to be you couldn't even rent to blacks. All that changed in the fifties when this here freeway was built and the whites started movin' out."

We took the downhill ramp into the heart of the neighborhood. The challenge would be finding a way back. Cabs were scarce in Anacostia, especially Simple City, but the witness's address was only a mile from the Metro.

A risky walk, but doable.

We turned left on Good Hope Road at the *Welcome to Historic Anacostia* sign, then right on 16th at Union Liquor. I'd had a dozen cases out of that liquor store: armed robberies, assaults, and one guy who spent an evening sawing a hole through the roof thinking he'd clean the place out. What he didn't realize was, the owner lived in an apartment above the store and called the cops when the saw punched through his ceiling. Rather than execute a risky roof-arrest, the cops waited and busted the fool when he dropped into the bedroom.

Sixteenth was a drive down memory lane. At 16th and U was King Convenience: two armed robberies, a dozen distribution cases, too many assaults to count. We turned left on W by Paramount Market, the scene of my first assault-with-intent-to-kill.

Memories.

We pulled to the curb at a public housing building. It was three stories of flat brick surrounded by a chain-link fence. A security camera dangled broken from the roof. In the courtyard, kids played in the dirt while their mothers sat in lawn chairs, smoking. Old men drank from paper bags. A cluster of young punks crowded the front door, their underwear blooming from their pants like mushrooms.

"Yuh-huh," said the cabbie. "Seventeen-oh-nine, Dubya Street. That'll be twenty-seven dollars even."

"We won't be long." I flashed him three twenties. "Need you to wait, okay?"

He looked at the cash, then at the punks eyeing us. "I'd sure hate to lie to you, young man."

The honesty was refreshing. I handed him two of the twenties, we got out, and the cab made a screaming u-bee.

"Guess he was in a hurry eh, Ro?"

"What's Witness One's name?"

"Janet Reynolds."

"Your friend tell you what apartment she's in?"

She consulted her napkin. "Nope."

We'd have to run the gauntlet. A white man and a black woman screams police, a misapprehension that normally afforded us a certain amount of protection in neighborhoods like this, but police don't show up in taxis. Several of the young men had moved closer and were eying us as if we were prey.

"I'll soften them up," Vicky said. "Wait here."

The drill was for Vicky to make contact, strike up a conversation with whoever looked like they might give us trouble, then call me over. It was safer that way.

"Hey baby!" Vicky called out.

Their heads perked as they watched her approach, swishing her hips. I couldn't hear what she said after that, but whatever it was had them smiling and staring her up and down. After a minute, she placed a hand on her ass.

The signal.

I got there just as Vicky was telling them, "This is Mr. O'Brian. We're looking for a woman named –"

"No way, baby," one of them said. "Ain't talkin' to no jumpers."

"He's not a jumper," Vicky said.

"Yeah," I said. "I'm not a jumper. I'm an attorney. We're looking for –"

"Ain't talkin' to no lawyers, neither."

They walked away.

"Bye baby," one of them said.

Vicky said, "You're a real party pooper, know that Ro?"

"Jumper?" I asked.

"Never heard that before? Cops are called jumpers because they jump out of their cars and arrest people. I should be charging you for this kind of info. Come on."

The front door was steel the color of gunmetal, and locked. Vicky turned to the lawn chair moms. "We're looking for Janet Randolph. Anyone know her?"

No response.

Vicky walked a few yards into the courtyard and shouted up at the building. "Miss Randolph! You home, Ms. Randolph?"

An elderly woman poked her head from a third floor window. She was dark-skinned, in her seventies, wearing a house frock with a bandanna strapped across her hair. "Yes?"

"I'm Victoria Bronco." Vicky beckoned for me to join her. "This is attorney Roman O'Brian. We'd like to speak with you."

"You here about the complaint I filed? About that police man?"

Vicky shot me a grin.

"Yes Ma'am," I hollered.

"My thritis is actin' up bad." She leaned on the windowsill and winced. "The buzzer is all the way in my livin' room. Knock on the door, why don't-cha. Young'uns' is always hanging in the hall."

The mood of lawn chair moms changed. "You sue police?" one of them asked. "Can I get your card?"

I pounded on the door. The lock released and it swung outward. I recognized the young man instantly. Shoulder-length dreads. Muscular, but skinny.

Prison will do that to you.

"Shit," he said.

"Whadaya say, Tray?" I tried to step around him, hoping Vicky was right behind. I had one foot over the threshold when he shoved me back into the courtyard.

"Fuck you doin' here, O'Brian? I did a nickel on that shit, know that?"

"You're beefing with the wrong guy," I told him. "That was Chaz's call, not mine. You want me to call the jumpers, I will."

He shifted his eyes, looking for cops.

"You let that man alone," Ms. Randolph shouted. "You don't live here, Trayon. Not supposed to be in here, anyways. You let that man alone."

He pulled a knife from his jacket and took a step forward.

"Time, Ro," Vicky said, grabbing my arm.

We ran across the courtyard with Trayon behind us screaming, "The fuck outa here, bitch ass lawyer!"

We ran down W, turned left on Martin Luther King and didn't stop until we got to the Metro station where we hopped on the green line toward Gallery Place.

"Who the hell was that?" Vicky asked, as the train lurched forward.

"Trayon Stokes."

"Well, I don't know him. And if I don't know him, you don't know him."

Normally she'd be right, but Vicky wasn't involved in the sordid work I did on that case.

"Remember Chaz Banks?" I asked.

"The guy who triple-nickeled his co-defendant a couple years ago? The one with the lisp?"

Banks was a former client, built like a tank, but with a speech impediment that made him sound like a five-year-old. He and Trayon were charged with armed robbery. The case against Banks was solid. The victim picked him out of a photo-array and the idiot confessed during interrogation. The case against Trayon was weak. No confession and the victim was fuzzy on Trayon's description. The government needed help to close it.

I advised Banks to triple-nickel Trayon. With a voice like that, there was no way he'd survive prison. Banks testified at trial and got probation. Trayon did five years.

"That guy back there was Banks' co-defendant," I told her.

"Ohhhhh," Vicky breathed. "Guess he's pissed."

"You think?"

"And I guess that means you're coming back to interview Ms. Reynolds on your own."

"Come on, it was a fluke. You heard what she said. He doesn't live there."

"Bull. She called him by name. He's a regular."

The train pulled into Gallery Place and we got off.

"Where you going?" Vicky asked, as I turned left toward the red-line platform instead of right toward the exit.

"Home." My head was throbbing. "Nap time."

"Don't forget, Ro. The Florida Avenue Grill. Nine

o'clock sharp. We're gonna find that graffiti ho tonight. And I gotta go to a *thing* after, so don't be late."

"That's right." I winked. "Saturday night. Johnny's back."

"Whatever, Ro, just don't be late."

"You heading to the office?"

"Dig it. There's got to be more in that evidence report we can use."

"Don't forget to call Ruffio's wife."

"You can't do it?" she whined.

"What I'm gonna do, is go back to my room, draw the curtains, put on a little soft jazz and snooze without distractions."

I walked away.

"Ro!"

"What?"

She had a hand on her hip, smiling. "Say hello to your mom and dad for me."

Damn.

I'd forgotten about them.

CHAPTER TWENTY-SIX

The Washington, D.C. Metro system is a sprawling web connecting every corner of the city. Modern and clean, it's a far cry from most of the neighborhoods it services. The Red Line platform was deserted, so I stretched out on a bench, closed my eyes and reassessed the situation.

What did Shelly have? Detective Tomlinson. The murder weapon. Physical evidence up the wazoo. DNA right around the corner.

What did I have? A few minor discrepancies in the evidence and a dirty cop who can't count gunshots.

And what did it get me? A thirty-year plea I can't take unless I prove my own client's guilt.

Embarrassing.

I checked my cell. Nine calls. Four from Ruffio. Three from Willie Benton of the Post. Two from Shelly, the last person I wanted to talk to.

The phone lit up: Ruffio.

"Mr. Roman, you talk to my wife?"

"Vicky's got that covered, Ruff. I just spoke with

her."

"You gotta do something. The police, they came to my brother's house lookin' for me. They say they got a warrant."

"Did you pay the extra –"

"Cristo! I gotta stay in a hotel now. How I gonna do that?"

I clicked off the phone and stepped to the edge of the platform as the train entered the station. The phone lit up and I snapped it to my ear. "I don't give a rat's ass *where* you get the money. Pay that bitch."

"Nice, Roman. Classy."

"Hello, Shells." The train glided to a stop in front of me. "Just gettin' ready to call you."

"We need a face-to-face."

"What's this all—"

"It's about you stealing evidence reports from the U.S. Attorney's office. We can handle this formally, or you can come to my office right now and we can work it out. Your call."

The train doors opened. An empty car. I'd have it to myself.

"On my way, Shells."

I stepped back from the train, took the Seventh Street exit and walked the four blocks to the Triple Nickel. It was easier to enter on Saturdays, but it still took ten minutes to wind through security. The elevator swished open on the ninth floor where Yolanda was at her desk.

"Sorry, Mr. O'Brian," she whispered. "She caught me putting the original back."

"You didn't get –"

"Nah." She flicked her eyes toward Shelly's door. "She ain't like that."

"Good," I said. "Tell me, darling. You have a nice time?"

She grinned.

"Roman!" Shelly screeched from her office.

Yolanda grabbed my arm as I passed. "You tell Mr. Stewart to call me."

Shelly was reading a file. I dropped my briefcase on her desk and took a seat. She ignored me, left me to stew like a kid called to the principal's office.

The walls were bare, except for a photograph of her shaking hands with the Attorney General at her admission ceremony ten years earlier. No diplomas. No art. No family pictures. She didn't wear a ring and I'd never seen her with a man, or a woman for that matter.

Shelly was all about the job.

"Removing documents from the U.S. Attorney's Office is a federal offense, not to mention an ethical violation." She looked up. "Christ, Roman. you want me to call a nurse?"

"I'm fine. And if you're suggesting I had anything to do with –"

"Save it. Is your client taking the Butner plea, or are we going forward with this pointless hearing on Monday?"

"That's what you called me here to ask?"

"Would you have come otherwise?"

Point, Shelly.

"My client is slightly hostile to the idea of eating thirty years," I said. "Things change, I'll let you know."

Shelly blew out a sigh. "In that case, I'm required to tell you that the Tomlinson investigation is before a grand jury."

"Since when?"

"Yesterday. More than that, I can't say. We're not giving up details."

I took it in. If the investigation was in front of a grand jury, they were dead serious about prosecuting Tomlinson.

"Just tell me this Shells, is it Brady?"

Brady is evidence that can be used to exculpate a defendant. Information the government acquired during its investigation of Tomlinson which would be helpful to Bushill's defense would have to be turned over when the discovery process began.

"That's debatable. Besides, even if it *is* Brady, it's discovery. You know the rule."

"And you know William Benton, I assume?"

"Post reporter. Why?"

"Guy won't stop calling me. He wants an interview. Bet he'd be interested to learn the star witness in the Bushill case is the subject of a grand jury investigation. I'd have to tell him our theory, of course, the reason the Tomlinson investigation is relevant to the Bushill case."

"Which is?"

I'd been fantasizing about springing Vicky's wacky theory on Shelly. "That it's possible Tomlinson killed his partner."

Shelly laughed.

"Why not?" I put on a serious face. "If Tomlinson and Knox were involved in unauthorized drug deals, then it's certainly possible Tomlinson clipped Knox for the drug money. Having the media snooping around, publishing trash about Tomlinson, that's gotta be worse than just Vicky and I."

Shelly gave me a hardball stare. "Speaking to the press about an outlandish theory, which the physical evidence says is *impossible*, would be reckless and irresponsible." She thought about it, then concluded, "Even for you."

I wasn't going to do it, but was curious to see how important it was for her to keep the details of the Tomlinson investigation secret. It was a barometer of what chances I had of getting her to budge on the plea.

"Just so you know," I said. "Given my new theory, I plan on asking Bearmond to reconsider, and to let me get into the details of the Tomlinson investigation at the hearing on Monday. Check out the case law yourself. Looks pretty solid."

I hadn't actually read any cases, but she probably knew that.

"Roman, all bullshit aside, you're serious about rejecting the offer? Going to trial? On these facts?"

"Not my call."

She hung her head and looked sick.

"Shells, you all right?"

She flopped a sheet of paper on the desk, face down. I tugged on it, but she wasn't letting go. I lifted my eyes to hers.

"I want you to know," she said, "I was ordered to give you this. Far as I'm concerned, the original plea offer was more than generous."

She lifted her hand and I snatched the paper. It was a plea offer. Voluntary Manslaughter. Ludicrous. The sentencing range was so small he would finish his time in the same pair of shoes. Bushill would have to accept, and Shelly knew it. I could hardly contain myself.

"And please," she said, reading my glee. "Don't flatter yourself by thinking you did anything to earn it. The only reason you're holding that offer in your hand is politics beyond my control and your understanding."

"Or . . . it's because your star witness is dirty."

"Or . . . because you Forest-Gumped a sweetheart deal which, as usual, you don't deserve."

"Or . . . I do deserve it." I thought about Tomlinson following us to the tunnel, and tapped a finger on my briefcase. "My investigation has you so shook up, you've got Tomlinson shadowing me."

"I couldn't care less what you do all day, you ego-maniac. If Tomlinson is following you, he's probably looking for a tip on where he can find a retro barber."

"All I'm saying is, there are unanswered questions.

According to the Evidence Report –"

"The one you don't have?"

Point two, Shelly.

"There's a third shell casing," I said. "Way outside the crime scene."

"If you had the foresight to steal the Firearms and DNA reports, instead of just the Evidence Report, you'd know that your client fired that shot. The third casing is a match to the one found next to your client and his DNA is all over the gun. Face it, Roman, your client's guilty!"

"Since when does that have anything to do with it? This case is about you proving it beyond a reasonable doubt." I held up the offer. "At least someone in your office realizes it."

Shelly eased back in her chair. "Not even denying it, is he?"

"Conversations with my client are protected by –"

"When I think of all the smalltime stunts you've pulled over the years. The last-minute dismissals. The witnesses who changed their stories after talking to you. The hookers you got off, God knows how. This offer makes me sick."

"We done?"

"I bust my ass to keep the streets safe from cop killers like Bushill. And when I'm forced to cut a deal that serves you up your job on a platter, you have the ping-pongs to play it off like it was your," she rapped a knuckle on my briefcase, "*investigation* that earned it?"

She snatched back the offer. "Spare me the Roman antics. Just take your offer . . ." she flipped the latches on my briefcase, lifted the lid and threw the offer in, smirking when she saw the briefcase was empty. "And be on your way."

I stood and looked out the window. "I can see why you want the streets safe. Got a pretty sweet view of them way up here."

"Same old Roman, making jokes. Don't you have a client to congratulate?"

"Getting old and cranky, Shells. Didn't used to take it personally when you got beat."

"Beat?" She stifled a laugh. "You actually believe that, don't you? What's worse, there was a time when it might've been true. When was the last time you beat anyone? Won a case on the merits? Argued the law?"

I had never seen Shelly so worked up.

"I know why you're so desperate to think you orchestrated that sweetheart deal. Thought this case was the one, didn't you? The high-profile murder case that would pull you back from the brink, take a burned out Fifth Streeter and turn him into a lawyer again.

"Well," she laughed. "This isn't the case. And that case? It's never coming. It's not the case that makes the lawyer, Roman. Other way around. Hardest thing about having to make that offer is, I have to make it to a guy who's so washed up he's the only clueless bastard in the courthouse who doesn't know it."

I tried to save what dignity I had left by heading

for the door.

"O'Brian!"

I froze, doorknob in hand.

"Roman," she whispered. "Just so you know. The offer expires Monday morning."

I yanked the door open and surprised Yolanda, eavesdropping on the other side. She glanced at me, embarrassed, and walked away.

I thought about going back to the office to grab some shuteye, but needed a break from the berber carpet. What I needed was my bed, or at least my couch. Hopefully Mom and Dad would be out shopping for their trip to Massanutten.

When I got to the Metro, I stood on the train to avoid falling asleep and missing my stop.

The offer was completely unbelievable. Voluntary Manslaughter. I couldn't process it. With Bushill's minimal criminal history, his sentencing range would between four and ten years, a midrange of seven. With time off for good behavior, he'd be out in six. Why?

On the other hand, what did it matter? I should've been happy.

But Shelly's words rang in my ears.

When I got home, I opened the door to find Mom watching game shows and Dad on the phone with Sal.

"Munchkin!" Mom looked at my face. "Hank! Call 911!"

"I'm fine, Ma."

"Did you get attacked? You look terrible."

"Ran into a door. I'll be fine."

"Hank, come look at this."

Dad hung up on Sal and joined us. "I have to say, son, your mother is right."

It was only the second time I'd heard him say that. First time was when I told Mom I was taking Brenda to the Jersey Shore for our fifth anniversary and she suggested it might help my marriage if I sprung for something more romantic.

Who knows? Might've worked.

"The shiner looks bad, son," Dad said. "Those cuts on your face infected?"

"Just need sleep. Maybe some Neosporin."

"I'll get it." Mom scurried to her pocketbook.

I stepped around Dad and dropped on the couch.

Mom hurried back and dabbed Neosporin on my cheek. "Oh, I almost forgot. Brenda stopped by."

"Here?"

"She is your wife, after all."

"Right," I said. "That Brenda. Ex-wife."

"She let her hair grow. Looked just darling. Didn't she look nice, Hank?"

"Swell, sugar." Dad hopped into bed to watch TV.

"Soooo . . ." Mom froze mid-sentence, the way she did when she had a surprise. "I invited her tomorrow for Sunday dinner. I'll order some meatloaf from that diner up the street and we'll have us a nice family meal. Isn't that wonderful?"

"Mom, why?"

"Oh, Roman. This has gone on long enough. I just think if the two of you –"

"Suuuugar . . ." Dad said.

"You get some rest, dear." She capped the tube and joined Dad in bed. "You want to look your best."

I pulled a pillow over my head to drown out the TV. Sunday dinner. Meatloaf from the diner. All of us cramped in a musty hotel room.

She did say Brenda looked good, though.

CHAPTER TWENTY-SEVEN

I woke to Mom shaking my shoulder, the room dark, except for the TV, and a teakettle whistling in the kitchenette. Didn't know I owned one.

"Munchkin, your phone's been ringing."

I played the last message. "It's nine o'clock, Ro," Vicky said. "Boston and I are waiting. No sign of Hatch. *Rooooman*, where are you?"

I stumbled to the bathroom and threw water on my face. The scars were still there, but the Neosporin had calmed them. The eye had bloomed into a classic shiner. Nice.

"Gotta go, Ma." I grabbed my jacket.

"Don't be silly. You just woke up."

"Work."

"At *this* hour?" She met me at the door. "Wait. I'll fix you some tea."

"No time, Mom." I kissed her on the cheek.

"Roman, your Neosporin!"

"Careful, son!" Dad called as I ran down the hall.

It was a five-minute cab ride to the World Famous Florida Avenue Grill, a holdover from the neighborhood's pre-yuppie days.

The first thing you noticed at the Grill was the smell. Country fried steak, catfish and cornbread. Like a grandmother's kitchen. The joint had been serving up soul food since the '40s and hadn't changed since the day it opened. A counter ran the length of the skinny diner with tiny booths taking up the remaining space.

The second thing you noticed were the pictures, celebrity headshots going back to the 1950s. Blues legends like Bobby Parker and Roy Buchanan. Jazz locals Billy Taylor and Frank Wess. Every mayor since Marion Barry in '79.

Vicky was in a booth with Boston, wearing her black leather over a red shirt, screeching into her cell. "Hatch! Call me!" She slapped down the phone. "Knew it, Ro. The little creep's gonna ditch us again."

"Good to see you, too, Vick."

Boston was dressed casually in jeans and a *Blues is Back* tee. He had what looked like a hickey on his neck.

"Boston," I said, taking a seat.

He nodded, angrily.

"Look, Boss. About last night –"

He silenced me with a quick wave and a discrete nod toward Vicky.

"What?" Vicky laughed. "You and Boston have a lover's spat? That where you got that black eye, Ro?" Her phone started blaring *Super Freak*, Hatch's ring.

She snatched it up. "Now, Hatch . . . No, not fifteen. Now!" She slid the phone back in her jacket. "Sorry. Can't help it. The creep brings me down."

"You talk to Ruffio's wife?" I asked.

"Oh, yeah."

"And?"

"Same nonsense. He called her, drunk off his ass. Left a message. Threatened to . . . lemme see . . ." She lifted a notebook from her pocket. "Kill you, you damn *beeeeeetch.*"

"I see. So you don't think you can –"

"Only thing's gonna calm that woman is a bag of dope." Vicky did her best Ruffio. "She peeeeesed, Ro, *peeeeesed.*"

The waitress brought a round of coffee. Vicky and Boston played the picture game.

"That one," Vicky said. "First picture, back wall."

"The Wicked Wilson Picket," Boston said, without thinking.

"Below that?"

"Shirley Horne, more jazz than blues, but totally awesome."

"And?"

"Raheem DeVaughn in the background and I don't see Reesa Renee, so she probably wasn't hungry."

I thought about telling Boston and Vicky about the new plea offer, that they should pack it in and call it a night. That we didn't need Repo. The case was over.

But the whole thing didn't sit right. Bushill was

facing first degree murder. Life in prison. When the government offered manslaughter in a murder case, it meant either the prosecutor was incompetent or there were serious problems with the case. I knew it wasn't the former, but with all the evidence against Bushill it was hard to imagine what problems she could be having.

"Above the first booth," Vicky said. "Third from the wall."

"Uhhhh . . ." Boston squinted. "Can't be Jelly Roll Morton. He died in '41, too early for this place."

"Looks like Scott Joplin," Vicky hinted, "but with a sound like Bo Diddley."

"Freddie Barns."

"Close . . ."

"Lonnie Barnes, Freddie's son."

"Disco."

"Damn," Boston said. "That was a tough one."

Shelly may have been factoring in an intoxication defense. First degree murder requires proof of pre-meditation. Even if the jury found that Bushill fired the fatal shot, it could easily be persuaded he was too drunk to have premeditated the act, reducing his culpability to Murder Two. But that would still be a life sentence for someone Bushill's age.

"Second from the door," Vicky said. "Black hat. Dark sunglasses."

"Please." Boston gave her a nudge. "Chuck Brown. Godfather of Go Go. Gimme a challenge."

Manslaughter was a sweet deal. And if there was one thing that made me suspicious, it was a sweet deal. Juveniles got sweet deals. Snitches who triple-nickeled their friends got sweet deals. Cop killers like Bushill got permanent, all expenses paid vacations from the world.

"Above the coffee station." Vicky pointed behind the counter. "One signed, *Loved the eats?*"

"Zola Taylor. Back up vocalist, The Platters."

"Wow, that's obscure. I already get you with that one?"

Boston smiled. "Ten minutes ago."

It had to be the Tomlinson investigation.

The Feds were involved and the investigation was before a grand jury. Hardly the routine inquiry Shelly originally claimed. Vicky's theory about Tomlinson shooting his partner was patent nonsense, but would details of the Tomlinson investigation be helpful in some way to Bushill's defense? Was that why Shelly's supervisors were acting like Santa Claus? Could they really be worried that, if the details came out, the jury would not only discredit Tomlinson's testimony but ignore gunpowder residue?

DNA?

It didn't add up.

"That one," Vicky said, pointing to a photograph of a young man with gold chains slung around his neck.

"Blues, jazz or R&B? Gimme a hint."

"Far out." Vicky laughed. "Never heard of Rayful

Edmond? You *are* a young'un."

"School me."

"Gangster," Vicky said. "Cocaine kingpin. Biggest thing in African-American organized crime since Frank Lucas. And he ran his business right here in this diner. Back in the late eighties . . ."

It was a favorite topic of Vicky's.

Rayful Edmond III was the most infamous drug kingpin the District had ever seen. Handsome and charismatic, Edmond was twenty-four when convicted of running a cocaine organization employing over one hundred dealers, distributors, and enforcers. In the '80s, the District's streets belonged to Edmond.

"Can't believe you've never heard of him," Vicky said. "What's Roman been teaching you?"

Edmund was still a subject of conversation among the older Fifth Streeters, who loved to reminisce about the cast of disreputable characters in the District back then. There was Mayor Marion Barry, who was convicted of cocaine possession then reelected mayor, and Johnny St. Valentine, an undercover narcotics detective whose escapades rivaled television super-cops, but who ended up behind bars himself.

Valentine infiltrated drug crews that were supplied by Edmond. His testimony as a narcotics expert was so effective he was used occasionally by the defense. It was later learned Valentine embellished his testimony, claiming to have a pharmacology degree from Howard University, a school he never attended. He pled guilty to perjury, putting at risk hundreds of convictions. A portrait of Valentine hung in the chambers of the Chief Judge of the Superior Court, exiting his Firebird wearing his trademark leather jacket, sunglasses and gold chains.

But the undisputed super-villain of the '80's was Edmund himself. Edmund applied volume-sales principles to the distribution of crack cocaine, principles he'd gleaned from his brief stint at the University of the District of Columbia's School of Business. Suppliers generally rule by fear and intimidation. Edmond ruled by weight. By establishing direct links to Columbian cartels, Edmond was able to undercut his competitors and offer his dealers more weight for their money. Toward the end of the decade, the Edmond organization controlled eighty percent of the District's crack cocaine trade and was responsible for over forty murders.

"But it wasn't Valentine who put the nail in his coffin," Vicky said. "It was one of his own . . ."

In the end, Edmond was triple-nickeled by one of his closest associates, a middle-age white woman he employed as a mule. Every upper-level figure in the organization, including Edmond's own mother, was convicted. Unprecedented security attended the trial. Jurors were seated behind bullet-proof glass, their identities kept secret. Edmund was held at a Marine base in Quantico Virginia and flown to court every day by helicopter to thwart attempts at armed rescue.

Edmund was convicted and sentenced to life. His

parting words were chilling. "I'll be back," he mouthed to the cameras as they ushered him to the helicopter waiting to take him to prison.

The words were prophetic. Edmond continued to orchestrate cocaine deals using the prison telephone system. Convicted again, Edmond cut a deal. He triple-nickeled his Columbian contacts in exchange for his mother's release, and according to some, was released himself. The U.S. Attorney's Office staunchly denied that Edmond was released. The official position was, although Witness Protection changed Edmond's name, he would serve out his life sentence – just like Bushill would if I couldn't find Repo, convince Bushill he's guilty, and get him to take that plea.

"The question is," Vicky said. "Where's Rayful? Sure, he's supposed to be in prison, but with his name changed, it's not like you can look him up. People claim to see him all the time. For all anyone knows, he's back on the street. And to think, he ran his empire from this little diner right here."

"That's absolutely right, honey," the waitress said, approaching with the check. The tag on her uniform said *Dora*. Paper thin with dark skin and impeccable posture, she looked old enough to have been there when the diner first opened. "Ray used to sit right there." She pointed to a booth by the window.

Vicky perked. "Can we . . ."

"Be my guest, honey."

Vicky grabbed Boston's arm and dragged him to

the Edmund booth.

I handed Dora a ten.

"Ro," Vicky said. "Join us."

"Maybe you should make a placard," I snarled. "Rayful Edmond, King of Cocaine, ordered his grits right here."

"What's with you, Ro? Not yourself tonight."

I couldn't get the meeting with Shelly out of my head. Most of what Shelly said was out of anger at having to make that sweetheart offer, but she was right about one thing. With me trying to prove Bushill's guilt in order to get him to plea, I sure wasn't working cases like I used to.

"Just tired," I said.

Vicky stretched her arms across the back of the booth. "Drag," she said, looking out the window. "The *creep* is here."

CHAPTER TWENTY-EIGHT

The streets were crowded with nightclub goers gearing up for the Saturday Night debauch. It was six blocks from the Grill to the Kafka House at 13th and U, a long hike for Hatch who had to push his bike with Vicky riding his ass the whole way.

"You don't talk to her, Hatch. Understand?"

"Cool."

"She takes off on her bike, she's yours. Follow her and report back."

"Cool."

"That's on the off chance she's there," I added.

"Downer, Ro. You're in one cranky mood."

We turned right at Bohemian Caverns, a jazz club at 11th and U, and walked past the Lincoln Theater, crown jewel of what used to be known as "Black Broadway." In the days of segregation, U Street was the only place African Americans could see live shows. The Great Satchmo. Duke Ellington. Cab Calloway. They all played there. Ironically, when segregation ended and blacks were given access to mainstream venues, the area declined. It wasn't until the real estate boom of the '90s, long after the Martin Luther King riots had decimated the neighborhood, that Black Broadway was revived. Except this time, it was for suburban yuppies.

"That the place?" Boston asked.

The Kafka House was a two-story building abutting an alley on U Street. The bottom floor was boarded and barred. Wallace said it was an abandoned coffee shop, but the façade was so layered in graffiti it was hard to make out what it had been.

"Dig it." Vicky pointed to *REPO* scrawled across the front door, then led us down the alley. "Here's the deal. One of us has to climb the fire escape and see if she's there."

The fire escape connected to a catwalk running along the outside of the building. It was metal-framed and floored with wood, rotted through in places. There was a four-foot gap at the top of the stairs. A row of boarded windows lined the catwalk. Third window in, the plywood had been ripped out. Music played from inside.

"She already knows what I look like," Vicky said.

"Me too." I said, taking note of the alarming gap in the flooring.

"Which means . . ." She shifted her eyes to Hatch.

Hatch looked at me.

I nodded.

"What's this chick look like?" he asked.

"White female," Vicky told him. "Five-foot-two."

"Is she . . ."

"She was wearing a mask," I said. "But she's thin, with really nice . . . Trust me, dude, your gonna love her."

"Righteous." Hatch leaned his bike against the wall and started up the stairs.

He didn't hesitate when he got to the top and leapt over the gap to the catwalk, showering us with flakes of rust and rotted wood. A metallic screech echoed down the alley, but the ancient contraption held.

Hatch flashed thumbs up and disappeared through the open window.

"First time I've had any use for that freak," Vicky whispered.

The noise from inside rose suddenly, young men chanting, "Toke, toke, toke . . ."

Revelers walked past the mouth of alley, mostly ignoring us, except two young men who stepped in for a pee. "YOLO!" one of them hollered, midstream.

Hatch reappeared at the window, flashing another thumbs up. He unleashed a cloud of smoke as he stepped onto the catwalk.

"Well?" Vicky hissed. "Any sign?"

"Sign?" He leaned on the railing and looked down, squinting.

"The girl," I said. "She there?"

"Oh, yeah. No sign of her, Ro. But my man Barfo? He's back! So if we're done, I'm gonna hang out."

Vicky whacked my shoulder. "Let's go."

We walked to the mouth of the alley and stood, shoulder-to-shoulder, watching the crowd.

"Was worth a shot," Vicky muttered.

"So . . . we're square, right, Ro?" Hatch hollered from above.

The Metro station on the corner unleashed a stream of night-clubbers. Taxicabs double-parked in the street, letting the sober out and taking the drunks in.

"What's the plan?" Boston asked.

"The plan?" Vicky sighed. "Hang out with Johnny, I guess. Share a cab, Ro?"

A bicycle swerved off U Street and pulled into the alley entrance. The rider was a young woman, skinny with blond hair, dressed in layers of black clothing. She skidded to a stop in front of us.

"Shit!" she blurted.

She pivoted on her rear wheel and took off down the street, the duffle bag over her shoulder clinking with what sounded like paint cans.

"Hatch!" I yelled.

Hatch bounded down the fire escape, grabbed his bike and met us on the sidewalk.

"You're on deck," Vicky said. "White girl. Blond hair. Black bike. West on U."

"Ummm . . ."

"That way!" Vicky pointed. "Christ, you reek of weed. Hit me on the cell when you find her."

"Stay with her," I said, as Hatch mounted.

"Done deal, Ro. Bitch is mine!" He cranked a pedal, slammed it, and peddled away like a fiend.

"Why do you use that freak, Ro?"

"Taxi!"

We piled into the backseat of a Capital Cab. "U-bee," I told the driver. "West on U."

He raised an eyebrow in the rearview. "You see this traffic?"

I tossed two twenties on the front seat and the cab took off, tires screeching as it crossed three lanes and turned west.

"Where now?"

"Straight," Vicky said.

Super Freak started playing on Vicky's cell. She put it on speaker. "I'm half a block behind her," Hatch said. "She just crossed Eleventh."

"Stay with her." Vicky leaned over the front seat. "Keep going, sir."

"Where?" The cabbie asked, slowing for a light.

"Straight!"

I tossed another twenty up front and he gunned it through the yellow.

"She just crossed Ninth onto Florida," Hatch said. "Straight . . . straight . . . no, right! She turned right!"

"Turned right, where?" Vicky asked.

"Yeah . . . right."

"Hatch, you miserable creep. Turned right *where*?"

The cabbie snatched the phone from Vicky as he barreled through another yellow, swerving around cars with one hand on the wheel. "Excuse me. This person turned right, yes?"

"Yeah," Hatch said "She turned right."

"Ayyyyyyyye see. And where? Where did she turn this right?"

"Who *is* this?"

"Hatch!" I yelled. "Where is she?"

"T Street, Ro. She's at the Howard!"

"Next corner," I said to the cabbie.

Across Ninth, U turned into Florida, where trendy restaurants and jazz clubs gave way to businesses that had been boarded up since the King riots of '68. The Howard Theater had been the lone holdout. It struggled through the late sixties and enjoyed a brief rebirth in the seventies, but was then shuttered and fell into disrepair.

"Nine dollars," the cabbie said, cruising to a stop.

I shot him a look in the rearview.

"Okay . . . all right." He snatched the twenties I'd thrown on his seat. "Have a nice night."

We walked past Central Communications, a cell phone shop blaring hip hop from a speaker above its door, then past Joe Caplan Liquor, the only other open businesses on the block. At T Street, Florida opened to a dark plaza where the Howard Theater sat in ruins.

Its three-story façade was crumbling. A dilapidated marquee drooped low above its doors. The *Howard Theater* sign, once a beacon of Black Broadway, hung cockeyed down the side of the building. The entire structure was in such danger of collapse it was girdled by a chain-link fence which had been ripped to shreds by the locals.

Hatch sat on a stoop beneath the marquee, blowing a joint.

"Wassup peeps?"

"Where'd . . . she . . . go?" Vicky asked.

Hatch nodded to his right. "Fire escape in the alley. Probably on the roof by now. What took you so long?"

"She spot you?"

"Get real."

"Hang out across the street. She takes off again, you know what to do." Vicky beckoned to Boston and I. "You two come with me."

We peeked around the corner of the building into an ally lined with abandoned warehouses. A fire escape zigzagged up the wall of the theater to an open door leading to its balcony.

There was a bicycle chained to a drainpipe at the foot of the stairs.

The fire escape looked more dangerous than the one at the Kafka House and clung to the building by rusty joints. Some of the steps had rusted through and hung detached.

"One at a time," Vicky said.

"No way," I said. "Three of us climbing separately? She'll hear it for sure. We'll make less racket if we go all at once."

"Fine."

"Ladies first."

"With you staring up my ass the whole way? Pass, Ro. I'll be right behind you." She nodded to Boston. "You after me."

With each step there was a crunch of rusted metal. Pieces of mortar tumbled downward with every shift of weight. But the best indication the operation might not go smoothly was the metallic screech as we hit the first landing.

"Easy, Ro," Vicky said. "Take it slow."

The stairs shuddered and I clung to the handrail, wondering what the last seconds of my life would be like with a ton of rusted steel crashing down around me.

In retrospect, one-at-a-time would have been the better plan.

At the second landing, the fire escape groaned and bowed from the wall. I cursed after cutting my hand on the jagged rail.

"Damn it, Roman." Vicky bumped into me. "Every time you stop, the stairs bend."

"You wanna go first?"

At the third landing, I was thinking seriously about bounding up the last flight, leaping through the door and leaving Vicky and Boston to fend for themselves.

A police cruiser turned into the alley and stopped below us with its siren off, but emergency lights on, lighting up the alley in alternating bursts of red, white and blue.

Go America.

I dropped to the landing, flush against the wall.

Vicky stretched out on the stairs below me with Boston on top of her.

A cop exited the cruiser and swept the alley with a flashlight. Vicky was breathing so hard I was sure he'd hear her, but after a minute he returned to his cruiser.

"Drag," Vicky said. "Didn't sign up for this."

I hadn't signed up for it either. Taking cover from police by clinging to a deathtrap, three stories above a dark alley, had been another subject missing from the Georgetown curriculum.

The cruiser let out a siren blast and shot down the alley. We stayed put for a few seconds, listening to the siren grow fainter.

"Boston," Vicky said. "How's about getting off my ass."

"Sorry."

We climbed the last flight and stepped through the door into darkness. I lit the place up with my cell. The six-row balcony was littered with bottles. Its tattered chairs reeked of mold. An old Weber grill sat in a corner surrounded by benches made of cinderblocks and planks.

"Over there," Boston said, pointing to a ladder.

We navigated through the darkness to the upper tier. The ladder extended through the ceiling to a trap door leading to the roof.

"Volunteer?" Vicky asked.

Boston raised a hand.

"You the man, Boss," I told him. "Hold the ladder

for you."

He started to climb.

"Lift that door slowly," Vicky instructed. "If she's on the roof, you don't want to –"

"Vick," I said. "He's not Hatch."

"Sorry. Can't help myself."

The door squeaked as Boston eased it open, just enough for a peek. "Someone's there, all right," he whispered. "Painting a wall. Far side of the roof."

"Is it her?" Vicky asked.

"I dunno." Boston climbed back down, looked at Vicky and laughed. "But the wall says *Repo*."

CHAPTER TWENTY-NINE

People who learn about the criminal justice system by watching TV are under the impression that the key to winning a case is investigation, that locating as many witnesses as possible is part of the search for truth. This is accurate when it comes to prosecutors, who are more-or-less in the crime-solving business.

Defense attorneys are in the crime *un*-solving biz.

For a defense attorney, less is more, particularly when it comes to witnesses. The more witnesses a defense attorney calls to testify at trial, the greater the odds they will contradict each other and highlight the fact that the defendant is dead guilty. The key to a successful defense is finding that one witness who will blow the government's case out of the water, or at least confuse the jury enough to raise reasonable doubt.

God bless her, that's what Vicky was trying to do.

"Let's coordinate," Vicky said. "First off, she'll assume we're with the press."

Boston said, "Why would she assume that?".

"Ask your mentor."

I smiled.

"So we're stuck with that," Vicky continued. "At least initially. We'll get her talking about graffiti, bring her around to the subject of the Hall of Fame, then ease her into the shooting."

"Bet," I said.

"The last time she cut and ran, so I'll go first. We don't want to spook her. If she's willing to talk, and I think it's safe to bring you up, I'll give the signal. But I take lead. You geniuses hang back and act like you're taking notes."

Boston nodded.

"Roman?"

"Your show, Vick."

She scaled the ladder, eased open the access door and climbed onto the roof. Boston followed, but hung at the top with his head through the opening, giving me the play-by-play.

"She's halfway there . . . Right behind her . . . Oh!"

"What?"

"Repo spotted her."

"And?"

"Nothing. They're talking." Boston looked down and frowned. "Kind of anticlimactic. How do I know when she gives the signal?"

"What's she doing now?"

"Just standing there with a hand on her ass."

"Right cheek or left?"

"Right."

"Let's go."

We climbed through the trap door. The roof was flat, bordered on three sides by a two-foot brick wall, and by a six-foot wall in the back. The Repo mural on the back wall was almost finished. There was a bench in front of it constructed from milk crates and two-by-fours with Repo's duffle bag and spray paint on top. To our right, the bright lights of the now-gentrified, former Black Broadway. The dilapidation of Florida Avenue was below. In the distance, the Capitol and the Washington Monument. All three D.C.'s in one view.

"I know you didn't ask to talk to us," Vicky was saying. "But just hear me out." She did the intros as we approached. "You remember Mr. O'Brian . . . from the fence, I'm sure."

Repo smirked.

"And this is Mr. Boston Stewart. He's –"

"On gig from Vice Magazine." Boston extended a fist. "Big fan. Been following your work for a year. It's deck."

Repo gave him a cautious bump.

Vicky fixed Boston with a stare. "Mr. Stewart's just here to –"

"I'll take it from here, Ms. Bronco." Boston pulled a notepad from his jeans. "Hope you don't mind if I take notes."

Repo nodded.

"Heard you gave my colleagues the frigidaire. Too bad. They're totally midtown –"

"That they are," Repo said, smiling.

"But they're on the level. In fact, I'm trying to do the same thing they're trying to do. Get your message out on the clothesline, but for real people. Nationwide. You willish?"

Repo considered Boston, then sat on her makeshift bench. Boston sat beside her, flipped open his notepad and shot Vicky a wink.

Vicky grabbed my arm. She walked me to the edge of the roof and we sat on the wall, looking on as Boston interviewed Repo. "Impressive," she said. "He speaks hipster, too."

Down below, Florida Avenue was empty, except for two homeless men dumpster-diving in front of the theater, and Hatch on his bike across the street, blowing another joint. A Crown Vick cruised slowly down the street, pulled into the alley and stopped next to the fire escape. I tapped Vicky on the shoulder and pointed.

"Crap, Ro," Vicky said. "How the hell does he *do* that? What is he, psychic?"

"Is that —"

Tomlinson stepped out of the Crown Vick, rubbed his bald head and started to look up. Vicky pulled me off the wall, out of view.

She slid out her cell and called Hatch on speaker. "See that jumper in alley?"

"Oh, shit," Hatch said.

I actually heard him spit out his joint.

"What's he doing?" Vicky asked.

"He's snoopin' around the fire escape, checking out Repo's bike."

"Let me know if he –"

"Sweet. He's back in his car . . . pulling out of the alley . . ."

"Is he gone?"

"He's . . . drag. Parking across the street."

"Keep outta sight." She turned to me. "What the hell is Tomlinson doing here?"

Excellent question.

"C'mon. Let's get in the game." I walked her back to where Boston had Repo chatting like a schoolgirl.

"Let's move on to why you do this," Boston was saying.

"You don't know?" Repo asked.

"Sure. Anti-gentrification is the basic theme, but it's better to get a direct quote."

"It's economic eviction," Repo said. "They take a crappy building, tear it down, and put up a craptacular condo. Urban renewal, right? Supposed to improve the neighborhood. But pretty soon, all the low-rent building owners start looking to sell. Before you know it, people who've lived in the neighborhood their whole lives have to leave."

"Let's talk about other writers. You ever write with Exist or Warp?"

"How is it you know so much about graff? What'd you do? Talk to Wallace?"

"Know him?"

She grimaced. "By reputation."

"Way I hear it, he's dying to sell your stuff."

"Fat chance. He takes legit writers and turns them into money grubbing hacks. Not that they ever get the cash. Exist sold five pieces, couple hundred each. After Wallace took his cut, Exist barely had bus fare. Guy's a leech."

"Who do you write with?"

"I mostly work alone, but sometimes with Nuk and Inca." She pointed to Boston's scribbling. "That's not their real names, you know."

"I'm square," Boston said. "Who else?"

"Crot, Nehi, Swabo . . . Met some of the old-head, too. Warp, Everclear, Seven . . . I met another female writer, Chelove. She's legit now." Repo shrugged. "It happens."

"What about Cool Disco Dan?"

"Heard about that. Heard he gave Wallace a piece. Breaks my heart."

"Who is he?"

"He bombed the city years ago. Got ups on the Metro, downtown, all over Southeast. It's mostly buffed, but the stuff in the poorer neighborhoods survived. He's a legend."

"Ever meet him?"

"Once, at a Go Go. He's in his thirties."

"Old, huh?"

"Vintage," Repo said with respect.

"Tell me some war stories."

"About what?" Repo grinned, enjoying herself. "You mean like the war with the Bethesda Bombers?"

"That a graffiti crew?"

"Yeah. I write alone, sometimes with a friend like Nuk, but steer clear of the crews. Idiots hopped up on testosterone, more interested in fighting than writing. But Nuk hung with Blitz 88 and when the war started with the Bethesda Bombers he asked me to help."

"You're joking. Graffiti wars?"

"Men," Repo said, tossing Vicky a soul-sister look. "Like friggin' boys. The Bombers started dissing Blitz tags all over town."

"Painting over them?" Boston asked.

"Nice pieces, too. So Blitz started dissing Bomber tags, writing 88 on every one they could find."

"Go on."

"Nuk asked me to go with him and his Blitz idiots to the Bethesda Metro. The night before, the Bombers hit the tunnel for a quarter mile. The mission was to diss the whole thing, a strike on their home turf."

"You went along?" Vicky asked.

"Stupid things we do for men, eh? We hopped off the platform after the last train and totally destroyed the place."

"You write *Repo* on any of them?" I asked.

"Why? So they could start dissing me? Anybody disses me, I'll kill em." She paused. "We were almost done when we heard voices down the tracks."

"Cops?" Boston asked.

"Bombers," guessed Vicky.

"Duru, Sky, Flame and Copycat. I didn't know them, except from their tags. They were just kids. Soon as they saw us, they chucked their cans and ran. Blitz chased them through the tunnel, up on the platform, and out the Metro. I just wanted to get the fuck out of there and go home. A police cruiser lit us up as we hit the street. The cop only caught one."

"Nuk," Vicky guessed.

Repo nodded. "Later, we got word he flipped, you know? Named names."

"That's harsh," said Vicky.

"Think you know someone, huh?"

"He rat on you?"

"Nah. Told on everyone in Blitz, though. Little fuckers kirked when they found out. Went to Nuk's house and wrote *Snitches get Stitches* across the front door."

"I remember that," I said. "It was in the Post."

"Cops took it serious. They all got charges."

"What happened to Nuk?" asked Vicky.

"Dunno."

"You don't still see him?"

"Right," Repo sneered.

"So . . ." Boston glanced at Vicky, then Repo. "Tell us about the Hall of Fame."

Repo smiled. "I was dying to get an up in the Hall, but waited till I got a reputation. Didn't want to be dissed as a toy, an amateur, you know?"

"Must have been a dream come true," I said.

"It was okay."

"Dangerous though, huh?"

"I don't want to talk about it," she whispered.

"Didn't run into any trouble, did you?"

"Why are you so interested in the Hall? Thought this was about me?"

"We're interested in that aspect of it," Vicky said. "For our readers."

I had to give it to Vicky. It couldn't have been easy for her to put on a ruse like that.

"I guess," Repo said. "Seen a few things, sure."

"Like what?"

Repo packed her things. "You wouldn't believe it."

"I saw a man get mugged once," Vicky told her. "Saw who did it, too. It was a young guy who lived down the street. Didn't report it, though. Guess I didn't want to get involved. Week later, I heard the same guy mugged an old woman, knocked her down and broke her hip. She uses a walker now. Know what I'm tryin' to say?"

Repo threw the last of her supplies in her duffle, tears starting down her cheeks.

"We'll keep it confidential," Vicky told her. "Like an anonymous source."

"It's already anonymous," I said "We don't know who you are."

"I was in the Hall," Repo said, brushing tears, "the night that cop got killed, doing my mural. Three men came walking down the tunnel, so I hid."

"Three?" I asked.

"They were arguing. Then that crazy fucker, he just started shooting!"

And there it was, the last nail in Bushill's coffin.

"I shouldn't have told you," Repo sobbed.

"It's okay." Vicky put a hand on her shoulder. "We knew you were there. You tied a rope to the man's –"

"How'd you know about that?"

"I . . . must've read it in the paper."

"Wasn't in the paper." She shot Vicky a betrayed look. "Who *are* you people?"

Repo grabbed her duffle, bolted across the roof and disappeared through the access door. Vicky ran after her first, then Boston, then me. By the time we got down the ladder and navigated our way through the dark balcony to the fire escape, Repo was peddling her bike down the street.

Hatch flew down the street behind her.

Then Tomlinson.

"You were right, Ro." Vicky craned over the fire escape railing, watching them disappear. "It's hopeless."

"So," Boston said. "What's the plan?"

CHAPTER THIRTY

Madam's Organ on a Saturday night is freak fest.
Three floors, not counting the roof deck, with
most of the crowd squeezed into the narrow space in
front of the first-floor stage. Since Vicky had a "date"
with Johnny, we were expecting the Johnny Hammond
Band, but there was a female trio on stage. A guitar, a
bass, and a front-woman in a cowboy hat belting out
Motown.

Bart was mixing drinks and taking orders. "Ro!"
he yelled, without looking up.

Vicky wedged through the crowd, stepped up to
the bar, and shouted in Bart's ear. Bart shook his head,
and told her something that had her fighting her way
angrily to the stairs.

Boston and I followed.

The second floor has a pool table, a balcony, and a
karaoke booth where a twenty-something was treating
the room to an off key rendition of *Sweet Child of Mine*.

Vicky took the narrow stairs to the third floor
salon, a tiny room with red walls. There's a small bar, a

handful of red velvet couches, and the uneasy feeling the space was designed for vampires.

Vicky and Boston claimed a couch.

It was a typical Madam's crowd: two Australian exchange students hitting on two Asian women, a couple in an armchair making out as if in a motel, and a group of jarheads at the bar, doing shots and yelling, "Whooo Waaa!"

"Yuengling, Boss?" I asked.

Boston nodded.

"Vick, I'll get you a –"

"Southern Comfort," she said. "Hold the ice."

"You don't drink. What's up with –"

"Don't wanna talk about it, Ro."

I stepped to the bar and signaled the bartender, an older woman, skinny with spiked hair, wearing a *Slayer* concert tee.

God Hates Us All tour.

"Two Yuenglings and a SoCo, neat." I looked back at the couch. Vicky was sobbing, her head on Boston's shoulder. "Make that SoCo a double."

My cell buzzed. It was Hatch. I put it on speaker.

"Ro, you . . . believe it . . . street . . . no kidding . . . over there for a . . . downtown."

"Say it again. Hatch?"

"Gotta go!"

I thought about calling him back and telling him to forget it. That it didn't matter who Repo was, or where she lived. I had what I needed. According to Repo, the crazy fucker did it. Bushill was clearly guilty, which meant he would take the plea.

Mission accomplished.

But I also thought about Judge Bearmond telling me the case required an attorney with my particular skills, that it had plea deal written all over it. I thought about Vicky reading me the riot act the other night and accusing me of sounding like Pockets.

Mostly I thought about my meeting with Shelly.

She slammed the drinks on the bar. "Twenty-seven fifty."

Steep. All of a sudden, I missed Bart.

I handed her a card.

"Back in a flash," she said.

Then again, where did Shelly get off saying I was washed up? The ability to recognize the futility of a situation? The foresight to perceive when there's a train coming down the tracks? And the good sense to get out of the way? Those aren't signs of being washed up. They're signs of being a rational man.

So why did it make me feel like I was you-know-who?

"Sign here."

I scribbled *Pockets* on the check, headed back to the couch, and handed out drinks. Vicky downed hers in one gulp.

"Maybe Johnny will show up later," I said.

"When? After his show in New York? Bart says he won't be back for a month. Forget it. I'm done."

"Maybe it's for the –"

"Don't wanna talk about it, Ro." She handed me her glass. "Maybe go with a little ice this time."

I headed back to the bar. Hatch called again.

"Downtown, Ro. She just went in the Harrington."

"The hotel?"

"Yeah." Hatch laughed.

It didn't make sense. Where would a street rat like Repo get the scratch for a downtown hotel?

"What about the cop?"

"Please," he said. "Ditched that bald fool fifteen minutes ago. She's talking to the desk clerk. I'm laying low in the lobby. When she's done, I'll see if I can figure out what room she's in."

Under normal circumstances, the Harrington would have been an incredible stroke of luck. Even if Repo paid cash, the hotel would require identification. We could subpoena her name. We could unmask Repo.

Not that it mattered.

But like everyone else in the city, I was curious.

"Shoot," Hatch said. "Scratch the hotel. She just left. No worries, dude. I'll wait in the lobby for a hot minute so she doesn't spot the tail, then grab my wheels and pick up the trail."

"Back so soon?" the bartender said.

"SoCo. On the rocks this time."

"Double?"

I looked at Vicky, slumped against Boston. "Nah."

"Dude," said Hatch. "You there?"

"Yeah. What's she doing?"

"Unlocking her bike . . . taking off . . . and the chase is on!"

"Make sure you don't—"

"Aw, friggin bitch!

"What?"

"That is *so* not cool."

"What, damn it?"

"Dude, she slashed my tires."

"Sorry, Hatch. Gotta go."

So much for unmasking Repo.

Just for kicks I went over in my mind how the trial would play out. Tomlinson testifying that Bushill shot Knox. Me grandstanding while discrediting Tomlinson. Shelly coming back with the gunpowder residue and DNA. And the big finish? Repo, who Tomlinson would eventually find, confirming that the "crazy fucker" had done the deed. Of course, there were discrepancies in Repo's story too.

Not that it mattered.

But in the interest of due diligence I considered them as well. Repo said she was painting when three people came walking down the tunnel, as if Bushill had been walking with Tomlinson and Knox. Her story was inconsistent with Tomlinson's.

Not that it mattered.

But playing devil's advocate, just as an intellectual exercise, I thought about what that might mean.

If Repo was lying . . .

"Nine even," the bartender said.

"On the card." I snapped up the drink and headed back.

Vicky was in a slightly better mood, the alcohol having taken effect. A teetotaler, Vicky got wasted just looking at alcohol. She was explaining the situation to Boston from a professional investigator's perspective.

"Screwed, screwed, screwed . . . That's what this case is, Boston, my boy. Screwed and tattooed. You know what?" She leaned in. "You got hazel eyes. Just like that tramp, Shelly."

I handed her the drink. What the hell. The damage was done.

"Tell him how screwed we are, Ro."

"Thing is," I said.

"We're so screwed," Vicky said, swirling her glass. "And correct me, Ro, if I'm wrong. That our client is, absolutely, for sure, gonna spend the rest of his –"

"I met with Shelly this morning," I said. "There's a new plea offer."

Vicky stopped swirling. Her ice came to rest with a *clink*. "How's that?"

"Voluntary manslaughter."

"You're kidding."

"There's a strict deadline, though. It's off the books Monday morning."

Boston said, "Voluntary manslaughter, what's that in terms of –"

"Thirty years," I said, "with a guideline midrange

of seven. Assuming he gets midrange, and factoring in time off for good behavior, he'll be out in –"

"Six," Vicky finished. "Jesus, you really must've beat Shelly up."

"Yeah," I said. "Gave her hell."

"My God, that's a sweetheart!"

"Sure is."

"A gift."

"Uh huh."

"Suspicious as hell."

"Exactly," I said. "Voluntary manslaughter? For killing a cop? According to Shelly, someone upstairs forced her to make the offer. So what I'm thinking is, there's gotta be a reason."

"What the hell does it matter what the reason is?"

"At first, I thought it has to be Tomlinson. That the Internal Affairs investigation must be bigger than we thought. That they don't want to risk Bearmond letting us introduce the details at trial. That somehow it would taint their case against Bushill."

"You beat them," Vicky said. "Who cares how?"

"But now I'm thinking, maybe there are discrepancies we don't know about. We keep digging, who knows? Maybe we –"

"You sniffin' glue? You heard what Repo said, Bushill did it."

"I know, but listen –"

"Monday morning that offer is dead. Dead as a doornail. Elvis dead. It'll be dead earlier if Tomlinson finds Repo, and he's all over that kid. He was there both times we found her. Probably tracking her cell."

"Can they do that?"

"Hell yeah they can. And you're going to waste time trying to be a hero again? There's only one thing to do. Go to Bushill and make him take it."

"I know, but I've been thinking. Repo's story? Actually full of holes."

"It's over, Ro."

"I know, I know. Just hear me out."

"Christ, Roman!" She flew off the couch, grabbed me by the lapels and pulled. "Are you so far gone, you don't even know when you've *won*?"

CHAPTER THIRTY-ONE

Sunday morning, I awoke to Mom making breakfast. She'd scored a few single-serving Frosted Flakes boxes from the bodega on the corner, and coffee from Tryst. Dad was in bed, sipping coffee, reviewing the latest issue of Timeshare World.

"Morning, Munchkin."

"Morning, Ma," I croaked.

"Lookie here," Dad said. "The Flamenco Suites is having its grand opening next month in Cancun. They'll be giving time away . . . *giving* it away."

"We already talked about that, dear," Mom said. "The airfare."

"Right, but say we get a good deal." He flicked the article with his finger. "Just look at that pool, will ya? Right on the beach."

"Yeah, dear." Mom set my breakfast on the coffee table.

"Forty-two-inch screens, complimentary HBO . . ."

"Uh-huh." She poured milk in my box of Flakes.

"That settles it," Dad said. "I'm calling Sal."

"You do that."

"They got pyramids in Cancun, sugar. I'm takin' you to see em."

"That's the spirit, dear."

An entire lobe of my mother's brain is devoted to responding to Dad.

"So, Munchkin. What's going on today?"

"Work," I said, starting on breakfast.

"On Sunday?"

"Big case, eh, son?" Dad asked.

"It's a case all right."

"Tell us about it," Mom said.

"It's a murder."

"Really? That does sound big."

"An honest to God murder." Dad shook his head. "What happened?"

"Well, that's the question. Sure looks like the guy did it, but there are loose ends."

Dad put down his magazine. "Guess you're gonna be investigating, huh?"

"Something like that."

"Interrogating suspects?" Mom asked.

"He's a lawyer, sugar. He doesn't interrogate. He investigates. Tries to figure the ins and outs, the ups-n-downs. Right, son?"

"Actually, I'm supposed to take a plea offer to my client today. See if he'll take it."

"Oh." Dad flipped open his magazine and adjusted his glasses.

Mom cleared the coffee table. "Whatever you think is best, Munchkin."

I took a long shower, then checked my phone and found three messages, each from last night, each from Vicky, each more drunkenly incoherent than the last. The general theme was clear, though.

Take the plea.

I gave Mom a kiss and headed out.

"Munchkin!" Mom called after me. "Don't forget. Dinner with Brenda tonight. Eight o'clock."

"Okay, Ma."

"Aren't you excited?"

I'd been giving Brenda the cold shoulder for so long I'd gotten used to it. She deserved it, though. You don't divorce someone, come crawling back, and expect to be welcomed with open arms. I wasn't dreading it, but excited wasn't the right word.

The word was 'apprehensive.' Brenda didn't mesh with my family. Mom graduated from Dunbar High. Dad dropped out in the tenth grade and spent forty-five years driving for UPS. Brenda's mother is a CPA, her father a senior partner at a K Street securities firm. She has a bachelor's in Nineteenth Century literature from Vassar and a master's from Penn, in addition to having graduated at the top of her class from Georgetown Law. Her conversations with my parents tended to be forced.

And, of course, there was the last time.

Two years ago, mom insisted on hosting Thanksgiving dinner. Dad had it catered by a local restaurant, even splurged on adjoining suits at the Ramada. They might have pulled it off had they not invited Uncle Sal and Aunt Terry. Sal met Terry at a Daytona strip club, got her to give up the life, and made a fairly respectable woman of her, except for her clothes. She showed up in spandex that would've fit twenty years earlier, tottering drunk, swearing like a roofer, and hitting on Brenda's dad. Practically gave the man a lap dance. Brenda was polite about it, though. She was like that. Forgiving.

Maybe I was a little excited.

I should've headed straight to the jail, but hailed a cab and told the driver to take me to Simple City. It was unlikely Trayon would be hanging around before noon on a Sunday, and I couldn't help be curious about what Witness One, Janet Randolph, would have to say about Tomlinson.

Not that it mattered.

"Slow down," I said as the cab turned onto W and passed her building. "I need to see if someone's here. Hang a u-bee, then come back down the street, slow."

The courtyard was empty except for a young man with a hoodie pulled over his head leaning against the front door.

A beat up Neon slowed to a stop in front of the building and we pulled behind it. The young man stepped from the building and walked toward the Neon, holding a finger to us as if we were next in line.

Trayon Stokes.

Just my luck. The building was Trayon's spot, the place he peddled whatever it was he was peddling these days. Street dealers are fiercely territorial and stake claim to specific locations so their regulars will know where to find them. Trayon was working the building.

"Forget it," I said, sinking low in my seat.

The cabbie gunned around the Neon. "Where to?"

"D.C. Jail. Nineteenth and –"

"I know where it is," he snapped.

There are few things defense attorneys hate more than the count: the tally of prisoners at the jail. The process takes an hour, during which time no inmates are brought to the visiting hall. Miscounts are frequent, and when they occur, double the dead-time.

The Sunday count was at one o'clock. Attorneys avoided the jail at that time as if it were Bearmond. My strategy was to arrive fifteen minutes before count-time, wind my way to the visiting hall, and have my client brought out before everything shut down. Five minutes before the count, Bushill still hadn't arrived, so I tapped the glass of the security bubble.

"Cage," the guard grumbled.

A bad sign.

The cage is a row of boxes on the far side of the visiting hall, each the size of a telephone booth, each wrapped in steel mesh, each with a plexiglass front. The inmate is shackled to a stool and has to speak to visitors through a phone. Tired of pulling Bushill off me, they'd ordered him to meet me in the cage. As I got closer, I could see his lip was swollen. He had a bandage over one eye.

I took a seat and put the phone to my ear.

"Find the ninja?" he asked.

"What happened to you?"

"Hmmph. Could ask the same of you."

"You did this to me."

"Sorry about your eye," he said. "You had that lip coming, though."

"Well?" I asked.

"Got in a scuffle."

"You all right?"

"What's it look like?"

"To be honest," I said, recalling the day we met. "Seen you worse."

He smiled, then winced. "This young'un thinks he can walk around with his jumpsuit around his waist."

"Okay."

"He's one of them underwear hangers."

"Huh?"

"Got underwear hanging out the back."

"Oh yeah, they'll get ya."

"Not me."

"What happened?"

"I sneak up behind him, snatch up his undies and yank. You should've seen him, grabbing for his ball bearings like they were about to be recalled by Chrysler. Decorum, I tell him. Got to maintain decorum, son!"

"Decorum's important."

"And that's it."

"End of story?"

"Well, except for the scuffle." He rubbed his chin. "Sent us both to the hole, thirty days."

The "hole" wasn't like in the movies, a tiny room with a stainless-steel toilet and a mattress. Being in the hole meant being on lockdown status: locked in a cell twenty-three hours a day. No social visits. No canteen. Shackled when transported through general population.

"Not that bad," he said. "Keeps me out of general pop."

"You want me to put in for PC?"

Inmates can request PC, protective custody, which pretty much means lockdown status permanently.

"Leave it be," Bushill said, quickly. "Don't want to be hot."

The danger of protective custody is that it causes other inmates to think the protected inmate is "hot," triple-nickeling other inmates. Snitching.

"A separation order, then," I suggested.

With a separation order, they would move him to another unit, lessening the chance of an encounter with the same inmate.

"Can take care of myself." He shifted painfully on his stool. "You find the ninja?"

I nodded.

His eyes held mine for what seemed like forever, then dropped to the floor. When he looked up, the life had gone out of them.

"She said you did it," I told him, confirming what he'd read in my eyes.

"Say why?"

"Don't think she knows," I said. "There are a few inconsistencies in her story, and we're tracking down a woman who has information about the investigation of Detective Tomlinson. Alternatively . . ."

His head went to his knees. "I'm sorry," he sobbed. "I'm sorry . . . Jesus, I'm sorry."

"Alternatively," I said. "There's a new plea offer."

"Take it."

"Manslaughter. It's complicated, but you could be out in –"

"Take it." He dropped the phone in its cradle and signaled for the guard.

"Alex." I knocked on the plexiglass.

They unlocked the cage and led Bushill away.

CHAPTER THIRTY-TWO

I took the Metro downtown, knocked out a nap in my office, then hailed a cab. When I told the driver Simple City, he gave me a disgruntled look, but took me there anyway.

It was stupid.

What did it matter what Witness One had to say? Tomlinson could've been the dirtiest cop in the history of dirty cops, the Pablo Escobar of the MPD. He and his partner could've threatened, maimed, even killed to protect an illegal drug empire spanning six states and it wouldn't make a difference. Bushill's plea deal could not possibly get any sweeter.

But I had to know. Watching Bushill breakdown in the cage made me feel sorry for the homicidal codger. And thinking about Tomlinson testifying, as if he and his partner were salt of the Earth, made me retch. If bringing details of their illegal activities to light would make Bushill feel better about what he had done, then I was all for it.

Not that it mattered.

The plan was foolproof. Park half a block from the building, wait until someone pulls up looking to score, then make a play for the front entrance while Trayon is making the sale.

Simple.

"Sir, you know the meter is running, right?"

I threw another five on the front seat.

The problem was, there were three of them hanging by the door: Trayon and two of his hoppers, juveniles who handled the sales so Trayon could keep his hands clean. Every time a car pulled up, one of the hoppers would run to the car, take the cash, then signal the order to Trayon who would send the second hopper to deliver the goods. Trayon never moved.

What's more, I was out of fives.

A police cruiser pulled up.

Perfect.

Trayon was taking cash from a hopper. He held a finger to the cruiser without looking. "With you in a minute," he yelled, stuffing two ziplocks of product in the other hopper's backpack.

The hopper tapped Trayon on the arm and pointed. Trayon looked up and the cop smiled back. Cop and drug dealer stared at each other across the expanse of their traditional battlefield, the front courtyard of a low-income housing project.

It was Trayon who broke the tableau.

He bolted right, up the walkway, then down W Street. The hoppers bolted left. The cop hit his lights and followed Trayon.

"Thanks for the ride," I said to the cabbie.

I looked back as I made my way to the entrance. Trayon had hung a quick turn and was running across the next courtyard, down the walkway that led behind the buildings. The cruiser screeched to a halt. The cop exited and stood with the door open as if contemplating chasing Trayon down, then got back in his cruiser and drove away.

I pulled on the steel door.

Locked, of course.

"Janet Randolph!" I yelled at the building. "You home, Ms. Randolph?"

She appeared at her window wearing a housedress, a bandana strapped across her wild hair. "Was hoping you'd come back. Where's your little girlfriend?"

"Just me today." There was a *clop clop* coming up the walkway alongside the building. "Can you buzz me in, Ms. Randolph?

"Ms. Janet . . . You call me Ms. Janet. Everybody 'round here calls me . . ."

Trayon rounded the corner of the building into the courtyard, looked up and down the street, saw that the cop had left, and smiled.

Until he saw me.

"Ms. Janet. Can you buzz me in?"

"Mother fucker!" Trayon strode my way.

307

"Oh my!" Ms. Janet said, and disappeared from the window.

The door buzzed. I yanked it open, jumped inside and slammed it shut. There was a bang on the other side a hot second later. I stood in the stairwell, panting.

"Ms. Janet!" Trayon screamed. "I need to visit my cousin. Can you let me –"

"You go on and leave that man alone!" she yelled. "I'll call the police, Trayon. Don't you think I won't!"

The stairwell was dark. Gouges in the plaster went all the way up, as if someone had redecorated with a medieval mace. The steps were wood, cracked and swollen in places, the result of some long ago flood. There were two steel doors at each landing. Apartment numbers hung crooked or were missing. The sound of Ms. Janet working her locks echoed down the stairwell as I made my way to the third floor.

"Hello again Mr. Brian," she said, waving me in. She was shorter than I thought she'd be, heavier. Grey hair twisted from the sides of her bandana in grey tufts.

The living room was sparsely furnished in an old woman's style with a paisley Victorian couch facing two easy chairs. One cream, the other blue. No TV. A copper tea service sat on a coffee table, steaming.

She settled in one of the chairs and motioned me to the other. Decades of photographs were displayed on the wall behind the couch. On the far left they were black and white, Forties and Fifties era family portraits. The Sixties began two feet in. Young people with bushy afros and tie-dye clothes, muscle cars in the background. In the center, the Sixties bled into the seventies. Tie-dye gave way to sequin dresses and platform shoes. Past that was the eighties and nineties. Baby pictures, then high school portraits and prom nights. On the far right, the babies started again.

"Guess you're here about that police?"

"Yes, ma'am."

"They told me they'd send someone." She raised an eyebrow. "A year ago."

I thought about letting her think I was there in an official capacity, but she had been kind. "Have to tell you, Ms. Janet. I'm not from the government."

"Who are you?"

"Defense attorney. The detective, the one you filed the complaint on? His partner was killed. I represent the man that . . . Well, you know."

"Hmmm . . ." She nodded.

"I don't expect you would know anything about that. We're just interested in –"

"Tomlinson," she said, her brow furrowing.

"Well, yeah."

"Hmmm . . ."

My eyes were drawn to the wall. "Your name came up as a witness and –"

"That's my grandson, Dartanian." She pointed to a photo, a handsome boy about eighteen. "He's the one helped me hang em like this, left to right, oldest to newest. Call it my time machine. The drugs took him, though." She frowned.

"Sorry," I said.

"His mother's gone . . . well, maybe she's still out there somewhere. I raised Dart myself. Tried, anyways. It's hard with people like your friend Trayon out there," she jerked a thumb at the window, "steering em the wrong way. That's all you can do is try, you know?"

"I know, Ms. Janet."

"Always told him, they start harassin' you? Tryin' to get you mixed up in the easy life? You tell me. I'll call the police. I'm not stupid. I know Dart couldn't do nothin' like that himself, not and keep living in this neighborhood. But I'm old, you know? Be surprised what an old lady can get away with."

She shot me a devil's grin.

"Come to find out," she said. "He ended up in the game just like the rest of em. Got shot one night over his stash. Couldn't have been much of a stash, him bein' so young and all, just startin' out."

She wiped a tear.

"So I asked around. Who did it? Who saw it?" She shook her head. "No one, of course. But I found out where he was *gettin'* his stash. Same place as your friend out there. From the same people I told Dart I was gonna call. Same people I thought would protect him."

"Tomlinson," I said.

"And from his partner, Knox. I sat right there at that window." She pointed. "Nights on end after the funeral. Saw em pulling up, callin' young'uns to their car, doing what everyone said they was doing. Supplyin' drugs. So I called it in. Told em everything I know. Nuthin happened." She grunted. "Till you came."

"They move kind of slow."

"Hmmm . . ."

"But they're investigating it now."

"Good." She eased back in her chair. "Anyways, that's all. Help your case any?"

I thought about Bushill agonizing over killing Knox, about how Tomlinson and Knox were supplying dealers in the neighborhood, how maybe they didn't pull the trigger themselves, but how a kid ended up dead, and how that might help ease Bushill's pain.

"In a roundabout way. Thank you, Ms. Janet."

"Where are my manners?" She reached for her tea service. "Cup of tea?"

"Thank you," I said, standing and looking out the window. "But I really should be . . ." Trayon was on the stoop with his hoppers, back in business. Dusk was turning to dark. "On second thought, I will have a cup, if it's not too much trouble."

"No trouble." She poured two cups. "Been drinkin' tea every evening for thirty years." She reached into the pocket of her housedress, pulled out a flask of Remy Martin, and topped off one of the cups with a double shot. "The doctor says tea is no good for sleep, but it don't bother me none. Capper?" She held the flask above my cup.

I stared at it.

"Mr. Brian?"

"Uh . . . no, thank you."

"Seen people turn down a capper before. Been a while since I seen anyone take that long."

"Guess I'm trying to cut back."

"Hmmm."

I took a sip. "It's good, Ms. Janet. Thanks."

We sat in silence, staring at her time machine.

I pointed to a black and white on the far left, a dark-skinned man in an army uniform, his arm around a young woman, her hands on the shoulders of a little girl in a bonnet and Sunday dress. "That you, Ms. Janet?"

"Oh my, yes." She laughed. "That's my mother, my father, and me. Years ago, yes."

A photograph near the center caught my eye, a white woman, the only white person on the wall. She looked familiar. It was a headshot signed, *To Janet Randolph. Thanks for the memories and keep fuckin' rockin!*

"My God, is that —"

"Yes," she said, shaking her head. "Janis had a mouth on her. Not much to look at, but an angel's voice, when she wasn't screaming, that is. The drugs took her, too. Terrible. Well, guess I got into the drugs myself a bit back then. Long time ago. I remember this one time —"

"You met Janis Joplin?"

"Phhht . . . Met her? Opened for her back in . . . back in . . . Lemme see, when was that?"

I stepped to the wall. Below Joplin was a group of musicians. "This was your band? You were a singer?" I pointed to a woman in her early thirties who reminded me of Vicky, the same mocha skin and puffy afro. "That's you right there?"

"Was me." She laughed. "Just a backup singer. Straight rhythm and blues. Nothin' fancy, but not like this mess they've got em singing today, if you could call it singing."

"Wow. You sure were one good lookin' woman, if you don't mind me saying."

"Well, I don't know about that." She grinned self-consciously.

I settled in my chair.

"You know, life is long," she said, draining her cup, her old eyes sparkling with tea and Remy. "Way you came in here, chased by them boys, you may need to slow down some. Can't get it all done in one day, you know."

I smiled and let her talk. I imagined it wasn't often she entertained.

"Can only do what you can do," she said, nodding off. "Do what you can do, and that's it."

"I know, Ms. Randolph."

"Call me Ms. Janet," she whispered. "What I'm sayin' is, as long as you keep tryin', well, God is happy. You keep tryin'. That's all you can do."

She closed her eyes and let her head fall back.

I stared at her time machine, wondering what mine would look like. Catholic School and Boy Scouts on the left. The high school debate team photo Mom had on the fridge for years. College photos in the middle, me with my head under a beer tap mostly, then law school. That picture of me raising a fist after passing the bar on the third try.

Keep trying, right?

Wedding pics. Our honeymoon in Florida. Marcus, the day we got him. The Christmas party at Sharden and Epps: the first one, where Brenda is kissing me on the cheek, followed by my mugshot after the last one.

The selfie I took that first night at the Sergeant.

There'd be a collage of criminal defendants, from Carlton Thomas, my first client, to Bushill. A close up of him weeping silently in his cage. Wondering what the hell happened. How he could have done such a horrible thing, and why? How the man he'd killed was a dirty cop who made money from the misery of others. How Tomlinson's story didn't match the evidence, and how Repo's story didn't jive with Tomlinson's. How none of it seemed to matter.

That's what my time machine would look like.

Dammit.

I fished out my cell and called Vicky.

"Ro," she answered. "You better be calling to say you talked to Bushill."

"You still got that crime scene evidence report?"

"Why?"

"Meet me in the tunnel. Bring it with you."

"I'm in bed, Ro. Rough night last night, remember? Besides, it's getting dark."

I heard the rustle of sheets and a deep voice behind Vicky say, "What's up, babe?"

"Is that Johnny?" I laughed, then checked to make sure I hadn't woken Ms. Janet.

"Don't wanna talk about it, Ro."

"See you in thirty," I said, and hung up.

I took the comforter off the couch and draped it over Ms. Janet, then let myself out and tiptoed down the stairs. At the bottom, I pressed an ear to the door jam. They were on the other side. Trayon and his four-foot henchmen.

Damned if I was going to wait there like frightened prey until Trayon called it quits for the night or decided I wasn't worth his trouble. I looked around for anything that could be used as a weapon. Nothing, except a fire extinguisher on the wall labeled, *Emergency Use Only*.

I could think of no greater emergency.

I undid the latch, removed the pin, and braced against the door with my hip on the release bar. It felt like a heart attack coming on. Drumming in my chest. Pressure behind my eyes. The things they don't tell you about in law school.

There would be a good ten seconds before they had time to react, I assured myself.

I burst through the door and it banged against the outside wall. They were on their feet in an instant, looking at me in disbelief. It has always been a source of pride that I took the time to stare Trayon down before pulling the handle.

The stoop exploded in white powder, a billowing cloud blotting them out.

"Da Fuck!" I heard, and shuffling.

Dropping the extinguisher, I ran through the cloud and up the walkway, but tripped over the curb and went down in the street, my face scraping against asphalt, my right knee striking the ground. I crawled to my feet and hobbled down the street, picking up speed as I adjusted to the pain.

I managed a limping gallop before turning to look. The ten second estimate had been generous. They were five car lengths behind and gaining, their faces covered in white powder. They would overtake me at the corner, and then . . . well, probably just a beat down.

Trayon didn't strike me as the homicidal type.

A garbage truck cut me off as I shambled into the intersection, its compactor filled with bags that had not yet been crushed into the interior. With a last burst of energy, I threw both feet forward and bounded off the asphalt toward that moving pile of garbage.

I landed half inside the compactor with my injured knee coming down hard on its rim. The bags exploded with a spray of pungent liquids. Trayon reached for my leg as he ran behind the truck, but lost a few inches as it accelerated. His resolve evaporated. Slowing to a trot, he shot me one last look of malice before he gave up. I flashed him the thumbs-up as the garbage truck carried me away.

What matters to God is that you try.

CHAPTER THIRTY-THREE

It was six o'clock when I hopped off the truck at Martin Luther King and began the five block limp to the Anacostia Metro. I'd picked up fresh abrasions on my face and the lip had reopened. The knee would almost certainly need surgery.

It's a snap to score a seat on a train after riding a mile in the back of a garbage truck. At the first stop, half the passengers made a dash for the next car. The only person left near me was an old man in a stained trench, wearing mismatched shoes and grungy pants, who either didn't notice, or smelled worse than I did.

I couldn't tell.

The odor wafting from my clothes was a blend of week-old chicken grease, sour milk, and peppermint. How the peppermint figured in was a mystery.

I got off at L'Enfant Plaza and gimped my way up D Street toward the tunnel. The gate to the parking lot was open. Good. It was unlikely I'd be able to climb in my condition. At the tunnel entrance I saw a flashlight down the tracks and heard Vicky's high-pitched laugh.

As I got closer, I could make out her silhouette, her arms wrapped around a man.

Had she really dragged Johnny down here?

She heard me crunching across the rails and hit me with her flashlight.

"Jesus, Ro. You all right?"

"What's it look like?" I held a hand to the light. "You gonna drop that thing?"

"Sorry." She lowered it and stepped away from her date: Boston, in the same *Blues is Back* tee he'd been wearing when I left the two of them at Madams.

"Mr. O'Brian," he said, guiltily.

"Oh yeah?" I smiled at Vicky.

"Don't wanna talk about it, Ro." She turned her flashlight on my leg as I limped closer. "What the hell happened to . . . Bogus!" She cupped a hand over her nose. "What's that crazy smell?"

"Remember our friend Trayon?"

"He toss you in a sewer?"

"Garbage truck. You got the evidence report?"

Pinching her nose, she fished it out of her jacket.

"If I may ask," Boston said, raising a hand. "What are we doing here, Mr. O'Brian?"

"I'm dying to know myself," Vicky said. "Christ, you stink."

"Investigating."

"Far be it from me to discourage this newfound enthusiasm, but why would we be doing that? Bushill won't take the plea?"

"He's thinking about it."

"Seen you sell a lot more time to harder-headed people. What's the problem? It's a righteous no-brainer. A sweetheart!"

"*That's* the problem." I snatched the flashlight. "Say you're Shelly. You've got a cop witness. Murder weapon. Gunpowder residue. DNA. What do you do?"

She rolled her eyes.

"Well?"

"Go for the throat," she muttered

"Exactly. But what if there's a problem with the case? A nuclear discrepancy. A hole so large a decent attorney will drive a freight train through it? Except, when you look across the courtroom you that see your opponent is a washed up Fifth Streeter just itching to take a plea. What do you do now?"

"Ro," she said, looking down. "I never said –"

"What do you do?"

"Don't tell him about the discrepancy. Make the lazy bastard an offer you know he'll take." She looked up and smiled. "A sweetheart."

I held her eyes until I could see she was with me, then shined the flashlight on Bushill's mattress. "That's Bushill," I said. "Walk me through the rest of it."

She took me through it, and with the evidence report there was no guessing this time. The crime scene was basically a triangle. At one corner was the mattress where Bushill was found lying next to the murder weapon. At another corner was where Tomlinson was standing, nine feet from the cartridge casing that had ejected from his gun. The final corner was Evidence Tag #12, the mystery casing which we now knew was also fired from the murder weapon. In the center of the triangle was Knox's body.

We ended up at Evidence Tag #12.

"What's Tomlinson's version?" I asked, handing Vicky the flashlight.

"The two cops are walking down the tracks." She traced their steps with the flashlight. "Bushill starts screaming, 'Get out of my house.'" She flashed the light on Bushill's mattress. "Bushill shoots. Knox goes down. Tomlinson returns fire, striking Bushill." She turned the light to where Tomlinson would have been standing. "End of story."

"Except?"

"Except Tomlinson was behind the wall and could not have shot Bushill from there."

"And . . ."

"And he makes no mention of the third shot." She illuminated Evidence Tag #12 at our feet, where the third casing had been found. "We already knew all of that, Ro."

"But what we didn't know before," I said, "is that the third cartridge casing, the one right here, matches the one found at Bushill's mattress, the one Bushill supposedly fired at Knox. According to Shelly, they were fired from the same gun. So, either Tomlinson failed to notice Bushill firing a shot here, then running thirty yards to the mattress and firing a second shot there, or he . . . or he . . ."

"Or he *what*, Ro?"

"I dunno. What's Bushill's version?"

"What's it matter?"

"Humor me."

"According to what he told you, he's drunk." She lit up the mattress. "Dead to the world. Next thing he knows, he's shot in the leg. Then a ninja," she flashed the light on the wall behind us, illuminating the Repo mural, "comes out of the darkness, ties a rope to his leg and vanishes."

"Right. Maybe not all that helpful. What's Repo's story?"

"Not that it matters," Vicky said. "But she never told us the whole story, just that she was doing her graffiti when she heard Knox and Tomlinson coming down the –"

"Nope," Boston said, taking the flashlight from Vicky and digging a notebook from his jeans. "Not quite accurate." He flashed the light on his notebook, then on the Repo mural. "Repo is there, painting her mural. According to her, she hears voices and hides." He swung the light down the tracks. "She sees *three* people coming down the tunnel, not just Tomlinson and Knox."

"It's dark," Vicky said. "She's scared. Confused." Vicky snatched back the light and shined it on Bushill's mattress. "But she also confirmed that the crazy man started shooting."

"Crazy *fucker*," corrected Boston, flipping closed his notebook.

"Now *there's* a discrepancy." Vicky said.

"Maybe we're looking at this the wrong way." I took the flashlight. "Vicky, go stand were Tomlinson would have been." I lit up the spot. "Boston, you take Bushill." I lit up the mattress. "Forget the witnesses. We focus on the physical evidence."

"All right," Vicky said, reaching the spot. "I'm Tomlinson."

"I'm Bushill," Boston said, at the mattress.

I remained where I was at Evidence Tag #12. "Each of us is standing where a shot was fired. Boston, if you're Bushill, who can you shoot?"

"Bushill can shoot Knox." Boston pointed to where Knox's body was found. "He can shoot you, but not Tomlinson." He nodded to the wall blocking Vicky.

"Vicky?"

"If I'm Tomlinson, I can't shoot Bushill from here." She pointed to the wall. "But I can shoot Knox, and I can shoot you. In fact, I'm thinkin' about it."

"Right."

Disregarding what witnesses say is often the key to an investigation. Witnesses get confused. Witnesses exaggerate. Witnesses lie. Bushill was too drunk to know what happened. Tomlinson's story couldn't be accurate, and Repo's version was highly suspect. It was dark and it happened quickly. Two of the witnesses were clearly confused.

One was lying.

In fact, why even entertain the idea that Tomlinson shot Bushill when it was absolutely clear he couldn't have shot him from where he was standing? On the other hand, why presume Tomlinson was lying? What if he was merely mistaken?

What if Tomlinson just *thought* he shot Bushill?

"Follow this," I said. "Way I see it, two people are shot. Knox and Bushill."

"Brilliant, Ro," Vicky said.

"But there are three cartridge casings, which means three shots were fired and one missed its mark. Someone missed. What if it was Tomlinson?"

"Come again?"

"He's walking down the tracks with Knox. He gets to the spot you're standing at now. A shot rings out. He returns fire in the direction he thinks it's coming from, but it's dark. The echoes in the tunnel confuse him. His shot goes straight down the tracks. He waits until the coast is clear, walks through the break in the wall to the next track, sees Bushill on the mattress and figures he shot him. Tomlinson discrepancy *solved*."

"Wait a minute," said Boston. "If Tomlinson didn't shoot Bushill, that means whoever shot Bushill had to be the one who shot Knox."

I hadn't actually done the math, but it made sense. If Tomlinson didn't shoot Bushill, then the same person who shot Bushill also shot Knox. According to Shelly, the cartridge casing at Evidence Tag #12 was fired from the same gun used to shoot Knox. So unless Bushill shot Knox from where I was standing at Evidence tag #12, ran thirty yards in the dark to his mattress, then shot himself, there was only one solution.

It was suddenly clear.

"Boston's right! If Tomlinson missed Bushill, then Bushill and Knox were shot by the same person and Bushill *didn't* shoot Knox."

"Who shot Knox then?" Vick asked.

"A person who had a clear shot," I lit up Evidence Tag #12 at my feet and traced a line to where Knox's body was found. "Who, after shooting Knox, ran this way." I limped across the tracks to the mattress. "Who shot Bushill, dropped the gun and fled while Tomlinson was still on the other side of the wall. When Tomlinson came from behind the wall and saw Bushill on the ground, he mistakenly thought Bushill shot Knox and that he'd shot Bushill. Meanwhile, the real shooter is somewhere down the tracks."

"Right," Vicky said. "What about the gunpowder residue? The DNA?"

"Ummmm . . . Obvious," I said. "Bushill struggled with the shooter for the gun, leaving his DNA and getting gunpowder residue on his hand."

She stood there thinking, with the hum of the transformer down the tracks and the sound of water dripping from the ceiling.

"Far out, Ro," Vicky said. "So Bushill didn't do it. Whoever shot Knox also shot Bushill. Makes sense."

"Really?"

"No. But swear to God, nothing else does."

"Boston?" I asked.

"I have to say, it's the only theory that matches the physical evidence. But who shot Knox and Bushill?"

"Well, that's the crazy part." I traced a line from Bushill's mattress to Evidence Tag #12. "It had to be the person who left that cartridge casing."

"Right, but who?" demanded Vicky.

I moved the light nine feet to the right, to where the person would have been standing when they fired the shot.

The light fell directly on a mural, which in metallic teal paint spelled, *R-E-P-O*.

CHAPTER THIRTY-FOUR

It was an awkward cab ride to Adams Morgan with Vicky up front and Boston in back, mashed against the door as far from me as possible. Windows open. Everyone with their head hanging out, gasping for air. Except me. I was getting used to it.

On the positive side, it was the same cabbie who abandoned me the night I meet Vicky at the tunnel.

Karma.

"Can you go any faster?" Vicky asked. "Jeez you reek, Ro."

"Yeah, but I feel great."

"Bet you do."

"Hate to play devil's advocate," Boston said, "but there are a few loose ends." Gulping air, he swung his head in the cab. "Why would Repo shoot Knox and Bushill? And even if she did, why on earth would she treat Bushill's wound afterward? Christ!" He thrust his head out.

"Simple," I said. "It was basically an accident. She carries a gun because she spends nights in rail tunnels and abandoned buildings. She's startled when two men come walking down the tracks. She shoots Knox, then runs across the tracks straight into Bushill, who wakes up screaming. In her panic, she struggles with Bushill, shoots him in the leg and drops the gun. Tomlinson shoots in the direction he thinks the shots are coming from, but misses. When he steps from behind the wall and sees Bushill on the ground, he puts two and two together and comes up with nine. Figures Bushill shot Knox and that he shot Bushill.

"And as far as the wound is concerned . . ." I was beginning to enjoy myself. "Maybe Repo looks back as she's running away, sees Tomlinson, and hides. After Tomlinson leaves to call for help, she creeps back to treat Bushill's wound because . . . who knows? Maybe deep down, she's a nice person."

"That aside," Vicky said. "It explains why Shelly made that sweetheart offer. She believes Bushill shot Knox, but knows she'll have a hard time proving it with Tomlinson's version being contradicted by the crime scene evidence."

"Exactly," I said. "In Shelly's mind, Tomlinson merely got it wrong about where he was standing, or his cartridge casing got kicked to where it was by the crime scene technicians. Remember, she doesn't know about Repo."

Boston gulped and swung back in. "We tell her, then? Clue her in to the defense?"

Vicky and I shared a look, then burst out laughing.

"Right," Vicky said. "You got a lot to learn about prosecutors, Mr. Stewart."

"So what's the plan?" he asked.

"Well, it's complicated," I said

"Short version." He exhaled and swung out.

The thing was, knowing that Bushill didn't shoot Knox and being able to prove it were two different things. Sure, a defendant is innocent until proven guilty, but if your trial strategy is to cross your fingers and hope the government won't be able to prove its case, you might as well take a plea, guilty or not. What a defendant needs, is a defense. And that would mean having Repo in custody and swabbed for DNA, having a lab match her DNA to the gun, hiring a crime scene expert to explain to the jury what we'd figured out in the tunnel, *then* crossing our fingers.

But that was the long version.

"The plan is to tell Bushill everything," I said. "It's his call. If he still wants to take the plea, he takes it. If not, then we've got work to do."

"Why would he ever take it?" Boston asked. "If he's innocent?"

"That's the problem with a sweetheart plea offer," I explained. "Sometimes it's so sweet compared to what might happen at trial, even an innocent man will hop on it."

"Dig it," Vicky said. "This is close enough," she said to the cabbie as we hit traffic on Columbia, a block from her building. "I gotta get out of this cab."

"Out of cash," I informed her.

"Wonderful. You owe me." She handed the cabbie a twenty.

Vicky and I bailed, but Boston stayed behind.

"I need to go home for some actual sleep," Boston said, winking at Vicky.

"Nine-thirty," I told him. "Bearmond's courtroom."

"I'll be there, Mr. O'Brian."

"Bye, Boss," Vicky said.

"Bonne nuit, mon cheri!"

I smiled at Vicky as the cab sped away.

"Don't start, Ro."

The knee had stiffened during the ride and I had to lurch along to keep up with Vicky. The Sunday night crowd was thick, mostly heading toward the strip at Eighteenth and Columbia where a group of musicians were serenading the intersection with a blues standard.

"Call it, Ro."

"Johnny Lee Hooker."

"Track?"

"Boom, Boom, Boom."

"You're on a roll."

"Yes I am."

"Hope you're not going to Madam's, looking like you are."

"What time is it?"

She glanced at her phone. "Eight-fifteen."

"Shoot. I'm late."

"For what?"

"Sunday dinner with the folks."

"That's nice."

"And with Brenda," I added, smothering a smile.

"Brenda your ex, or Brenda your . . . whatever?"

"Ex."

"Really? She's there now?"

"Woman's never late."

"You know what?" She stopped short. "Maybe you should take a raincheck. I'll call your mom. Tell her we were out on a job and you got hurt, that I took you to the E.R. In fact, that might not be a bad idea."

"I'm fine." I limped forward. "Nothing a shower can't fix."

"Roman."

"What?" I stopped and looked over my shoulder. She had a hand on her hip.

"Love ya, Ro, and I want things to work out with Brenda. But truth is, you're not looking your best right now. Know what I mean?"

"Funny. I feel great."

"So you keep saying."

"Love you too, Vick." We locked eyes. "Call me in the morning. We'll share a cab."

I turned left on the strip at Eighteenth. There was a performer swallowing flames, dreadlocks pumping to Jamaican rhythms at Bukom, and half-drunk pedestrians clogging the street.

Adams Morgan, and the night was young.

"Ro!" Bart shouted from the balcony of Madam's.

"Not tonight, Bart," I yelled, as I shambled past. "Got a date."

"Uh huh," he said. "Good luck with dat, mon."

I was going to miss that neighborhood.

The concierge desk at the Sergeant was staffed by a young woman covered in tattoos: sleeves on both arms and a teardrop below one eye. Whatever she had inked on her chest swirled up her neck to her chin.

"You okay, Mr. O'Brien?"

I thought about asking her the same thing.

"Absolutely fine," I said.

Alone in the elevator, I gained an appreciation for how rank I smelled. A scarred face stared back at me from the smoky mirror on the elevator wall. I shuddered to think of the contaminants from the garbage truck that had seeped into those wounds. The eye was black and the lip swollen, but lucky me, the cheek lacerations from the other night were healing nicely.

I practiced walking as I made my way down the hall to my room. If I shifted my weight, touching down with just the ball of my right foot, I could manage a fairly normal gait, so long as I kept under a mile-per-hour. The plan was to say hello from the doorway, then one-mile-an-hour it straight to the shower.

Simple.

The second I put the key in, Mom swung the door open. "Hank!" she screamed, after taking a look at me. "Call 911!"

"I'm fine, Ma."

They crowded toward me, then recoiled.

"Whew," Dad said.

"Oh my," Mom said.

"Hello, Roman," Brenda said, a hand on her nose.

Mom was right. She looked fantastic, her hair had grown down to her shoulders and she was squeezed nicely into a black dress. Simple, but classy. Marcus was cradled in her arms, struggling to break free. The only one not covering his nose.

I loved that mongrel.

"You need to see a doctor," Mom said.

Dad said, "Your mother's right."

Third time.

"I'm gonna hit the shower, folks." Abandoning the plan, I limped full-speed toward the bathroom.

"Your leg, Roman!" Mom exclaimed. "Oh, Hank. Call 911!"

"He says he's fine, sugar."

The shower felt great. Could've stay in there an hour. After, I wrapped in a towel and ran hot water over the knee, hoping I could get temporary use out of it. It had turned a deep purple and the swelling was just getting started.

Mom brought clothes. "Hurry, Munchkin. We have a special guest, you know."

Navy blue khakis and a lime-green shirt.

Perfect.

Marcus went nuts when I left the bathroom, yelping and wagging his tail in Brenda's arms. She let him go and he jumped on the bed, leapt in my arms and licked my face.

"Hey, buddy."

"Come join us, Roman." Mom said.

They were sitting on pillows on the floor, Mom and Dad with their backs against the couch and Brenda against the bed. Styrofoam containers were set out on the floor.

I eased down next to Brenda, using the edge of the bed for support while extending my leg.

"So, Roman," Brenda said, pointing to my face. "What –"

"Don't ask."

We ate as best we could with Marcus bouncing around for handouts. Mom started in with her Roman stories: the time, when I was ten, a swarm of Maryland State Troopers pulled us over because I'd put a sign in the back window of Dad's Volvo that said, "Help! I've been kidnapped!" And the time I skipped school in junior high, got picked up by the truant squad, but convinced them I was a child prodigy enrolled in my freshman year of college.

"It was then," Mom said, "I knew our little munch-kin would grow up to be a lawyer."

Brenda smiled, dutifully. She'd heard it all before.

"Sugar," Dad said, pushing his empty styrofoam forward. "How's about we take Marcus for a walk?"

"We haven't had our dessert yet," protested Mom. "They had the most wonderful cheesecake at that diner. There's a slice for each of us in the –"

"Suuuugar." Dad nodded at Brenda.

"A walk sounds nice, dear."

Brenda directed them to a bag of doggie supplies. Mom fished out a leash, and after fussing over what to do if Marcus broke free, Dad managed to get her out the door. I could hear Marcus yelping his way down the hall and Mom saying, "Hush, Marcus. The neighbors!"

"So," Brenda said. "How are you, really?"

"Good," I said. "Ran into a few problems working a case, but I'm fine. Really."

"Must be some case."

"A murder," I said, offhandedly.

"Really?"

"Fairly interesting. This cop gets shot while –"

"Get out!" She rested an arm on the bed and leaned closer. "The one killed by that homeless man? The one on the news? That's yours?"

"Yeah," I said, playing it cool. "So what've you been up to?"

"The usual," she sighed. "BP doesn't want to settle on the North Sea oil rights claim, so it's been back and forth to London once a month."

"Rough."

"Sidanko Oil is driving me nuts with this merger, so when it's not London, it's Kiev or Moscow. Ever been to Kiev in the fall?"

I laughed. She knew I hadn't.

"On the bright side," she smiled proudly. "Guess who finagled season tickets to the Baltimore Opera?"

"You didn't."

"Did," she said.

"Love those guys."

"Box seats. Through the firm, of course."

"I figured."

"Which brings me to why I've been calling."

"Brenda." I crooked an elbow on the bed and leaned in. "I'm sorry for not calling you back. This new case, well, it's been crazy."

"I understand." She looked me in the eyes. "And I'll understand completely if you say no. There's no pressure."

"Go ahead."

"With all this traveling, and with the opera season coming up, I just can't handle Marcus any longer. I know how you love the rascal and I checked with hotel management. It's not a problem, so long as you pay a pet deposit." She looked around the room. "Which I would absolutely insist on paying."

"I see."

"I'd hate to have to take him to a shelter."

"Of course."

"Would you mind?"

CHAPTER THIRTY-FIVE

I woke Monday morning to Marcus jumping on my chest with the leash in his mouth, Mom asleep, and Dad snoring like an ogre. I hopped on one leg to the bathroom and soaked my knee before getting dressed.

I checked my phone. Three messages, all from Ruffio, and a text from Vicky wondering how it went last night. I texted her to meet me out front in twenty minutes, then leashed Marcus and headed downstairs.

Kalorama Park is four blocks from the Sergeant, but with my knee like it was, it would have taken most of the morning to limp there. I unleashed Marcus and he ran up and down the strip, peeing on parking meters, and gutter-feasting on food from last night's fete.

Way I figured it, Adams Morgan being what it is, I might never have to buy dog food.

When Marcus finished, he ran back and jumped in my arms. I carried him to my room, opened the door, let him in and closed the door behind him.

"Christ!" I heard Dad say as I gimped down the hall toward the elevators.

"Bad, Marcus!" Mom yelled. "Get off your grand-father!"

Vicky was out front in a Red Top cab wearing her court duds: a black pantsuit and a white blouse with a black beret to hold down her fro.

Nice.

"Well?" she asked, as I eased into the back seat. "How'd it go with Bren?"

"I got the dog."

"I'm sorry, Roman."

"Courthouse," I told the driver. "Fifth and Indiana."

Vicky gave me her consolation look. "Your eye looks better, though."

"Thanks."

We ran into traffic three blocks from the court-house and the cabbie said we had to get out.

"Take me to the front door." I glared at him in the rearview. "Been thinking," I said to Vicky. "Why wait for Bushill to tell us whether he's going to take the plea before we track down Repo again?"

"Because it's his call," she said. "You know that."

"Sure, but let's say he wants to reject the plea. Isn't the preliminary hearing our only opportunity to have Repo answer questions before trial? To get her under oath and force her to testify?"

"What would be the point? She'd only lie."

"Exactly."

One of the advantages the government has is the grand jury. The system was designed as a procedural safeguard, a way to ensure citizens are not charged without sufficient evidence. What it ended up becoming was an investigative tool, a way for prosecutors to lock in the testimony of witnesses, defense witnesses even. It's common practice for prosecutors to call defense witnesses at the grand jury so they can later point out differences between their grand jury and trial testimony.

It's all about creating the impression that defense witnesses are lying.

Defense attorneys don't get a grand jury. But why not use the preliminary hearing to do the same thing? With any luck, the lies Repo told at the preliminary would be inconsistent with Tomlinson's testimony and with the physical evidence. We could lock in her lies, then whack her with the inconsistencies.

"Hear me out," I said. "We force Repo to testify at the preliminary. She lies, so what? She gets locked in. Every detail recorded under oath. Every misstatement. Everything she says that's inconsistent with Tomlinson and the physical evidence preserved in a transcript we can use against her if she testifies at trial."

"Like a grand jury," Vicky said, intrigued.

"Exactly."

She shook her head. "We still don't know who she is or where to find her. And you can forget about the Bear granting another continuance. No way, Ro."

"Unless . . ."

"What? She happens to get arrested in the next thirty minutes?"

I smiled. "You still have that text message Repo sent you?"

Vicky nodded.

"Give me Repo's number.

Vicky searched for it.

I dug out the barfly's business card and called her on speaker.

"Brenda Bowles," she answered.

"Darling, how've you been?"

"Vito," she whispered, seductively. "Told you not to call me on this number."

Vicky laughed. "Classy, Ro."

"It's Roman, Bren. Got a minute?"

"Roman, what are you doing calling me?"

"Business."

She breathed heavily. "What kind of business?"

I had no choice but to tell her everything.

CHAPTER THIRTY-SIX

Getting inside the courthouse was rough. Reporters buzzed the plaza like insects and swarmed the cab as we stepped out. I leaned on Vicky's shoulder and limped to the entrance where the marshals were holding the media horde at bay. Boston was waiting in the lobby.

"Hey, Boss," Vicky said.

He nodded.

"Showtime," I told him.

"Same plan?"

"Not exactly." My phone lit up and I put it to my ear. "What'd you find out, Bren?"

"Not convinced I should help you, counselor. Tell me again why I'm doing this?"

"Can't tell you more than I know, and I've already told you everything."

"I'm fine with making certain we've arrested the right guy for killing a fellow cop, but if this ends up being some defense attorney trick –"

"It's not."

I waited her out. If Brenda wasn't convinced I was on the level, there was nothing more I could say.

"This is hard, Roman."

"I know."

"I'm gonna trust you." She sighed. "Don't let me down. And don't mention to anyone where you got the info."

"Promise."

"I checked," she said. "If Tomlinson is tracking the number you gave me, there'd be a warrant application filed with Special Proceedings."

"And?"

"Nothing."

"You're telling me that Tomlinson is not tracking Repo's cell phone?"

"Bingo."

"Check again."

"I did. He's definitely not tracking her. Doubt he even has her number."

"How can that be? Tomlinson showed up every time we found her. He was even there when . . . Wait, he's tracking *me*?"

"Bingo."

"No way."

"I just ran the search."

"How could he –"

"It's not legal, of course, but it's not hard either. He files a warrant application and attaches an affidavit swearing the request is based on probable cause, that he needs to track a suspect, except instead of listing a suspect's number, he lists yours. A judge signs off and your cell-phone provider gets an order to provide the location of the cell towers on which your phone is pinging. It's not highly accurate, but can pinpoint a phone to within a block or two. Point is, in twenty minutes he's got you tracked."

"So he lied to the judge."

"Bingo."

"Dirty bastard."

"Unethical for sure, but I wouldn't go so far as to call the man dirty."

It wasn't that hard to believe, really. Tomlinson sees his partner killed. He's convinced Bushill did it. Maybe he even sees Repo running down the tracks and figures she's an acquaintance of Bushill's, a witness who can help put him away. He doesn't mention her in the Gerstein because he has nothing to go on and never makes the Repo connection. He files a bogus warrant request to track my phone assuming that, with Bushll's help, I'll find her. And when I do, he's right there. It's an egregious constitutional violation. Totally illegal.

Then again, it's Tomlinson.

"I need you to do one more thing."

"Before you start," she whispered. "I *know* what you're going to ask and –"

"Come on. You've got probable cause up the ass. Don't even need to lie on this one. Will you do it?"

I waited out the silence.

"Call you back," she said, and hung up.

"Well?" Boston asked.

"Let's go see Bushill."

It was nine-thirty on the dot when the clerk opened the courtroom. After the line of attorneys shuffled in, we were told Bearmond wouldn't take the bench for another twenty minutes.

Good to be the judge.

There's a door in every courtroom leading to the cellblock where defendants are held. The marshals let us through to see Bushill.

"You all right, Mr. O'Brian?" one of them asked.

"Never felt better."

Bushill was alone in the cell.

"Frenchie," he said, clutching the bars. "I wish to apologize for my behavior last night. Especially for giving you that shiner."

"That was two nights ago," I told him.

"So it was."

"Far out," Vicky said, laughing.

"Nevertheless, I apologize for my rudeness. After you explained that I'm guilty . . . when the full force of my actions were made clear . . . the monstrosity of my crimes laid bare for me to –"

"You didn't do it."

"Say what, now?"

"You didn't kill Knox."

"Hmmm . . . Didn't kill him." Bushill pondered the implications. "Didn't kill him in what *sense*?"

Vicky pushed me aside. "I'm Victoria Bronco, Mr. Bushill. Roman's investigator."

"Finally," Bushill said. "Someone with authority. This man's confusing in the extreme."

"A common complaint. I've investigated this case thoroughly, Mr. Bushill. Left no stone unturned. And I can tell you unequivocally that you did not kill that cop."

"Unequivocally?" he said, tears forming.

"You don't have to take a plea."

Bushill looked to me for confirmation.

"I need to speak to Alex alone," I said.

Vicky looked hurt, but grabbed Boston's arm and led him back to the courtroom.

I didn't like kicking Vicky out, but what I told Boston about the dangers of a sweetheart plea deal is no joke, especially for an innocent client. It's not a legal decision so much as a gambling decision. Take the deal and do time for a crime you didn't commit, or reject it and run the risk of doing even more time.

In Bushill's case, life.

And as convinced as I was of Bushill's innocence, we were far from proving it. We'd have to find Repo and get her to confess, which seemed unlikely, or somehow prove her guilt. A thousand things could go wrong.

I laid it out for Bushill. The crime scene evidence. How Tomlinson could not have shot him. How the person who shot him had to be the same person who shot Knox. And, most important, how we'd have to give up the potential for a six-year sentence just to get a chance to prove it.

"Judge is on his way," the marshal yelled, poking his head through the door.

"Decision time," I said to Bushill. "I need crystal clear instructions. What are you going to do?"

"I'm gonna . . ." His eyes met mine and he nodded. "Ride with you."

Wonderful.

"All rise!" Ms. Harrison announced. "Come to order. The Honorable Jeremiah Bearmond presiding. God save the United States and this honorable court."

I went back in the courtroom and took a seat with Boston and Vicky while Ms. Harrison went through the Ghost Docket.

"Well?" Vicky asked.

"Said he's riding with us."

"What the hell does *that* mean?"

Someone placed a hand on my shoulder. "William Benton, Washington Post. Can I ask you a question, Mr. O'Brian?"

"Get your ferret paw off me, Willie."

"Simmer down, Ro," Vicky said.

"On Your Honor's preliminary hearing docket, the United States versus Alexander Bushill!"

Shelly stepped up to the prosecution table. "Shelly Jarvis for the Government, Your Honor."

The marshal led Bushill to his seat. I tried to suppress the limp as Boston and I made our way to the defense table.

"Roman O'Brian for the defendant, along with attorney, Boston –"

"Are you okay, Mr. O'Brian?" Bearmond looked at me, concerned. "You're limping."

"I'm fine, Your Honor. Bicycle accident."

"And your eye?"

"Handle bars. Straight to the face."

Bushill grunted. I thought I heard Vicky snicker.

"You should be more careful, Mr. O'Brian."

"Yes, Your Honor."

"Very well. This hearing was continued to give the defense the chance to locate a witness. Is the defense ready to proceed?"

"Your Honor," Shelly interrupted. "Over the weekend, the government extended an offer to the defense, which expires if the defendant goes forward with this hearing. I might add, Judge, that the offer is *more* than generous. Voluntary manslaughter." She shot me a glance. "The defense has yet to respond."

"Well, well," Bearmond said, smiling. "That was quick work, Mr. O'Brian, and a manslaughter plea at that. What are we doing today, counsel? A hearing, or a plea?"

Shelly leaned on her table and stared. Bushill looked up with hope. Boston and Vicky teetered on the edge of their seats. Even ferret-faced Willie seemed caught in the moment.

My phone vibrated

"Court's indulgence," I said, drawing it from my jacket.

"Mr. O'Brian!"

It was a text message. One word: *Bingo*.

"Your Honor!" I said. "The defendant is rejecting the government's plea offer and will be going forward with the hearing."

"You're sure?" asked Bearmond, shaking his head.

I nodded.

"Call your witness, then."

Dammit. A witness.

"The defense calls . . . Alexander Bushill."

"Hot damn!" Bushill rose with a clink of chains. "About time."

"There's one administrative issue," I said, as the marshal led Bushill to the stand.

"Which is?" Bearmond asked.

"My colleague will be conducting the hearing."

Boston grabbed my sleeve, terror in his eyes.

"I have an emergency matter to attend." I tried to step from the table, but Boston wasn't letting go.

"As lead counsel," said Bearmond. "Wouldn't it be prudent to remain?"

"Mr. Stewart is a skilled litigator, Your Honor, well versed in the case. And he was approved under the Superior Court Attorney Buddy Program."

"Attorney Buddy *what*?" Bearmond scoffed.

"Mr. O'Brian," Boston whispered. "I ummmm . . . made that up."

Hilarious.

"Hope for you yet, Boss." I whispered back. "The point is, Judge Bearmond, I have every confidence in Mr. Stewart."

"At this point," Bearmond said. "I don't care who does it, so long as one of you *buddies* step into the well of this court right now."

"Go get em, Boss," I said.

"What do I do?"

"Stall."

CHAPTER THIRTY-SEVEN

I hobbled down the corridor toward the exit with an arm over Vicky's shoulder. Vicky had my phone in her hand, ringing the barfly on speaker.

This is Detective Brenda Bowles. At the sound of the beep . . .

"Hit it again," I told her.

"You gonna tell me what's going on?"

"Good news or bad?"

She shot me a look.

"Bad news is, we just flushed a sweetheart down the toilet, banking on proving Repo is a cop killer."

"And the good?"

"We just found Repo."

"Where is she?"

This is Detective Brenda Bowles. At the sound of the beep . . .

"Hit it again."

"Where?"

"Don't know yet. Brenda filed –"

"Brenda?"

"Detective Bowles. She filed for a track on Repo's phone."

"You know," Vicky said. "I liked you better when you weren't cozying up to cops."

"Bowles sent me a text. I think she found Repo."

"What'd it say?"

"Bingo."

"You rolled your client's future on *bingo*?"

I smiled. Guess I had.

The phone picked up. "Roman?"

"Brenda," I yelled. "You find her?"

"Here's the deal. As far as I'm concerned, this was a graffiti investigation. Had nothing to do with your case."

"Of course. Where is she?"

"Far as anyone knows, you stumbled on her yourself."

"Yes, yes. Where?"

"You locate her, you let me know right away. I'll give you five minutes before I call it in, but as soon as I do, they're going to show up and swat-team her ass."

"Dammit, Brenda. Where?"

"New York and L Streets, Northwest. Two block radius."

"Two blocks?"

"Based on the cell towers. Best I can do."

"Thanks, sugar."

The phone went dead.

Vicky helped me through the front doors, then left me to limp through the media jackals while she ran to hail transportation.

"Mr. O'Brian! Is it true your client turned down a plea offer?"

"Is the Bushill case headed to trial?"

"Roman!" Vicky yelled, holding open a cab door.

I snatched a boom mic from one of the gaffers and used it to crutch the last twenty yards to the curb. Vicky jumped in the cab and I fell in behind her, tossing the boom to the gutter.

"New York and L," I said.

The cab took off up Fifth Street toward New York Ave.

"How you holding up, Ro?" Vicky asked.

"Never better." I grimaced digging out my wallet.

Vicky tossed a twenty on the front seat. "That's forty you owe me."

"Gotcha."

We hung a right at New York and the cab pulled over at its intersection with L. "Have a nice day," the cabbie said, pocketing his twenty.

New York Avenue is four lanes, and was bordered on both sides by abandoned row homes and shuttered businesses. I couldn't see anyone who might be Repo.

"Once around the block," I told the driver. "Slow."

He turned right on L and cruised past a series of low-rent apartment buildings. No Repo. At the end of the block was a boarded up high-rise, ten floors, with a

banner hanging from the roof that read: *Coming Soon.
Hide Park Vista Luxury Condos.*

Repo territory.

"Whadaya think?" I pointed to the banner.

"Dig it, Ro."

We exited and Vicky helped me to the building
entrance, covered in plywood and Tyvek. Someone had
pried the plywood back creating a small entry. Vicky
squeezed through and I followed.

The lobby was gutted and dark. What remained of
the front desk was piled in splinters. The sheetrock had
been removed exposing wiring and plumbing. The floor
was an inch thick with plaster and sawdust.

Vicky lit up the lobby with her cell. Repo's bike
was leaning against what used to be a phone booth.

"Bingo is right," she said.

"Think she squats here?"

"No way. She's probably writing. My guess would
be the roof."

The elevators in the main lobby weren't working,
but the maintenance elevator by the emergency stairs
was in service. Vicky pressed Roof Deck and it lifted us
with unbelievable slowness, creaking and bellowing as
if, at any moment, it would plunge back down. The
lights in the elevator were out, but the Muzac was on,
playing an orchestrated version of a vaguely familiar
R&B tune.

"Call it, Ro."

"You're kidding, right?"

There was a muffled *ding* as the elevator reached the roof.

"What's the plan?" Vicky asked.

"Plan?"

The doors slid open with an explosion of light and we stepped out onto the roof.

CHAPTER THIRTY-EIGHT

It's not that I didn't have plans. I had elaborate plans. One was to quit this job which had me climbing fire escapes, humping through abandoned buildings, and getting assaulted by my own clients. Maybe I'd sign up with a corporate firm. Spend my days writing contracts, my nights with shallow women. The type who value men for their money.

I'd need a car, of course. Something sporty.

A new apartment, while I was at it. With Marcus joining the team, the Sergeant wasn't going to cut it. Something with a backyard. The burbs, maybe.

And while I was on the subject of The Team, it'd be nice to recruit a new member. A woman. One who didn't confuse me with an opera fan, or with guys named "Vito."

So yeah, I had plans.

Just not for Repo.

We crouched behind an air conditioning unit. Repo was on the far side of the roof. She had her duffle slung over a shoulder and four sheets laid out on the ground, sown together to form a long banner. On each sheet was painted a letter in metallic teal spelling, R-E-P-O.

One end of the banner was tied to a lightning rod with the same yellow rope we'd found in the tunnel, the other to a fire escape ladder poking over the edge. My guess was, she'd roll the banner over the edge and unfurl REPO down the side of the building for all to see.

Then run.

The selfish brat was starting to piss me off. There she was, doing her thing, unleashing her self-righteous bullshit on the city while Bushill sat in a jail cell for a crime he didn't commit, or at least on the witness stand spouting nonsense to Bearmond.

God, I wished I was there.

I sent Brenda a text: *Found Repo. Hide Park Vista. The roof. Thanks, sugar.*

Vicky said, "This is going to require finesse."

"Uh huh."

The arrogance. Sure, Repo had been frightened in the tunnel, had no intention of doing what she'd done. But to let a man, even a waste of oxygen like Bushill, take the rap while she went on with her sad crusade?

Despicable.

"We talk to her," Vicky said. "Accuse her even, but the main thing is to keep her in place till the cops arrive."

"Uh huh."

"Last thing we want to do is spook her."

"Uh huh."

I leapt from behind the air conditioner and lurched across the roof, my knee radiating flashes of pain. Repo had her back to me, rolling the banner toward the edge.

"Roman!" Vicky screamed.

Repo turned and I caught her broadside, the both of us collapsing in a pile of twisted arms and yellow rope. Terrified, she broke my grip and tried to crawl away, but I snatched the rope and lassoed her legs.

"You're gonna tell me what happened, you little witch." I grabbed her by her shirt and shook. "Or, swear to God, I'm chucking you over the side!"

"Roman!" Vicky had me by my jacket, pulling me off.

Repo scrambled for her duffle, whipped out a paint can and let loose a ten second burst of metallic teal in my face. "Fuck you, old man!"

Paint in the eyes is a pain unlike any other. The upside was, it made me forget the knee. I have no idea what happened while I laid there in agony. When I came out of it, Vicky had Repo sitting on the ledge with the rope still tied around her legs.

"We just want to talk," Vicky was saying.

"I told you everything!"

Vicky caught me staggering toward them out of the corner of her eye. "Chill, Roman!"

"I'm good." I said, collapsing on my butt in front of them. "Please, continue."

"Look," Vicky said. "We know you were scared. We know it was an accident."

"Accident?" Repo looked at her incredulously, tears forming. "That's what you think?"

"Manslaughter at best."

"Fuck this." Repo yanked the rope.

I grabbed it and pulled. "Here's what happened. You're doing your stupid graffiti. Two cops show up. You panic. Shoot one of them in the head. On your way out, you panic again. Shoot the homeless man in the leg."

I yanked the rope. Repo yelped.

"Then," I said. "For the first time in your miserable life, you feel sorry for someone other than yourself. You tie a rope around the homeless man's leg when the other cop leaves to –"

"He wasn't a cop!" Repo Yelled.

I went to yank, but Vicky stopped me.

"What do you mean?" Vicky asked.

"The bald man –"

"Guy who looks like Mr. Clean?"

"Right. Baldy and this Hispanic guy come down the tunnel. They're with the cop who got killed, except I didn't know he was a cop. Read about it later. Baldy, he's talking to the cop who got killed."

"There were *three* of them?" Vicky motioned for me to stay out of it.

"Yeah. Baldy, the cop who got killed, and the Hispanic dude. They're talking about making a deal."

"Who is?" I asked.

"Chill, Ro." Vicky said. 'Who's talking?"

"Baldy and the cop."

"What kind of deal?"

"I dunno. I'm crouched in the dark in front of my mural. Baldy and the cop are down the tracks. But the Hispanic guy, he walks up the tracks and leans against the wall, practically on top of me. I'm on the ground, laying low. I ain't tryin' to eavesdrop, know what I mean? I'm tryin' to *hide*."

"What did you hear?"

"All I know is, the cop wants to make some kind of deal, but Baldy, he don't want to. That's it."

"Think," Vicky said. "What did they say, exactly?"

Repo dropped her head in her hands, burying her fingers in her dirty blond hair. "The cop who got killed keeps saying he has to do some kind of deal. He has family. Something like that. Keeps saying that Baldy should do the deal with him, but Baldy keeps trying to talk him out of it.

"I think . . ." She lifted her head. "I think it was over the price. The cop who got killed says he wants to do it for three nickels – five hundred fifty-five dollars, or thousand. I don't know drug lingo."

"Three nickels?" Vicky asked.

"Something like that."

"*Triple* nickel?"

"That's it!" Repo wiped her face on her sleeve. "The cop says he's going to make a deal with the triple nickel, whatever that is."

"Then what?"

"After he says that . . ." Repo teared up. "After he says that, Baldy nods to the Hispanic guy and the Hispanic guy pulls a gun from behind his back and shoots the cop!"

She dropped her face back in her hands.

"Then this poor old man – I didn't even know he was there – he stands up in the middle of the tunnel and starts screaming, 'Get out of my house!'"

Repo gulped air.

"Breath." Vicky dropped a hand on her shoulder. "You're doing great."

"Baldy and the Hispanic guy run over to the old man. Baldy takes the gun from the Hispanic guy. They're talking about what to do, but I can't hear. The old man's just standing there."

"And then Baldy," Repo whimpered. "He wipes down the gun, puts it in the old man's hand and bam! He makes him shoot down the tracks, then makes him drop the gun to the ground. Baldy pulls out his own gun, takes a step back and shoots the old man in the leg. Oh, God! The old man is screaming. He falls to his mattress, just screaming and –"

"What happens next?"

"Baldy, he's hunting on the ground for something."

"His cartridge casing?"

"I dunno. Whatever it was, he picks it up, walks back to where he was standing before, and drops it on the ground. What the fuck was *that* about?"

"And then?"

"Baldy and the Hispanic guy go back the way they came. I freak the fuck out, start running down the tracks the other way. They must have heard me. I hear them running after me. It's pitch black. I'm not gonna beat them to the end of the tunnel, so I crawl into a big cardboard box on the middle track and hide under this nasty blanket. They run past me, up the tracks, then back."

"How'd you get out of there?" Vicky asked.

"After a while, I can't hear them. Just the old man, still screaming."

"You went back?"

Repo nodded.

"Tied that rope around the old man's leg?"

"Then I left."

"Brave," Vicky said.

"That's the worst Goddamn bullshit I ever heard," I said. "A mysterious Hispanic guy shoots the cop. Then to cover the Hispanic guy's tracks, *another* cop makes the homeless guy take a shot with the same gun? That's your story?"

Repo turned to Vicky, "What the hell is he babbling about?"

"It makes sense, Ro," Vicky said. "The cartridge casing by the mural at Evidence Tag Twelve is the one the Hispanic guy used to shoot Knox. The one by the mattress is from Tomlinson making Bushill shoot the same gun. Bushill has gunpowder residue on his hand and his DNA is on the gun because Tomlinson rigged the scene, made it look like Bushill shot Knox. Even Tomlinson's cartridge casing makes sense now. He picked it up after he shot Bushill and dropped it where it would corroborate his Gerstein version, except he wasn't careful, didn't realize he'd put himself behind a wall without a clear shot at Bushill. It all fits."

"Yeah, right."

"Ain't it obvious? Tomlinson and Knox are in the tunnel with the Hispanic guy who must be one of their regular dealers, or another cop for all we know. They're dirty. They're under investigation and they know it. Just a matter of time before they're indicted. Knox wants to make a deal."

"Why would Knox tell Tomlinson he's going to make a deal?"

"They're partners. Blood brothers. Knox wants to give Tomlinson the chance to come in on the plea deal. Do it together. That way, no one has to triple-nickel anyone else and they both get a better deal. But Tomlinson doesn't go for it and Knox gets whacked."

"Bullshit."

"Think, Ro!" She slapped me on the side of the head. "Where the hell would she get all that accurate info about the crime scene? How would she even know to claim Tomlinson moved his cartridge casing? And where would she possibly have heard the term *triple nickel*?"

She had me there.

There was a muffled ding. On the far side of the roof, the elevator door slid open. Out stepped Detective Tomlinson. Big. Bald. Gun in hand.

A shot rang out.

Repo's shoulder spurted blood and she fell back over the ledge. The rope went taught. I lunged forward and looked over the edge. Repo was hanging upside-down a foot above the fire escape landing.

There was a second shot. Then footsteps.

Vicky swung over the edge and dropped to the landing. I went next, but hung there clutching the ledge.

"Drop!" Vicky yelled from the landing below, her arms extended as if to catch me.

Another shot. Bits of concrete sprayed in my face from the bullet grazing the ledge. I let go and Vicky jumped back, screaming. I hit the landing in a blizzard of pain.

"Sorry, Ro," she said, helping me up.

Vicky pulled the knot on the rope. Repo dropped to the landing, face first.

Karma.

I braced against the railing and, with my good leg, kicked the plywood over a window. We leapt through into the building.

The floor was dark, a cavernous space with sheets of opaque plastic hanging from the ceiling, forming a series of intersecting passages. Vicky propped Repo on her left shoulder, then me on her right. We stumbled through the passages like three drunk rats in a maze.

"Repo," I said. "Why did you tell us the *crazy* man did it?"

"Fuck, asshole!" She nodded at the roof, toward Tomlinson. "He don't seem crazy to you?"

Excellent point.

We wound our way through the plastic maze to the far wall, the service elevator and stairs. Vick hit the call button and the elevator started its squeaky trek from the roof. A loud thud reverberated as Tomlinson dropped to the fire escape landing.

"O'Brian! I've got a warrant for the girl! You're harboring a fugitive!"

"Fuck you!" Repo shouted.

A shot *pinged* off the elevator door. Tomlinson started ripping through the plastic sheets, bulldogging our way.

"Take the stairs, Vick." I lifted my arm off her shoulder.

Her eyes locked with mine. "I gotcha, Ro."

The elevator chimed and the doors opened. We piled in. The doors hissed shut as the last sheet of plastic fell. There were two shots, and two dings in the elevator door.

We could hear Tomlinson's footfalls on the stairs as the elevator started its slow descent, a cheesy Chris De Burgh number playing on the speakers.

Lady in Red.

My phone vibrated and I snatched from my jacket, illuminating the elevator with dim blue light. Repo slumped on the floor. Vicky backed into a corner.

"Hello?"

"Munchkin! Your father and I are on our way to Massanutten. Don't you worry, we left plenty of food for Marcus."

"Mom! I'm at New York and L. Send police!"

"Hank!" Mom screamed. "Call 911!"

"He's fine, sugar," I heard Dad say.

I hung up and started to dial 911 myself, but the elevator came to an abrupt stop on the fifth floor. The door chimed. Vicky and I slammed against it, stopping it from opening.

Three shots. Three dings in the metal door. The elevator continued down with Vicky and I braced against the door.

It ground to a halt at the lobby. Vicky and Repo retreated to the corners. I positioned myself at the door with my arm cocked, ready to throw all my weight into the one shot I'd have at the bastard. The whole thing happened in slow motion.

The elevator chimed.

The door slid open.

I lunged forward in the darkness and swung, the crunch of bone confirming I'd hit my mark. He tumbled backward as if hit with a hammer, arms extended crucifixion-style. There was just enough time to register the fact that it wasn't Tomlinson, that I'd punched out a uniformed police officer, before the rest of the swat team dog-piled me into oblivion.

CHAPTER THIRTY-NINE

Central Cellblock is a facility at police headquarters next to the courthouse. From there, prisoners are walked through a tunnel to the Bullpen in the basement of the Superior Court where they wait to be presented before a judge in Courtroom C-10.

But that's not where they took me.

No sooner had they shoved me in the back of a police cruiser, the officer driving got a call from his sergeant instructing him to bring me directly to courtroom 103.

Bearmond.

We entered the courthouse through the security entrance on C Street. With my hands cuffed and my knee wrecked, it took two of them to lift me from the cruiser. I was escorted to the elevator and helped down the hall to Bearmond's courtroom.

Boston and Vicky were waiting in the corridor.

"Congratulations, Mr. O'Brian," Boston said. "It was an honor to work with you."

"Proud of you, Ro," Vicky said.

They handed me to two marshals who practically carried me into the courtroom. The gallery was packed. Shelly was at the prosecution table speaking to an MPD detective.

Bearmond turned to his clerk. "Call the Bushill case, Ms. Harrison."

"Shouldn't we bring out the defendant?"

"God no," he said.

"United States versus Alexander Bushill!"

The marshals brought me to the well of the court and stood me before the Bear.

"Well, Mr. O'Brian." Bearmond shook his head as the marshals removed my cuffs. "Suppose it was only a matter of time. Shall I call a nurse?"

"I'm fine, Your Honor."

"Ms. Jarvis," said Bearmond. "After the hearing, the government demanded that Mr. O'Brian be brought here and that the case be recalled. Does the government have representations?"

"The government does," said Shelly, joining us at the bench. "There have been recent developments in the case. The government located a witness. She's being treated for a gunshot wound at Washington Hospital Center and thereafter will be taken into custody for vandalism, but has given a statement."

"And?" said Bearmond.

"The statement of the witness has led us to develop an alternate suspect in the Knox murder case. In fact, that suspect is in custody right now, pending charges of murder, assault with intent to kill, and obstruction of justice for shooting the witness. The government is still investigating, of course –"

"Of course, but?"

"But pursuant to these developments . . ." Shelly looked at me and smiled. "The case against Alexander Bushill is dismissed."

There was a resounding "Whoo Hoo!" from the back of the court.

"Mr. Stewart!" Bearmond slammed his gavel. "I'll remind you to respect the dignity of these proceedings."

"Sorry, Your Honor."

"I'm impressed, Mr. O'Brian." Bearmond feigned concern. "Now go home and get some rest. You need to take better care of yourself."

"There is one . . . complication." Shelly shot me an embarrassed look.

"Complication?" said Bearmond.

Shelly nodded to Bearmond's clerk.

"The United States versus Roman O'Brian!" Ms. Harrison announced. "The defendant is charged with one count of assault on a police officer."

"Emerson Rathbone for the defense, Yah Honor." Pockets stepped up and gave me a wink. "Mr. O'Brian waives formal reading of the charges, asserts his Fifth Amendment rights and demands his *immediate* release."

A young woman stepped up to take Shelly's place. "Sharon Davis for the government, Your Honor. The government is asking that Mr. O'Brian be held in jail and that the matter be certified to courtroom C-10 so that it can be assigned to a felony-two judge."

My luck. It was the special I'd scammed in Ruffio's case.

Karma.

"Sorry, Mr. O'Brian." Bearmond shrugged. "This case will be certified to Courtroom C-10."

Clack!

The marshals re-cuffed me and escorted me to the cellblock. I passed Tomlinson being led into the courtroom in shackles, his belt gone, his tie taken, his eyes blazing. He gave me the same look of hatred he'd given Bushill at the preliminary hearing.

"The United States versus David Tomlinson!" Ms. Harrison announced. "One count of first degree murder, one count of conspiracy to commit murder, one count of obstruction of justice, three counts of assault with intent to kill . . ."

The cellblock door swung shut behind me.

"Hang on a minute," I said to the marshal as we passed Bushill's cell.

Bushill jumped from his bench.

"Congratulations, Mr. Bushill," I said. "It's over. The case is dismissed. They're going to release you."

"Whatever you say, Frenchie." He clutched the bars, leaned forward and whispered, "You find the ninja?"

"Take care of yourself, Alex."

I nodded to the marshal and they led me away.

We wound our way to the basement. It was too early for presentments in Courtroom C-10. I had to wait it out in the bullpen. It was crowded as always. As we approached the cage, someone started yelling, "That's my lawyer! My lawyer!"

"Pipe down," the marshal said, inserting his key.

"Mr. Roman! Thank God you're here. My wife is lying!"

The marshal opened the cage, shoved me in, and slammed it shut.

"Hello, Ruffio."

"Mr. Roman, my wife is . . . My wife is . . . You *arrested*?" He shook his head and walked away.

"Hey, man," someone said. "You a lawyer?"

I dispensed free legal advice for a half hour. Some interesting cases, too: an armed robbery where the only witness was a senior citizen with cataracts, and a simple assault where two transgender Russian hookers were duking it out over turf.

I actually couldn't wait to get out there and put the gloves on again.

"O'Brian," a marshal called. "You have a visitor."

Detective Brenda Bowles walked up to the cage in a pinstriped suit. Butch, but sexy.

"Why am I not surprised?" she asked.

"It was an accident. How is he?"

"The officer? Pissed off, from what I hear."

"You know what I mean."

"Broken nose. He'll live."

"Tell him I'm sorry, okay?"

"You can tell him yourself." She smirked. "He'll be testifying at your preliminary hearing."

"I can't believe they're going forward with this assault-on-a-police-officer bullshit."

"For what it's worth, the MPD recommended they drop the charges, given the situation with Tomlinson."

"So what happened?"

"That prosecutor, the one handling your case? The special? What's her name?"

"Sharon Davis."

"Man, she's got it in for you. Seems you have that effect on women."

"It's a skill, like anything else."

"I'm sure you'll get released at the preliminary, so that gives you what? Three days first-class accommodations at D.C. Jail?"

"Could be worse," I said. "Make friends. Talk law. No interruptions."

"Excuse me," an old man said. "Lemme ask you a question."

"With you in a minute," I said.

"Don't let me interrupt your work." Brenda tapped the bars. "Call me when you get out. We'll go on that proper date you were asking about."

I smiled. "Like an actual, out-in-public date?"

"Let's not get crazy." She winked. "How about we iron out the details when you're not behind bars."

I watched her walk away.

"Here's what happened," the old man said. "They arrested me, see?"

"Uh huh."

"But turns out, I'm innocent."

"Of course."

"So my question is, can they *do* that?"

They gave Repo a pass on the graffiti charges in exchange for her testimony against Tomlinson. She was accepted into the art program at Georgetown, then expelled for vandalizing the faculty lounge.

Tomlinson went to trial, was found guilty, and scored thirty years at Butner.

That's justice.

Ruffio was finally convicted for threatening his wife. Judge Alvarez took it easy on him, though, and gave him probation with anger management classes. I heard from his probation officer his wife took him back and they had another girl.

Vicky got over her infatuation with Johnny and fell for Boston. He's a nice enough guy, I suppose. Really seems to care. Even gets jealous when Vicky and I go on late-night investigations.

I moved out of the Sergeant and rented a ground floor apartment in Adams Morgan with a backyard. Marcus loves it. Brenda too. The barfly, not the ex. She dumped her boyfriend and bought a condo. We date, sort of.

It's complicated.

Hatch gets busted now and then and still pays my fee in messenger service.

After more than ten years prosecuting criminal cases, Shelly quit the U.S. Attorney's Office and took a job with a private firm. I see her around the courthouse from time to time and we always talk about Bushill, whose whereabouts are unknown.

They set him up at the New York Avenue shelter the day he was released. He checked in, then out within six hours. Every once in a while I go back to the tunnel looking for him.

Pockets died.

They found him slumped over a crossword puzzle in the lawyer's lounge. Heart attack. It was the largest funeral I ever attended. The entire courthouse turned out: lawyers, judges, even former clients. Bearmond delivered the eulogy himself, referring to Pockets as a dedicated public servant, a true Fifth Streeter.

Other than that, we're all still here.

Mike Madden is a criminal defense attorney in Washington, D.C. His work has been published in *Pulp Metal Magazine*, *The Saturday Night Reader*, *Thuglit* and in the *Baltimore Sun*.

His collection of short stories, *Savage Journey,* is available on Amazon.com.

Connect with Mike Madden at:
www.MikeMaddenAuthor.com
Twitter/ @MikeMadden999
Facebook/MikeMadden

717 D St., NW
Suite 400
Washington, DC 20004

Made in the USA
Monee, IL
13 August 2020

37463030R00213